MY KINDA
Player

USA TODAY BESTSELLING AUTHOR
LACEY BLACK

My Kinda Player
Summer Sisters Book 5

Copyright © 2018 Lacey Black

Cover Design by Y'all. That Graphic
Editing by Kara Hildebrand
Format by Integrity Formatting

This book is a work of fiction. Any reference to historical events, real people, or real places are used fictitiously. Other names, characters, places and events are products of the author's imagination, and any resemblance to actual events or places or persons, living or dead, is entirely coincidental.

Published in the United States of America.

ISBN-13: 978-1-951829-24-7

MY KINDA Player

AJ

1

It's a Summer sister tradition that on the first Saturday of each month, the six of us get together. We take turns picking the location or activity, anything from margaritas and a movie to wine and painting classes at the small gallery uptown. One thing, though, is as certain as the sun rising over the Chesapeake Bay every morning: there will be alcohol involved.

Always.

It's what I like to call the last hoorah of summer. The time where nights are warm and the breeze blowing off the Bay feels muggy. And with every tick of the clock, I get closer and closer to returning to the classroom. Not that it's a bad thing, because I really do love my job, but I'm sure as most teachers will attest, I just wish summer vacation lasted a little bit longer.

When June hits, you're just so damn excited to finally be out of school that you decide to enjoy a few weeks of sunbathing and relaxing. Then July hits and you start to compile the to-do list of all the things you want to get done on your break. Repaint the cabinets, stain the porch, clean out the yard shed so you can finally find those stupid hedge trimmers that you swear you have.

But then you're reminded that you're still on summer break. Why do all of this crap when the temperatures are at their highest and the beach is calling your name?

That's when August hits, and you're like, "Holy shit, I didn't get anything done that I swore I'd complete this year."

That's where I'm at.

It's the first Saturday in August (Sisters' Night) and I have nothing to show for my vacation except a killer tan and extra copper highlights.

Before I can let the guilt creep in about not getting anything done over my three-month teaching reprieve, I turn my attention to my sisters. We're all here, beachside as our favorite local band, Crush, plays on the makeshift stage.

Jupiter Bay, home of eight thousand busybodies who know everything about everyone. It's the place I've called home for all twenty-nine years of my life; well, except for when I went to college. But I came back, just like I knew I would.

Nine months out of the year, I'm the eighth grade math teacher at Jupiter Bay Junior High, home of the Hawks! I also tutor before school, and was roped into being the cheer sponsor a few years back. Go team! It hasn't been easy trying to keep my good girl facet in place, especially when the bad girl in me is begging to take over. But if there's one thing I've learned about living in a small town, it's that the rumors will fly and the stories will be elaborated regardless.

So I let my inner vixen come out and play every once in a while.

Tonight, we're celebrating two things: the end of summer and the end of Crush. It's their final performance as a group, and the mood has been a mixture of melancholy and anxiousness. That's why the alcohol is involved. One of my twin sister's boyfriend has played lead guitar with this band since they started fresh out of high school.

Let's talk about my sisters, shall we?

I'm right smack dab in the middle of the six Summer sisters. Yep, all girls.

The oldest is Payton, recently married to Dean McIntire. She owns Blossoms and Blooms uptown, the small floral and gift shop. I've helped man the front counter a few times over the years, but my thumb is as brown as they come, so I stay as far away from the flowers and plants as possible. Dean is an accountant and has the cutest little girl from a previous relationship. My niece by marriage, Brielle, is amazing. Even though she's not Payton's biological daughter, she is hers in every way that matters. In fact, they go to court next month to finalize the adoption.

Payton and Dean were married last month in Vegas. Basically, they hopped on a plane (that my dad flew), bought some rings, and were married in a chapel on the strip. They were home before they missed dessert. Well, that's not true, but they give new meaning to the phrase *shotgun wedding*. It's all good though, especially in light that it was going to happen anyway.

Next in line is Jaime. She's married to Ryan Elson, a local contractor. She works for a local not-for-profit called Addie's Place, where kids can go after school to receive help with school, a snack or meal, and socialize with other kids. I had heard about it through school, but never really knew the ins and outs of the organization until Jaime started working there.

They were married this past April, and while there are no kids on the way yet, I fully expect her to be knocked up sooner rather than later. These two are like rabbits on Viagra and have been busted getting freaky more times than anyone ever should.

I'm next in the order, but we'll jump over me to Meghan.

Oh, sweet Meghan. It's been a rough year for the sister who wears her heart on her sleeve. A year ago this past February, her fiancé, Josh, was killed in a car accident. It wrecked her, as well as the rest of our family, who has had to watch her grieve and mourn his loss. She's doing well, though, all things considered. She works full time at a dental office in town, and has been keeping herself busy crafting everything she can get her hands on. I think it's her way of just staying active so that her mind doesn't wander back to a time when everything was right. She'll get there. I know it.

Rounding out the Summer clan are the twins, Abby and Lexi. Abby is an editor for a big publishing company in New York and works from home. She lives with Levi, the hottie guitarist up on stage, who has been her best friend since, well, forever. I think they were ten when they started their friendship, and even though it remained safely tucked in that platonic, no-sex stage for way too long, they've finally figured out they're better together, having all the sex. Levi is also an EMT and volunteer fireman in town, which just adds serious points to his hotness factor. Well, if I were keeping points.

Finally, there's Lexi. Mouthy, knocked-up Lexi. We'll skip over the fact that she was married to douche-y Chris and focus on the fact that she's now with Linkin. Tall, muscular, gives lap dances as good as they come, Linkin. He's a mechanic and was living next door to Lexi when she left her ex. Now, they have babies on the way–yes, two–and I'm anxious to be an aunt to babies. Lexi's a full-time beautician at Hair Haven uptown, or at least she was until a week ago. At not quite seven months, her belly has gotten too big and her feet too swollen to work as many hours as she has been, so she had to cut back to part time. Sitting at home is killing her.

That's why she's here now, nursing a bottle of water, and trying to ignore the alpha man hovering in the corner, ready to pounce at her first sign of discomfort.

"That man is driving me crazy," Lexi mumbles, glancing over her shoulder to where Linkin is standing with Dean and Ryan. "He won't even let me sit down by myself anymore. It's like he's afraid the whale might fall and not be able to get back up," she adds, making a face that includes sticking out her tongue at the man not too far away.

"Aww, I think it's sweet," Jaime coos at the way Linkin dotes on Lexi. "He's going to be an amazing daddy."

"I agree. If I ever have a baby, I hope my man is half as attentive as yours," Abby adds.

"Levi will be a terrific father," Lexi adds, her eyes tearing up. "Don't mind me. These stupid hormones have me crying over toilet paper commercials."

Abby blushes. "Well, I didn't say anything about Levi, but if that were to happen, I think he'd be a phenomenal father."

"Definitely. And think of all the sex, Abs. You'd be like Lexi, humping everything like a Chihuahua," I say before sticking my straw into my mouth.

"Not *everything*, AJ. Just one specific *something*." Lexi gets that ornery smirk on her face and I can tell exactly what that *something* is, and it's attached midsection to the man standing not fifteen feet away.

"Are we going to start talking about sex now? I feel like I need another drink for this," I say, turning and looking for my cooler.

"What's the matter? You no longer a fan of *the sex*?" Payton asks, calling it *the sex* the way our grandma always does.

"Oh, I'm a huge fan of it. Just wish I could find some worth talking about," I grumble as I mix the pineapple juice in with Malibu Rum.

"Well, don't look now, but I think Dexter is making faces at you," Meghan says, trying not to giggle.

When I glance up, the drummer wiggles his tongue suggestively and throws me a dirty grin. My stomach actually clenches and the contents consider making a reappearance. "Gross."

"What, not interested in another ride on the Dexter pogo stick?" Payton laughs.

"Maybe you should. I bet you could get a good two or three minute power nap in again this time," Lexi adds, wiping tears of laughter from her eyes.

"Ha ha," I grumble, trying to push that horrible night out of my mind. It was last year when I finally decided to give in to his constant advances. Little did I know that he'd be maxed out at two minutes of grunting and pounding before finding his own release. It was so bad, I dozed off there about halfway through. Shit, even trying to pretend he was Chris Hemsworth didn't do anything but ensure I had to rename my vibrator to Channing Tatum when I bought him. Chris was so out after that.

"Wait, what happened to that guy you left with last month?" Abby asks.

Oh. Him.

The night is a bit foggy, but I could never forget him.

Sawyer.

"Oh, you know, just another guy in town for the summer," I say blasé, trying to look for a quick subject change. "So are you ready for the shower next month?" I ask my youngest, most pregnantest sister.

Lexi's eyebrows shoot into her hair, but she doesn't call me on the blatant subject change. Thank God. "I'm ready. Linkin has been so amazing, getting everything set up and ready."

"Did you really make him paint the room three times?" Meghan asks.

"It's not my fault that the first two shades of yellow looked like smashed bananas and pee," Lexi defends.

"I heard he didn't complain once when she changed the color three times," Jaime says with a smile.

"He didn't," Lexi says, a soft blush staining her cheeks.

"Looks like someone's getting road-head tonight," Payton chides, grinning like a fool.

"Can't," Lexi pouts. "There's no more car sex until after the babies. I can't bend over the console."

They keep debating the pros and cons of car sex, but my mind wanders elsewhere. To that night.

The truth is I could never call Sawyer a summer fling. First off, you'd have to have sex to constitute a fling, right? And, well, I'm just not ready to spill the details of that fateful night, one month ago, to my sisters. It's too embarrassing.

When I close my eyes, I can still picture his ocean blue eyes and feel the way his brown hair slid through my fingers. I followed him from the bar, eager to spend a little naked alone time with him. When we stepped onto the sidewalk, his fingers were warm and slightly rough as they wrapped around mine. He pulled me gently toward a car, a nice one that said rich trust fund. Inside, I melted against the butter-soft seats, high on hormones and anticipation.

We didn't speak as he drove down the beach to a nice hotel. The nicest hotel in town. He hopped out of the car and came around to my side, extending his hand to help me out of the car in a total gentlemanly move I hadn't seen in a long time. My head was swimming and my stomach churning, but I kept praying it was because of the man beside me.

Unfortunately, it wasn't.

I remember everything about the kiss. It started sweet and soft, even as electricity started to course through my blood. His hands, *my God those hands*, swept up my jaw, caressing my skin before making their way into my hair. I've never wanted someone to pull my hair as badly as I wanted him to.

The kiss quickly turned ravenous. It was wild and electric and everything a kiss should be. His tongue stroked mine, probing into my mouth with so much expertise and efficiency that my knees started to get weak. My back pressed firmly into the side of the car. His powerful thighs framed my legs, keeping me from melting into a pile of hormonal mush at his feet. He was tall–so freaking tall–towering over me like a possessive giant.

And my Lord, that hard-on. It was long and hard and pressed into my stomach, ensuring that I'd remember the way it felt against me for years to come. Hell, probably even a lifetime. It was that memorable of a cock.

My hands gripped at his shirt. I was afraid of breaking the connection or that he'd disappear altogether, leaving me alone to wallow in my loneliness and self-pity. But he didn't. He was there, holding me tight and kissing me like I was the very oxygen he needed to breathe.

"Will you come up to my room?" he asked, his hands still threaded into my hair.

"Yes." It was the only answer I could give. I was drowning in his blue eyes, captivated by his being. I *needed* more.

Unfortunately, that's when my current state of drunkenness reared its ugly head. My stomach pitched like I was lost at sea on a dingy and I started to sweat. How much had I had to drink? Too much. The answer was entirely too much.

"You okay?" he asked, taking in my chalky green complexion and stomach-clenching tremors.

I knew what was about to happen, and apparently so did he.

Sawyer spun around, pulling me to the bushes just as my stomach decided to unleash hours' worth of alcohol and food. If I wasn't too busy puking my guts up all over the sidewalk and the evergreens, I'd be completely mortified. Instead, I spilled everything I ate and drank that day, while the man held my hair and whispered sweet words in my ear. Of course, it wasn't what I had hoped he'd be whispering. You know, "Fuck, you feel so good" or "I'm gonna fuck you until you can't remember your name."

Instead, I was hearing, "Shhhh, sweetheart, it's okay," while he rubbed circles on my heaving back.

When I was finally done retching, he picked up my boneless body and carried me off as if I weighed nothing. I remember hearing the elevator ding. I remember feeling him juggle my body as he unlocked his room. I remember the feel of soft sheets against my clammy skin.

But I couldn't open my eyes.

The last thing I remember before I slipped into unconsciousness was a cool rag placed on my forehead and the feel of his fingers against my cheek as he moved my hair. In the morning, I woke up alone. He was gone, and if it weren't for the fancy hotel room, I'd think he was a figment of my imagination.

But he wasn't.

I know it.

Now, here I am, surrounded by my family, having a great time as we celebrate our last sisters' night before school starts up again in a few weeks, and I'm lost in the memories of blue eyes and fantastic kisses. They haunt me in my sleep almost nightly, ensuring that I wake horny and yearning for more.

But more will never happen.

He was gone when I woke up and left no further way to make contact. I mean, would you leave your name and number for the woman who puked all over the sidewalk outside your hotel?

So now I'm left with those pesky memories that won't go away and an overactive imagination of what could have been if not for the pukepocalypse. I guess that just proves that I'm destined to be alone. I'm always going to kiss frogs who don't turn into princes. I'm never going to find my person the way Payton, Jaime, Abby, and Lexi have.

And that's okay.

I don't need a man.

I don't need a relationship.

Relationships are nothing but hurt and pain.

I'm fine on my own.

I got this.

Sawyer

2

I glance around the house trying to figure out where in the hell to start. Boxes are stacked everywhere, my furniture still wrapped in plastic. The movers did a hell of a job, considering I was relocating from practically one side of the country to the other. Okay, maybe not quite that far, but Texas to Virginia is quite the distance.

And that suits me just fine.

A little distance never hurt anyone. In fact, I reached the point in my life where I craved it, along with the familiarity of home. Sure, people might occasionally recognize me, but nothing like in Arlington. This should be a walk in the park compared to where I called home for the past ten years, which I'll gladly take.

The house is a new beachfront home with big windows and private access to the Bay. The realtor said it was prime real estate, which, of course, came with a prime price tag. It was still affordable, at least compared to the mortgage I left in Texas, and the view is killer. I can't wait to find my old running shoes and start pounding the sand.

But that'll have to wait. Right now, I need to find the box that was shipped here from the bedding store. The realtor said it was delivered a few days ago, as well as a few other items that I needed, right before we pulled out of Arlington.

The sun is starting to set, bright orange light filtering in through the bare windows at the front of the house. It reminds me that I'll have to buy curtains, probably sooner rather than later. I take off into the living room, searching for the box and am pleased to find it, along with a few others, by the fireplace. I rip off the packing tape and retrieve the goodies inside. The sheets go straight into the washing machine, which along with the other appliances, were all delivered and hooked up before I arrived.

My stomach growls, reminding me that I haven't eaten since we arrived early this morning. The movers took a quick lunch, but for the most part, we worked hard unloading the truck and getting everything moved inside my new place. They were off, headed back to Texas, by four, which has left me staring at mountains of boxes and wondering where to start.

Instead of doing what needs to be done, I grab another bottle of water from the fridge and slip out the sliding back door. This is actually what sold me on the house. The large deck, hand-laid brick walkway, and the built-in grill and fire pit. It's a perfect place for entertaining, if I had friends here or knew anyone. There's a decent sized grassy yard before you hit sand. The Chesapeake Bay is maybe fifty yards out, just a stone's throw away from my back door. Hell, it wasn't that long ago that I'd be able to toss a stone pretty fucking far into that big body of water. Now, even after surgery and months of therapy, my shoulder isn't what it used to be and I'd be lucky to hit water after it bounced in the sand.

But enough of the pity party, I have shit to do and very little time to do it.

School starts in less than a week, and I'm anxious to get into a routine that doesn't involve physical therapy and appointments with various doctors. This is a whole new norm for me, complete with new job, new house, new town, hell, a new state.

As I dive into one of the boxes labeled kitchen, I can't help but wonder how much of the new is a front. Am I running from the past, from the memories that trail me everywhere I go? Probably a little. But I need this clean slate. I need it like I need air. Some place where I'm not followed and hounded. Some place that doesn't hold painful memories.

I'm counting on this fresh start to help get my life back on track.

I needed Jupiter Bay.

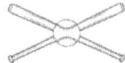

I drive through downtown, shaking my head when I discover pretty much everything is closed. This place is nothing like Arlington, which had nightlife on every corner. It's well after nine and my stomach just couldn't take being empty any longer. Plus, I needed out of the house pretty desperately. Even after two full days on the road, I was feeling the familiarity of restlessness sweep in. When I finally spy neon lights, I pull my car into a familiar parking lot. A smile tugs on my lips as I slip from my car and head inside.

Lucky's looks exactly the same as it did a month ago, except now there are only a handful of customers. The tables are empty compared to the way it was last time I was here. An older man works the bar and a handful of stools are taken, eyes moving from watching the baseball game on the television to scoping out the new guy who just walked in.

As I approach the bar, I can't help but glance over to the large table in the back. It sits empty now, not like it was that night when I was completely entranced by a brunette with stunning green eyes. I watched her for several minutes before her eyes finally collided with my own, and in that moment I knew.

I had to have her.

Adjusting the sudden discomfort in my pants, I take a seat, coincidentally in the same seat I sat in the last time I was here. A few of the guys throw nods my way, but for the most part, they leave me alone, which I'm grateful for. The last thing I need is to be recognized and forced to relive the moment that changed my life forever.

"What can I get ya?" the old man asks, a warm smile on his face and a bar towel thrown over his shoulder.

"Is the grill still open?" I ask, my stomach choosing this moment to remind me that it needs food.

The guy chuckles. "Could be. Won't take me but a minute to fire it up. Though, the pickin's will be pretty slim. I think I can cook you up a burger and fries," he offers.

"That sounds perfect, actually. Thanks."

"Anything to drink?"

"Miller Lite," I answer, grabbing a few peanuts from the bowl set in front of me.

"Be right back."

"Thanks," I reply, watching him head back into the kitchen.

A few minutes later, he returns and gets my beer. The Rangers are playing the Cubs tonight, but I already knew that. I know that schedule like the back of my hand. Swartz swings on a high pitch and hops it up into center. That familiar mix of anxiety and anger starts to creep in as I watch the fielder catch the ball and fire it to second base. The second baseman misses the tag, but keeps Carter on base.

I have to glance away.

My gut churns and I play it off as lack of food, but deep down I know better. It's regret. Anger. Longing.

My sport. The one I had to give up after one bad play. One split-second decision took it all away.

Just like that.

"Here ya go," the old man says, setting the hot plate in front of me.

"Thanks," I say, snapping myself out of the memory. Wiping my clammy hands on my pants, I grab a fry and pop it into my mouth. A bottle of ketchup and some mustard are pulled from the cooler behind the bar and set in front of me. I load up my burger with condiments, squirt a big glob on my plate, and dive in.

As I eat, my eyes return to the television. I can't help it.

The old man hangs around, resting his elbow on the bar and relaxes, watching the game. By the time I'm halfway through my burger, he asks the question I've always dreaded. "You miss it?"

Glancing his way, I see his eyes still focused on the TV. But I know he's talking to me. Besides the fact that I'm the only one on this end of the bar, I'm probably the one former pro ball player in the joint. "Yeah," I answer honestly.

The man nods and turns his hazel eyes on me. "Name's Lucky," he says as he extends his hand.

"Sawyer," I reply as I shake his hand. "But you probably already figured that out."

He shrugs before standing up and turning his attention back to the bar. "Holler if you need anything."

I nod before returning my attention to my burger, which he lets me finish in silence. My mind drifts back to the game, but not the one on TV. I relive the hit over and over again, like some horrible instant replay. The crack of the bat. The line drive that sails straight down the third baseline. The dive. The landing. The catch.

The pain.

It was like nothing I had experienced before, shooting straight through my body, hitting every nerve ending. I wanted to puke, but was afraid to move. The replays showed the dive on every sports show for the next two weeks, following the story through every surgery and every hospital visit. They stayed with me until that moment I was cut from the team.

Now, here I sit, in an old bar, watching my team play without me.

My food settles like concrete in my belly and the beer isn't helping much either. Pulling a twenty from my wallet, I toss it on the bar, throw a wave at Lucky, and head back out into the warm August night.

My past trailing closely behind me.

AJ

3

"Aren't you glad to be back? How was your summer? I'm so excited for this year! Did you hear about Coach Becker?" Laney Porter smiles widely, her bleach-blonde hair teased high and her lips painted bright pink.

"Hey, Laney. How was your summer?" I ask, knowing that she'll ask me the same questions again shortly. That's just how she is. She talks a mile a minute, nonstop, and sometimes it's a bit hard to keep up. Can you imagine being in her English class?

"It was awesome, of course. I went to visit my dad who lives down the street from the Indianapolis Motor Speedway, so of course, we got tickets and went." Breath. "Have you heard if they've replaced Coach yet? I mean, Ruby called me over the summer and told me he took early retirement because of that issue he had with Mrs. Dorsch. You know the one I'm talking about right? Of course you do. Everyone knows. It's not every day the

PE teacher gets caught with his pants around his ankles with one of the student's moms. Oh, and she's twenty years younger than him! Can you believe it?"

This is the point in the conversation when I usually tune her out. She means well, I know, and she really is a nice lady, but having a conversation with her is like trying to train a beagle to tap dance. It's just not happening.

"Anyway, so our first staff meeting of the year. There are two new teachers, from what I've gathered. They replaced Connie Jameson, the sixth and seventh grade math teacher, which you probably know that since it's your department. I hear he's a younger guy, probably close to your age, which I guess is really close to my age too! And then there's Coach Becker. I haven't heard who they replaced him with. Have you?" She blinks repeatedly, waiting on my response.

"Nope, I haven't heard yet, but I'm sure we'll find out in a few minutes." I glance down at my watch, cursing myself for not waiting a few extra minutes to come down to the teachers' lounge. "Excuse me a second, Laney," I say, getting up from one of the worn couches and heading to the back of the room. The coffee pot is calling my name.

"Good morning," Ellen Morris (she teaches Science) says as she hands me the pot.

I pour myself a cup of coffee, doctoring it up as best I can to camouflage the actual coffee taste, but even then my options are limited. There's some powder creamer, which is basically like adding chalk, and a handful of sugar packets. I hoard all of it, tossing it in my paper cup, and stirring it with a little plastic stick.

The room gets louder as more bodies cram inside. When I turn around, I'm thankful that my seat beside Laney is occupied. That leaves just a few open seats at the back of the room. Taking one in the corner, I grab my phone from my bag and make sure it's set to silent. The last thing I want is to be the person in the staff meeting whose phone goes off during the principal's speech about keeping our phones in our desks during the school day.

I'm checking my email when Mr. Stewart enters the room. He greets the room warmly, his voice welcoming and friendly. It's always like this before school starts. Near the end of the school year, he'll sound a bit more like Darth Vader. Working with teens and preteens takes a toll on all of us come mid-April.

"If you'll all take a seat, we'll get this meeting started," he instructs.

I slip my phone into my bag and reach for my coffee cup on the floor. As I'm bent over, a shadow falls over me and someone sits in the chair next to me. I hope it's Brandy. I'm just starting to sit back up when his leg moves, barely hitting my hand. But it's enough to send the contents in my cup splashing over the rim and spilling on me.

"Ah!" I say, moving the cup from one hand to the other.

"Shit," my neighbor mumbles, reaching for my cup and taking it from my hand. I have enough additives to my coffee to help cool it down a bit, so it's not scalding hot, but it's still pretty warm. I reach over to my right and grab a napkin off the counter, blotting at the residual beverage. When my hand is wiped clean, I dab at the droplets on the floor, making sure no one will slip.

"Thank you," I say, reaching blindly for my cup.

The man places it in my hand. "I'm so sorry about that. I wasn't paying attention," he says. His voice is warm and apologetic, and oddly familiar.

When I glance up, I'm struck by hypnotizing blue eyes and dark brown hair. He has a bit of facial hair that resembles more of a five o'clock shadow than a beard. His lips are full and soft and remind me of amazing kisses that promised an equally amazing night.

My heart hammers in my chest and my mind blanks.

This can't be happening.

"Fuck."

4

Sawyer

She's here.

The woman from the bar. She's sitting next to me in the teachers' lounge on the first day of my new career. That can only mean one thing. I almost slept with a coworker.

Of course, at the time, she wasn't a coworker. I was here merely for the interview–for a job I thankfully received.

Leaving her in my bed that morning was the hardest thing I had ever done. She looked like a goddess, brown hair fanned out on the pillow, and pert little mouth slightly agape. Okay, so maybe it was more like wide open, with a soft snore slipping from her throat, but whatever. She was cute as hell, and it did a number on me.

Unfortunately, when I returned from my interview, she was gone. The damn thing took longer than anticipated as the principal took me on an extended tour of the school and wanted to talk baseball. When I finally got free and could get back to my hotel room, I was disappointed to find the bedding slightly rumpled and the room empty.

She was gone without so much as a trace left behind.

And now here she is. Sitting right next to me, cute little reading glasses perched on her nose. She looks just as gorgeous as I remember. Her hair hangs loose around her shoulders, free and begging for my fingers. Her green eyes are the color of emeralds, sparkling and bright. Her mouth gapes open, plump and ripe for my own lips. She's a wet dream, and for the past month, she's been mine.

"AJ." Just saying her name, even after a month, is already causing all of my blood to rush south.

"Sawyer." My name on her lips comes out a croak. It also makes my dick twitch in my pants.

"Welcome back, everyone. We have a lot to cover today, including the introduction of a couple new teachers. Let's go around the room and introduce ourselves. Name and what subject you teach," Mr. Stewart directs, filling up his own coffee cup.

I listen as we go around the room, each new coworker sharing a name that I won't remember today. Finally, we get to the woman sitting next to me. It should be embarrassing how quickly my heart rate escalates in anticipation. I also hold my breath.

"AJ Summer, eighth grade math."

That's all she says, but the words go straight to my cock. I glance her way, unprepared for the reaction my body has to hearing her voice. She stares straight ahead so I take the opportunity to study her features, refreshing my memory of how delicate each curve and feature of her face is while she sleeps. She has no idea that I stayed up for hours that night watching her sleep.

Creepy? Probably.

But I don't give a shit. I felt something the moment my eyes connected with hers back in July. The moment she feels my eyes on her now, she turns my way. Electricity sparks between us, alive and powerful. Her hypnotic green eyes search mine, for what, I'm not sure. But I can tell the moment she seems to recall our previous meeting.

"Sawyer Randall, PE," I state without removing my eyes from my neighbor.

AJ blushes a pretty shade of pink that spreads from her neck down and disappears into the collar of her flowy purple tank top. My own flashbacks assault me, one right after the other. The connection. The invitation. The car ride.

The kiss.

My God, I relived that fucking kiss like some lovesick loser for weeks. Hell, I'm still enjoying the instant replays. Her lips were soft and urgent, her taste as sweet as sin. I was instantly hooked, craving more.

But then she turned that weird shade of green. I had a split second to move her to the bushes before she puked all over the place, including my shoes. Thank God I've always had a strong stomach because as soon as she was done, the fight and every ounce of energy she possessed just seeped from her small body.

Carrying her up to my room felt a little too good. Almost like I was carrying her over the threshold.

Wait.

What?

No. No threshold. No romance or relationship.

Sex. That's what that was.

Well, almost sex...

And now here she is, sitting beside me and trying to pretend like I didn't watch her vomit alcohol like a college co-ed after her first kegger. Well, too bad, AJ Summer, eighth grade math teacher. I don't forget. I'm *not* going to forget. Not the way she felt in my arms and definitely not the way her lips tasted.

The problem is... what do I do about it?

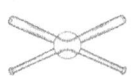

After an hour of sitting on a hard chair, listening to my new boss drone on and on about policies and procedures (which I've already reviewed in great lengths with my welcome packet), we're finally dismissed. Teachers jump up eagerly, excited to start another school year. For me, I'm excited to start my first.

"Hey, man, it's an honor to meet *the* Sawyer Randall," the other newbie teacher says, his eyes shining with eagerness as he comes over and shakes my hand. I glance over to AJ, hoping that she'll hang around a few minutes, but find her quickly slipping from her seat and heading to the door.

"I can't believe I'm teaching with *the* Sawyer Randall." My attention is pulled back to the man in front of me.

"I'm excited to be here," I tell him honestly.

"Shouldn't be too hard from what you're used to, right?" he asks with a snicker. "I mean, aren't major leaguers like wrangling adolescents sometimes?"

I don't find his joke humorous, but I smile the same. "Something like that."

I try to politely excuse myself, but the guy just isn't having it. "How do you think the baseball team will be this year?"

"Well, I'm not quite sure yet." You know, considering school hasn't even started yet.

"I did a little research. Last year's team went ten and six and we only lost three eighth graders. We seem to still have solid swingers and pitchers," he states, lightly hitting my arms with his knuckles. "You know, I was interested in the head baseball coach's position and applied. They told me they'd keep me in mind, but then I found out they hired you for PE, and of course, gave you the baseball coaching job. I mean, they're not about to give it to me over a former pro like yourself. I wasn't bad back in the day. I played college ball, man. So when you're ready to pick your assistant, I'd be more than willing to help. I played centerfield. I have a lot to offer the team," he says, eyes eager and hopeful.

"Oh, well, I'll keep that in mind. It was great meeting you," I start, leaving it open to fill in his name.

"Bryce. Bryce Lehman. Sixth and seventh grade math." Again, he offers me his hand.

"Bryce, right. Well, Bryce, I'm gonna head to my office and try to get a calendar set for the first few weeks of school. Gotta keep our youth active."

"True, true. Well, it was great meeting you, Sawyer. Mr. Randall," he corrects in a rush. "Anyway, we're both new here so we should stick together. Anytime you need a friend or want to grab a beer after work, let me know."

"Sure, Bryce. Talk to you soon," I say, trying to pull myself away from the young, energetic teacher. He's a different character, that's for sure, but the one thing I pick up right away is that he'll be working closely with AJ in the math department.

It takes me another twenty minutes to get out of the teachers' lounge. I'm used to being recognized most places I go, and I expected no different in Jupiter Bay. Though, I'll admit an opportunity to be inconspicuous would be welcome right now. I wonder how it's going to be on our first day of school? Has word gotten out yet that Sawyer Randall, former Major League Baseball All-Star, is coaching high school baseball and teaching PE?

I'm sure it hasn't since I'm not being hounded for interviews or being trailed by jackasses with cameras. Even after my injury and being cut from the team, sports broadcasters and tabloid hounds still love to snap a pic of me having coffee or leaving physical therapy. The sports reporters don't bother me as much, though I'd prefer them to focus less on the end of my career and more about the stats I had while I played.

The tabloids can take a hike, though. Throw my name on *People*'s Sexiest Man Alive list a few years in a row, a trending hashtag in the Twitter-verse calling me #SexySawyer, and one very high profile relationship, and suddenly I'm tabloid fodder right next to Miley Cyrus.

Everyone seems to want a piece of me.

Everyone except a certain brunette with the brightest green eyes and the lips of an angel.

AJ Summer didn't seem to care who I was. Either she doesn't know or it's an act. I've met my fair share of gold diggers, pretending to not care about my fame or fortune, yet only to discover that's all they really cared about in the first place. Being someone's arm candy and looking good for the press. My gut tells me that's not AJ.

I make my way back to my new office, nestled right in between the gym and the boys' locker room. Barb Jordan is the girls' PE teacher and is already in her office on the opposite side of the gym. I met her first thing this morning when I arrived at the school and dropped my bag off in my new office. She's easily in her fifties and holds quite a few coaching records at the school for girls' basketball and volleyball. I could learn a lot from her.

Sitting down behind my desk, I can't help but wonder what kinda teacher I'll be. I have dick for experience when it comes to teaching, but have more than enough to contribute to the baseball team.

My goal is to be firm, but fair, while having fun. Athletics can be enjoyable; you just have to find the things that spark and hold their interest.

I get to work, but can't help the way my mind occasionally wanders back to AJ.

Miss Summer.

After months of surgeries, recouping, rehab, and public scrutiny, I think my luck is finally changing. The thought of seeing her five days a week? Yeah, I'd say things are definitely starting to look up.

5

AJ

"My God, that man is smokin' hot," Brandy Kohl says, fanning her face as she dramatically falls back against the chalkboard in my classroom.

"Oh, Brandy, not you too. That's all I heard from Laney and Phyllis as I left the meeting earlier," I reply, abandoning the label maker and giving my friend my full attention.

"He's freaking tall and sexy and gorgeous and sexy. I'm going to look for every excuse possible to get him down to the principal's office on a regular basis," she adds, a mischievous grin on her pretty face.

Brandy and I met my first day on the job. She works in the office and directly under Principal Stewart. Not *under him* under him, though I don't think it's not from lack of want. If it weren't in the employee handbook that relationships between the principal and staff is strictly forbidden, Brandy would have been all over him like he was catnip and her kitty was ready to play.

"He's all right," I mumble, turning my attention back to the folders I was labeling for my new filing system so she can't see the lie written all over my face.

"All right?" she exclaims loudly, walking toward my desk. "Are you blind or just plain mad? Maybe the fact that you haven't gotten laid in months has your hot guy radar off a bit?" she asks, reaching over and placing her hand on my forehead. "You don't appear to have a fever."

"Knock it off," I grumble, pushing her hand away.

"He sat by you. Does he smell as good as he looks?" Her eyes twinkle with excitement as she awaits my answer.

Yes, Brandy, he smells incredible. He smells so good I wanted to climb him like a tree in the middle of the teachers' lounge, coworkers and boss be damned.

Instead, I go with, "I didn't notice."

"Didn't notice?" Again, she reaches for my forehead.

"Stop!"

"I'm starting to get a little worried about you."

"I'm fine, Brandy. Just trying to get my room ready to go for Tuesday. It's difficult, though, having an *interruption* bothering me."

"Yeah, yeah, yeah. I know I'm keeping you from your color coding files and your fancy schmancy label maker, but aren't you at least a little bit interested in the hot new teacher?"

Oh, I'm interested, all right.

"Whatever, Brandy. He's decent looking, sure, but he's no Channing Tatum."

No, Channing Tatum has nothing on Sawyer.

"You're nuts."

"What's the big deal, anyway? Why does everyone have their panties in a tizzy?" I ask.

"You mean, besides the fact that he's hotter than Mount St. Helens after its eruption in nineteen eighty?"

I can't help but crack a smile. "Yeah, besides that."

"I hear he played baseball or something. Not sure. No ring on his finger, though, I definitely noticed that." Me too. "And besides, my panties aren't in a tizzy, they're soaked." Brandy gives me a wide wolfish grin, her blonde hair framing her heart-shaped face.

"I don't need to know anything about the state of your panties."

"Anyway, at least we'll have a little more eye candy to help get us through the school year, right?"

Understatement of the year.

"He's definitely an improvement over Mr. Burton and his coffee-stained ties," I smirk.

"God! How does one man miss his mouth so much?" she laughs, shaking her head. "All right, I'm going to head back down to the office and stare at Mr. Stewart's ass."

"Enjoy," I holler as she throws me a wave over her shoulder and exits my classroom.

The girl is crazy, but I love the hell out of her. We've become good friends over the last six years, and she definitely makes my time at school a little more entertaining.

Chuckling, I shake my head and get back to my color coded labels, but it doesn't hold my attention. Instead, I find myself booting up my computer and bringing up the Google search engine.

Sawyer Randall.

Enter.

It takes only a second to start bringing up stories and articles and pictures. I stare, awestruck, at the headline of the first article. With shaky fingers, I click on the link and start to read. My eyes devour the feature, my mind spinning as I try to process this shocking new data.

This can't be right.

Can it?

"Holy shit."

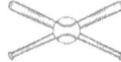

"Do you follow baseball?" I ask as I approach the counter at my sister's floral shop.

"Grandpa stole third base earlier this afternoon, if you know what I mean," my grandma says, a dirty smirk crossing her face.

"I think I just threw up in my mouth," I grumble, turning to find a mirrored disgusted look on my oldest sister Payton's face.

"Oh, there was nothing gross about it," Grandma adds. "He does this thing with his tongue and it–"

"Stop talking!" I proclaim before sticking my fingers in my ears.

I stopped in after school to see how Payton was doing at the shop, needing maybe a little advice from my oldest sister. Just my luck that she has a shop full of people. Linkin's mom, Karen, is here, making up a small bouquet of yellow and white daisies for the display case. She started working here full time earlier in the summer and seems to be enjoying it.

And of course, Grandma is here. It's like the woman can sniff out the potential for gossip and latches on to even the smallest thread like a pit bull to a bone.

My grandparents, Orval and Emma, are, well, different. Okay, fine. They're batshit crazy, but I mean that lovingly. At almost eighty-two, they bring new meaning to the phrase public displays of affection. They're constantly groping each other, are caught in compromising positions, and are the givers of the world's most inappropriate gifts.

But even with their own brand of sexually charged crazy, I love them to death.

They were there for us when our mother died.

I was just about to turn thirteen when our mom lost her fight with ovarian cancer. She left behind her husband and their six daughters, ranging from ten to eighteen. Dad is a pilot and used to fly commercial jets back then. When Mom passed, he took a step back from the large airlines that took him to all corners of the world, and started flying small charter planes for the rich and fancy out of a smaller airstrip not too far away.

His trips were shorter and he was home most nights, but it was still hard.

Enter Grandma and Grandpa.

They moved in with the seven of us and quickly became a strong tie that kept the family together. It wasn't easy, especially with six hormonal girls, but we managed because we had each other. I honestly believe we're a closer family because of that bond we formed, which started with our Mom. Trish Summer was an amazing woman.

I miss her so much.

"Why do you ask about baseball, Alison Jane?" Grandma asks, not even bothering to hide the fact that she's nosing around at the papers on the counter.

I contemplate on how much to tell them, but it's not like it's not going to get out sooner or later. I mean it's not every day a former professional baseball player starts teaching physical education in Jupiter Bay. Once school is back in session, everyone and their brother will know, even those who don't follow baseball.

"The new teacher is a former ball player," I decide to tell, casually.

"I once dated a professional baseball player, you know," Grandma says, a far-off look on her face.

After several seconds, Payton finally speaks. "You did?"

"Yes, yes. Joe. What a young stud that man was."

"What happened?" Karen asks, stopping what she's doing and listening to the conversation.

"It ran its course. He ended up marrying Marilyn." She goes back to straightening up the rosebuds that don't need straightening.

"Marilyn? As in Marilyn Monroe?" I ask, completely dumbfounded.

"You dated Joe DiMaggio?" Payton whispers, her shock as plain as the look on her face.

"Anyway," Grandma says, waving her hand as if it's no big deal. "You're working with one? What's his name?"

"Sawyer Randall." Just saying the name makes my heart start to beat a wee bit faster.

Grandma pulls out her phone and starts to type. I glance over at Payton, curious as to what she's doing. Did we bore her enough that she decided to check her email?

"There," she says with a victorious smile.

"What did you do?" Payton asks, stepping up beside Grandma and glancing down at her phone.

"I went to that Twitterbook. He has a stellar ass, AJ. I made sure to tell him," she says, clicking around on her phone.

"You told him?"

"She did," Payton confirms, reading the screen. "What a magnificent ass on that @sawyerrandall. I've seen plenty in my day and can't wait to get my hands on it. #SexySawyer #BestAssEver," Payton glances my way, fighting laughter.

"You're incorrigible."

Grandma continues to click through her phone. "Have you seen the *Sports Illustrated* spread he did wearing only his cleats and a backward ball cap? His glove is in the way of the goods, but I can tell he's packing. I have a nose for these things," she says, turning the phone to show me the picture she found.

And there it is.

Sawyer Randall standing at third base, his legs spread wide, as he crouches down to catch a ball. And yes, that glove is positioned *just right*. I can't imagine how many takes it took to capture this shot.

Lucky photographer.

"That's hot," Payton chimes in, a wide smile on her face.

"Knock that off. You're married now."

"Married, yes. Dead, no. There are no rules against looking, AJ."

"Truth," Grandma adds with a decisive head nod.

"Wait a minute," Payton says, grabbing the phone from Grandma's hand. My stomach starts to tighten as she studies the photo. It's only a matter of time now, and fortunately, I don't have to wait long before my torture begins. "That's him!" she proclaims.

I turn my attention to Karen beside me, helping her clean up small scraps of greenery and baby's breath from the large stainless steel workstation.

"Holy shit! You slept with Sawyer Randall?" She just couldn't keep this shit to herself, could she? Now she opens her big mouth in front of Grandma, who won't let this thing slide on a cold day in Hell.

"AJ! You were feeding the kitty with this gorgeous ball player? How? When? Why didn't you share the deets?"

"Thanks a lot," I grumble at my traitorous sister. She gives me an apologetic look as she shrugs her shoulders. "There's nothing to tell."

"Liar," Payton smirks. "I saw the way you were eye-fucking him at Lucky's that night." She turns and glances at Grandma. "It was so hot, even I needed a cigarette."

Rolling my eyes, I keep my attention on the little clippings of waste. "It wasn't what you think." I can feel their eyes on me as I pretend to dust off the remains of nonexistent leaves. "We didn't actually sleep together, though we might have slept together."

"Wait, what?" Karen asks, glancing to Payton to see if she understood.

"Can you explain?" Payton asks, crossing her arms over her chest and leaning back against the counter.

"Fine," I grumble, tossing the towel onto the clean table and turning their way, mimicking Payton's stance. "We left together. I'm pretty sure we both had every intention of... you know."

"*The sex*," Grandma chimes in with a grin.

"Yes. Anyway, I started to feel ill. I had been drinking a lot and, well, I ended up getting a little sick and passing out in his bed," I say in one quick breath.

"So, you slept *in the same bed* but didn't have *the sex*?" Payton fights the smile that threatens to take over.

"I had been mixing alcohol and there were shots involved, Dr. Watson," I defend.

"Oh, I remember," Payton says, snickering. "I can't wait to tell everyone," my double-crossing sister says, grabbing her own cell phone from her pocket and firing off messages to each of our sisters. Hell, she's probably making the announcement in the group text.

"No sex? You had that hunk of man-meat in bed with you and you didn't once dip the corndog in the batter? Have I not taught you anything, AJ?" Grandma gives me a total *I'm disappointed in you and can't even believe we're related* look.

"So, you slept in the same bed, but didn't actually sleep together. That must make working together a little awkward," Karen chimes in, slapping me upside the head with her reminder of the huge mess I've created.

"Slightly." I can't help my sarcastic tone.

"Well, you're just going to have to sleep with him then. That's the only way." Grandma gazes up at me with a proud smirk, kinda like she just solved the world hunger problem.

"Yes, because sleeping with a coworker *now* wouldn't cause any issues, I'm sure. At least back in July he wasn't technically a coworker yet. At least, I don't think he was." At this point, I'm not sure I trust my instincts when it comes to the opposite sex. In fact, I'm sure I don't. Not when you look at the long line of frogs I kissed that turned out to be total toads.

My phone starts to chime, letting me know the Summer sisters have seen whatever messages my big sister sent and are now responding. Awesome. Conversation seems to happen around me as I grab my phone. Yep, group text. And Grandma was included.

Jaime:	Holy shitballs! Sawyer Randall?! I just Googled him. *flame emoji*
Lexi:	Did you get a glance at the goods at least? A hand on it? What size bat is he swinging for the fences with???????????? MUST. KNOW. SIZE. OF. BAT.
Abby:	I'm sorry you got sick. *sad face emoji*
Meghan:	I Googled too. Yowzers, AJ! *insert gif of ovaries exploding*
Grandma:	He just responded to my Tweeterbook post. I'm inviting him to dinner. Tagged you too, AJ!

I glance up to see Grandma's nose in her phone and what could possibly be pure evil radiating from her pores. Don't let the sweet old lady charm fool you, folks. This woman is a mixture of crazy, wicked, and disobedient, all wrapped up in a Viagra-laced bow.

The Twitter notification appears on my screen as she grins victoriously at her device before slipping it into her pocket.

Jesus, Mary, and Joseph, is this really my family?

Sawyer

6

What to do in a small town where you don't really know anyone?

Good question. When you find the answer, let me know.

I'm practically climbing the walls with anxiety, needing to get out of the house a little bit. I made it through my first week of school fine, but am a little disappointed to report I didn't get a chance to steal a few moments alone with AJ. The only time I saw her in the teachers' lounge, she was having what appeared to be a private powwow with the school secretary. When I came in, they lowered their heads and seemed to whisper. I'm man enough to admit that I was seriously hoping it was me they were talking about. In fact, I was pretty certain it was about me, but I'm just not sure if it was for the reasons I wished for.

You know, that she found me crazy attractive and was going to ask me to share a cup of coffee sometime.

The attraction isn't the issue. I know it and she knows it. I felt it that night back in July, and if the way my cock stirs to life in my pants when she's near, I'd say it's still alive and thriving. And it sure as shit wasn't one-sided. You can't turn off that kinda attraction with the flip of a switch.

Now I just need to decide what to do with it.

AJ appears to be fine with ignoring my existence, pretending that I didn't have my hands down the back of her pants, the taste of her lips on my own, or the sound of her gasps filling my ears a mere month ago. Well, Miss Summer, I can't forget, and I sure as shit don't want to.

This isn't a game, but I'm filled with this sudden and all-consuming desire to win. And the prize? One brunette with invigorating green eyes and the mouth of a sailor. She's sin wrapped in proper khaki pants and sensible flats. She probably causes wet dreams for half the male student body with her button-downs that reveal just a hint of cleavage.

Miss AJ Summer, eighth grade math teacher.

Challenge accepted.

When the clock hits nine, I decide it's time to get out of the house. The air is warm, yet feels refreshing coming off the Bay as I climb into my Mercedes and practically peel out of the driveway. I can feel the tension evaporate with every mile I put between myself and the house, where it's quiet and, well, quiet. My mind starts to wander and the doubts start to creep in. Can I do this? Can I transition from one career to another without giving myself ulcers in the process? Fuck knows I've stressed enough over the interview, move, and first week at school.

But this is what I've always wanted.

I knew playing ball wouldn't last forever, and even though many will transition into broadcasting or a sports reporting position, I knew I wanted to do more. I wanted to work with the kids early in life, guiding those with a love for sports and nurturing their passions the way my old coaches did for me.

That's why I made sure I completed school before turning pro. I needed to have my ducks in a row when the time came.

And that time is now.

As I pull into town, a route that's becoming very familiar, I look for people. I don't need a big crowd, but I wouldn't mind shooting the shit with a few guys right about now over the game and drinking a few beers. Before I even realize it, I'm pulling into the lot next to Lucky's. Maybe the owner will be here again tonight and want to chat.

There's a handful a patrons inside, but not nearly as crowded as it was that fateful July night a month ago. I'm not quite sure what constitutes Saturday nightlife, but I don't really think this is it. Those same older gentlemen sit at one end of the bar; guys I'd probably consider the regulars of the joint. On the other end, I spy a handful of younger guys shootin' the shit with the bartender, who is not Lucky.

I head in their direction, but leave an empty stool between the guy at the end of their group and myself just in case they're not game for entertaining a stranger.

The guy behind the bar nods and walks my way. "What can I get ya?"

"Miller Lite bottle," I reply as I get comfortable on the stool.

My attention is pulled to the television above the bar where the Braves and Phillies are tied at one a piece at the bottom of the ninth. Bases are loaded and the closer is stepping up to bat for the Phillies. My heart starts to race as I recall moments like this. This is why I played the game. The thrill, the excitement, and sometimes even the letdowns. But in the end, it was still just a game, even if it had been my whole life.

Well, not my whole life, but for a while, pretty damn close.

"Sawyer Randall," I hear from the guy beside me, his face lighting up with recognition. The guy is tall with dark hair and eyes, and a friendly disposition. He's broad and tan, like maybe he spends time outdoors, and wears laugh lines around his eyes well.

The man reaches over and extends his hand. "Ryan Elson. I'm a big fan. Not of the Rangers, though, sorry. I'm from New York."

"Ahhh, Mets or Yankees?" I ask.

"Fuck the Yankees," he replies with a wide grin, which makes me laugh.

"You're all right, Ryan Elson," I confirm, patting him on the shoulder.

"This is Dean, Levi, and the one behind the bar is Linkin."

"Nice to meet you all," I say, suddenly feeling at ease with these guys.

Obviously, they know who I am, or at least Ryan does, so I sit back and wait for the next series of questions to come. They always do. What was it like in the pros? Carrie Doherty, huh? What was she like to wake up next to? How's the shoulder? Tough break about being let go from the Rangers. Any chance you'll be able to play ball again someday or have you reached your expiration date at thirty-three years old?

But those questions don't come.

"So, a teacher, huh?" Levi asks from the far end.

"Guilty," I reply, tossing some popcorn into my mouth.

"That's cool. It's not every day someone with your stats decides to head back to junior high," he says with a grin.

"No, definitely not. I had a few offers from Fox Sports and ESPN, but I didn't really want that. I'd always liked working with kids, so I thought PE and coaching was a better fit."

I wait for the next question in this series. Why teaching? It's not like you need the money.

And that would be true. I don't need the money. I was never into overspending on all the elaborate shit most other pro athletes seem to indulge in. I invested early on, paid off all of my parents' debt, and could live comfortably for the rest of my life playing golf or tennis at a country club.

But that's not me.

And I hate golf and tennis.

There's no way I could do that shit. I'd be bored and ready to crawl out of my skin after the first day.

"Our sister-in-law works at the school," the guy in the middle, Dean I think his name was, says.

"Yeah? Who's that?"

"AJ Summer."

Well, if that doesn't get my attention.

"Yeah? Sister-in-law?" I ask casually, yet my heart is racing in my chest.

"One of the middle ones. I'm married to Payton, the oldest. Then there's Jaime, Ryan's wife," Dean says.

"I'm dating Abby, one of the twins," Levi adds.

"And I knocked up the other twin, Lexi," Linkin chimes in as he dries off a glass.

"So there're five of them?" I ask, committing every tidbit of detail to memory.

"Six. There's one more. Meghan." Ryan glances down at his beer, a look crossing his face that I can't decipher before it becomes obscured. Solemn looks seem to appear on all of their faces, which lets me know something bad happened, probably to that other sister.

"Anyway, have you met AJ yet? She teaches math," Dean asks, the sadness on his face quickly pushed away.

My mind flashes to hungry lips and a wicked tongue that makes my cock start to harden in my pants. "I have. We sat next to each other at the staff meeting this week."

They each nod, but no one gives me any more dirt. I mean, is it too much to ask for these dudes to start spilling all of her dirty little secrets right now?

Yeah, probably. Guys usually could give two shits about that stuff.

"So are you rooting for the Rangers to go all the way or do you secretly have a favorite team?" Ryan asks as another beer is placed in front of him.

We end up chatting and watching sports highlights for the next hour, until the clock hits ten.

"Are you guys ready?" Levi asks, tossing a few bills on the battered bar top.

"Yeah, I'm surprised my phone hasn't gone off yet," Ryan says, pulling his phone from his pocket and lighting up the screen.

"They're probably all drunk and haven't even realized it's already getting as late as it is," Dean answers, pulling his own wallet and phone from his pocket.

"Tell Firecracker that I'll be home as soon as I close down at one," Linkin says behind the bar. He seems legitimately torn about having to stay and runs his hands through his hair.

"Will do, man. I'm sure she'll be fine. Grandma's staying," Ryan says as he stands up.

"Shit, don't remind me. I'm afraid I'm going to have to lock the bedroom door when I sleep tonight," Linkin quips with a subtle smile and the shake of his head.

"At least Orval isn't staying and you don't have to worry about hearing them screw in the next room," Ryan throws at him.

"No shit," Linkin says with a hearty laugh.

I must be wearing my confusion on my face as I try to follow their conversation. Levi steps up to me and fills me in. "Lexi was put on partial bed rest yesterday at her appointment to keep her off her feet. Linkin had already told Lucky he'd fill in for him this weekend, so the sisters are all over at their place keeping her company."

"Pizza and margaritas were on the menu. My guess is so is road-head," Ryan adds, slapping his hands together in victory and wearing an excited grin.

"And since I'm working until one, Grandma made herself comfortable in my guest room."

"Plus, he's opening in the morning at noon." Dean adds.

"Which is why I feel more comfortable with someone staying at the house. She's already starting to dilate, and even though the docs say the babies will be okay to come a little early, I'd feel a hell of a lot better if they'd stay inside Hotel Lexi for another month."

"Babies?" I ask.

"Yep, two," he confirms, a proud smile on his face.

"A twin is having twins," Levi adds.

"And Linkin has twin brothers," Ryan throws in.

"Wow, you guys don't slouch on getting the job done," I say with a laugh.

"We don't," Linkin says before turning to the guys. "I'll see you guys soon. Drive safe."

"I'm driving. I stopped drinking a while ago," Dean says before turning to me. "It was nice meeting you, Sawyer. Maybe we'll catch you again sometime."

"Yeah, I'd like that," I find myself saying and meaning it.

"Definitely," Ryan says, reaching for my hand. "We're having a cookout next weekend for Emma and Orval's anniversary. If you're not doing anything, you should come."

I almost ask if AJ will be there, but I bite the words back before I can let them fly. Of course she'll be there. It's her grandparents.

"Sounds good, actually. I don't really know too many people in town yet," I say.

"I figured. The party's moving from our place to Lexi and Linkin's since she's supposed to rest. Get the address from Linkin before you leave," Ryan says before heading out into the mid-August Saturday night.

When I turn my attention back to Linkin, he slips a napkin across the bar. Not the first time that's happened to me. Hell, not even the first time it was a dude. But I'm still thankful it's not a phone number with a big red lipstick kiss above it.

It's his address.

To a party.

One that AJ will be attending.

My night just started looking up even more.

I shove the napkin into my pocket and finish my beer.

"Have you met Grandma yet?" Linkin asks, a hint of a smile on his lips.

"Nope," I answer, then recalling a Twitter tag I received earlier in the week. I would have completely skipped over it, like I do the thousands of other tags and posts, but something in the post had me stopping. The old woman was talking about my ass in the first post, which caught my attention and begged for my standard thank you reply. But it was her response with a tag and talking about dinner that really drew me in.

@AJSummer.

I didn't click to follow her, but was tempted. Her page is set to private so I was unable to see anything besides her profile, which was your typical smiling photo.

"Well, Sawyer, you're in for a treat," Linkin says with a wide smile before turning his attention back to his work.

Something tells me he's right.

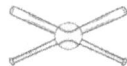

The first official day of school with students in attendance came and went in a flurry of teenage hormones and baseball stories.

The kids were excited, especially the athletic ones, when they discovered who their new PE teacher was. I tried to keep their focus, but it was too difficult. They all wanted the story, the draft, the injury, the lifestyle. The girls wanted to know about Carrie. I mean it's not every day your physical education teacher is a former pro baseball player who was married to a Victoria's Secret model, right?

Yeah, that's something I wasn't getting into with them.

Besides the fact that it was the first day back and everyone was hyped up on excitement and anticipation, throw me into the mix. I'm good-looking. I'm not being modest, just stating a fact. I've been named to *People*'s Sexiest Man Alive more times than I can count, been featured in *Playgirl* magazine, and posed nude for *Sports Illustrated*.

Shit, my ass has its own hashtag.

And I work hard in the gym to maintain that rating.

Now the halls are empty. School dismissed early for its first day, which is a welcomed reprieve. I knew the first day would be intense, but it was almost overwhelming. Kids everywhere, running, chatting, and trying to catch up on what they all did during the summer, and I can't remember a single name.

Except one particular name that I can't seem to forget.

Most of the teachers are either in the lounge, discussing the students in their classes, or still in their classrooms prepping for the next day. I don't see AJ congregating with the others, so as soon as I can slip out, I head down the empty hall that leads to the math classrooms.

Through the doorway, I see my new favorite teacher sitting behind her desk, writing on what appears to be a desk calendar. She's wearing those khaki capris that seem do as much for my overactive imagination as some skimpy overpriced lingerie. Add a pair of brown sandals and a light, flowy top that matches her eyes and she's a walking fantasy that I could watch all day long.

My reaction to her should scare me, but for some reason, it doesn't. I have a reputation of being a playboy that has followed me since I was signed. Young, good-looking, dated his share of models, actresses, and even a few Grammy-nominated singers. Then I met Carrie, and the tabloids were always looking for the dirt. Over the course of our relationship, I was a liar, a cheat, and a womanizer on more occasions than I can count, but that's what happens when you're in the spotlight.

In reality, I was anything but. I was never really into the party scene, even when I was young and women were throwing themselves at me like beads at Mardi Gras. Sure, I might have partaken in a little no-strings sex (hey, I'm a guy) when I was young and dumb, but it was never my MO. And never when I was married. I was always a one-woman kinda guy, and that didn't change while I was with Carrie.

But I'm not interested in reliving my past, nor thinking about my ex. Instead, I'd like to focus on the woman in front of me, filling out upcoming events on her calendar. Her long dark hair is pulled up in a ponytail, leaving the long, slender column of her neck exposed. Suddenly, I want to kiss and lick that neck more than I want my next breath.

In fact, I crave it.

I must make a noise (probably a groan) because her eyes the color of brilliantly cut emeralds turn and focus on me standing in her doorway. If she's surprised to see me there, she doesn't show it. "Hey," she says, her voice as smooth as butter.

"Hey. How was your day?" I ask, taking a few steps into her classroom.

"It was good. Yours?"

"Not too bad. I probably gave a hundred autographs and was asked to senior prom."

"Prom?" she asks.

"Yeah. Apparently, she wanted to go ahead and lock me in as her date for when she's a senior in high school," I chuckle.

"Wow, that definitely tops the request I had for an extra hall pass this afternoon." Those full lips I've often pictured wrapped around my cock smile widely and make my dick twitch and start to harden.

"Naw, I bet he just wanted an excuse to chat with the hot teacher," I state bluntly as I approach her desk. She looks so tiny when she's sitting in a chair, but I know from personal experience that she fits ever so fucking perfectly against my body.

She glances up, her gaze slightly humorous beneath long lashes. "Actually, it was girl."

"Hmmm, well, that might change things a bit." I click my tongue inside my cheek and gaze down at what I could easily dub the most beautiful woman in the world. She doesn't need a spread in a magazine or to wear practically nothing while walking the runway to earn the title. She just has to be herself, looking up at me with humor and question in her eyes, the damn long, slender column of her neck begging for my tongue.

Devine.

I want her.

The room seems to fill with a sexual charge that steals my breath and makes my heart race. She must sense the change. Those intoxicating eyes darken and her breathing quickens. That mouth I had my lips all over opens, forming the most dick-hardening little O. Damn, this woman is sexy.

She stands up, the top of her head hitting just below my chin. My legs move, completely on their own accord, until I'm invading her personal space. She looks up at me, eyes wide, her hands forming tight fists at her side, as if she's struggling to keep from reaching for me.

Well, join the fucking club, sweetheart.

A wisp of hair escapes her ponytail and hangs down along her cheek. My fingers move, grasping that tendril of hair and moving it behind her ear. Of course, I make sure my fingers graze along the softness of her skin, heating up my blood clear down to my toes. The sweetest gasp slips from her lips and goes straight to my cock. The bastard is impossibly hard right now with no relief in sight. Not as long as AJ Summer is in the vicinity.

She licks her lips right before my eyes, and I take it as a sign that she wants the kiss as much as I do. And holy fuck do I want this kiss.

I bend down slowly, making sure to keep eye contact. Her plump lips get closer and closer, and I can practically taste her already. Her eyes flutter closed, her chin lifted upward as she waits for me to claim her lips with my own. There's only one thing left to do, one simple, pure craving, and that's to claim her in a kiss.

My lips hover over hers, my body igniting and desire taking over, when the moment is broken like delicate crystal on a tile floor.

"AJ, how was your... oh, I didn't realize you had a visitor already."

She pulls back quickly and stumbles into her desk. Her eyes are wide as she runs a shaky hand over her button-down shirt, in an effort to smooth away wrinkles that aren't there. "Hi," she gasps, her voice crazy-high and full of nerves.

"Randall," he says with a bite, taking in our closeness and starting to do the math.

"Bryce, good to see you," I say, leaning back against the chalkboard and crossing one tennis shoe covered ankle over the other. I put my hands into the pockets of my gym shorts, not even caring that my cock is unmistakably hard against my stomach. One pair of tight boxer briefs is the only thing keeping it from tenting my basketball shorts.

"Sorry to interrupt," he says, his eyes volleying back between AJ and me.

"You didn't," she insists. "Sawyer just stopped by to see how my first day went," she adds, turning her attention to me and noticing my pants. Her eyes do her best impression of a cartoon, bugging out of her head, as she quickly turns her full attention to Bryce. "How was your day?"

"Good, good," he says, walking over to where she's standing a few feet from me. He completely ignores my presence as he proceeds to tell her all about his day, including those students he feels will make great additions to her Honors Math class next year.

AJ tries to pull me into their conversation, which doesn't seem to make the other man in the room happy. He looks tense every time I speak, which makes me smile inwardly a bit. He's threatened by me, as well he should be. I'm not about to step aside and let him flirt and ask her out.

Fuck that.

And fuck him.

She's mine.

She just doesn't know it yet.

7

AJ

The backyard is set up with tables and chairs, streamers and balloons. There's enough food to feed an army, thanks to Levi and Abby, and coolers on the porch filled with water, pop, and beer. A few friends of my grandparents' mill around, chatting about the warm weather and the approaching end of summer, as we all wait for the guests of honor.

Where are they?

"The guests are arriving," Payton whispers.

"They were supposed to be here almost thirty minutes ago," Jaime says nervously, stirring the meatballs in the Crock-Pot.

"You don't think anything happened to them, do you?" Abby asks, worrying her bottom lip between her teeth.

"I'm sure they're fine, babe," Levi says as he comes up behind her and places a kiss on her cheek.

"Yeah, they probably got tied up in their red room," Ryan laughs, making us all groan in disgust. It's not every day your eighty-something year old grandparents construct their own red room of pain after seeing *Fifty Shades of Grey*.

"Why did you have to bring that up? I had blissfully forgotten all about the fact that my childhood bedroom now houses a Saint Andrew's Cross and ball gags," I reply, choking down the bile threatening to come up.

"Watch out or you'll end up getting just that for Christmas this year," Meghan says, a rare smile on her face. Not that she doesn't smile, but they're rarer than they used to be before Josh's death. So when you see a real Meghan smile, it melts your heart and reminds you that as difficult as it can be, life goes on.

"Or I could get a sex swing, like Abby and Levi," I sass.

"Stop talking," Abby begs, her face turning a gorgeous shade of fuchsia.

"Yes, please stop talking," Dad says as he joins our group and gives hugs to each of his daughters.

"They will be here shortly, I'm sure. I'd rather not think about what they could be doing in the house that would have kept them," Dad says, shivering as he joins Dean and Ryan at the grill.

"Oh, I forgot to mention that Nick ended up staying in town, so I invited him to stop by," Meghan tells us.

Nick would be Dr. Adams, her boss. She's worked for him since she graduated college and came back to Jupiter Bay. Nick had just started himself at one of the few dental offices in town, and recently purchased the business from Dr. Zastrow when he retired.

"Ohhhhh, how is the good doc?" Payton asks, waggling her eyebrows suggestively.

"He's fine," Meghan shrugs. "But he broke up with Collette last week. He's been moping around the office, so I invited him to get him out of the house."

Dr. Adams has been absolutely wonderful where Meghan is concerned. After Josh's accident, he gave her as much time off as she needed to grieve, and still continues to be a friend. We've silently wondered if maybe something more could come of their budding friendship, but there was always the factor of Collette.

But now…

"He's here," Jaime says, nodding to the side of the house where Nick Adams has just emerged.

He meets Meghan in the yard, offering her a friendly smile. He's a great looking guy, with dark hair just long enough to tangle your fingers in and hazel eyes. In fact, there was a time where I wouldn't have said no to the good doctor if he had asked me out. Meghan actually planned to set us up once, but then he started dating Collette Cartwright so nothing more became of it.

Now, even knowing that he's single again, I don't feel anything toward him. Yes, he's hot with those hard muscles you can only achieve by spending time working out, but he just doesn't do anything for me.

At least not anymore.

Now, my panties seem to become useless just by conjuring up the image of one certain baseball player. The way he kissed me back in July, like he was about to devour me and provide orgasm upon orgasm for as long as he could dish them out, is enough to keep me up late into the night. I've relived that kiss so many times, it's tattooed onto my brain and shows no sign of ever going anywhere.

Then there's the way I can feel those sexy blue eyes watching me at school. I can feel them in the teachers' lounge and when I'm walking down the hall. It's so intense, it's as if I could literally feel him reach out and touch me. And then there's the fact that he's so freaking tall. I've never been attracted to someone who's six six (that's his height, according to his Wikipedia page). He's like a skyscraper, all broad shoulders and rippling muscles.

I'm completely enthralled with a coworker, and there's nothing I can do about it.

And the object of my late night self-induced orgasms just walked around the side of the house.

Shit.

"Oh my God, is that who I think it is?" Lexi asks when she waddles out the back door. Linkin is there, guiding her down the step and to the lounger he bought just for the day so she could come out and enjoy the party without having to lift a finger and be off her feet.

My heart is suddenly in my throat with excitement and nerves. Mostly nerves. Or maybe anticipation.

Sawyer stops and talks to Dean, Nick, and Ryan, and as soon as Levi and Linkin see him, they head over too. They're all chatting and laughing like old friends, which makes me wonder how in the hell the new guy in town is suddenly buddy-buddy with my family.

"My word, that man is so much hotter in person than spread across the glossy pages of all those magazines," Grandma says, startling us with her sudden presence.

"Grandma," Abby chastises. "It's your anniversary," she reminds.

"I'm aware, Abs. And your grandpa is in a very good place right now. See that smile?" she asks, pointing to the grin my grandpa wears as he walks over to the guys. "That's the look of a very sated man who spent the afternoon harpooning the salty longshoreman."

"What?" Jaime asks.

"Which part did you not understand, Jaimers? The part about your grandfather being very well sated or the euphemism I used to describe *the sex*? That's why we're late, you know. When Orvie takes one of his pills, well, he turns into a ravenous madman, hell-bent on jamming the clam with his fishing pole."

"Jesus," I groan, looking to extract myself from this conversation.

Quickly.

"Oh, don't be a stick in the mud. I promised Grandpa oral for our sixtieth. That's much better than the traditional diamond gift we should give."

"Oral. The gift that keeps on giving," Lexi giggles, holding her massive stomach while it shakes.

"You better watch it, Lexi, or you're gonna pee your pants," I retort, making my sister stop laughing immediately.

"Shit, you're right," she grumbles.

"Seriously, ladies, check out the ass on that man. Do you think he'd give us a private replay of that naked photo shoot?" Grandma asks, fanning her flushed face.

"Us, probably not, but AJ? I'd say the chances of that happening are looking pretty good," Meghan says, taking her eyes off the celebrity long enough to glance my way.

"I agree with Meggy. He keeps glancing over here with that *I want to fuck you against the side of the house* look, and I'm pretty sure it's only directed at one of us," Jaime adds, giving me a wink and a smile.

"He probably just wants to finish what he started before the puking," Lexi chimes in, reminding us all of the reason I didn't sleep with him the first time.

"You should be lucky he's even still interested, AJ. Puking usually makes men run the other direction," Jaime says.

"How do you know he's interested?" I ask, glancing back at the guys and finding those blue eyes still on me.

"He's interested," they all say in unison.

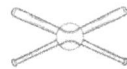

"Hey." His deep, husky voice sends shivers down my spine.

"Hi," I reply with a squeak, turning my attention away from the food and toward the tall drink of water standing beside me.

"Beautiful day," he says, reaching forward and grabbing a handful of pretzel sticks.

"It is." I feel his eyes on me as I keep stirring the pasta salad that doesn't need to be stirred. The silence stretches on for one minute, then two, and starts to unnerve me. "So..." I start, and let the word trail off.

"So…" he mimics, giving me a cocky smile.

"So, what are you doing here?" I finally blurt out.

"I was invited," he says, popping another pretzel stick into his mouth with a smile.

"Invited?" I ask, trying to recall if I ever talked about my grandparents' anniversary celebration while at school. I know I talked about it with Brandy while we ate lunch earlier in the week, but I don't think any of the other teachers paid us any attention, and I don't recall Sawyer being in the lounge at the time.

"Yeah, I had beers with the guys last Saturday night, and they invited me. Since I'm new in town, and all, they thought I'd enjoy coming over and hanging out for a while. Is that a problem?" he asks, his gaze intent as he stares down at me.

"No, no problem. I was just surprised to see you, is all." My voice sounds unnaturally pitchy and breathy.

He leans forward and invades my personal space. I can smell the detergent on his shirt and the soap on his skin, and it takes everything I have not to lean forward and run my nose along his neck and inhale. "A good surprise, I hope."

I don't confirm or deny, which makes him smile. I, of course, find myself grinning back with a wily little smirk.

"Come on, buttercup, I'll let you sit by me at dinner," Sawyer says, sliding his very large hand along my lower back and escorting me to the food line.

My family gathers around, along with the extra guests here to help celebrate, and it's like no one cares that we're eating dinner with a former pro baseball player. I mean he has a World Series ring in his jewelry box, for crying out loud. Yet my family is chatting with him about the difference between an inlaid brick patio and stamped concrete, and whether Lexi's twins will be boys or girls.

"So, Randall, what are your intentions with my granddaughter?" I hear my grandpa ask from across the picnic table.

"What?" I gasp, my eyes as wide as the paper plate holding my hamburger. "There are no intentions," I insist, everyone in the yard suddenly paying close attention to our conversation.

"Actually, there are, sir. I intend to date your granddaughter," Sawyer replies casually, yet directly to my grandpa.

Grandpa stares down the man sitting beside me with a critical eye. My face flushes with a rare blush while I watch, mouth agape, as they continue to stare each other down. Hell, even my sisters sit back and watch the show.

"Good deal, son. Make sure you don't skimp in the bedroom department. Women love a good wine, dine, and romp in the sheets, you hear?"

I make a gargly, gaspy noise that resembles me choking. "I'll make sure not to withhold, sir," I hear Sawyer reply over the blood swooshing in my ears. And, damn it, if I don't catch the humor in his voice.

"Oh, I'm pretty sure a big, strong man like yourself would *never* disappoint in the bedroom. I've seen your stance and that big Louisville Slugger you carry," Grandma practically coos.

"Dear God, kill me now," I grumble over the laughter of my sisters. "This is what you went through?" I ask Jaime, seeking confirmation. "I laughed when we all showed up at Ryan's place and Grandma called the Coast Guard, and now this is my payback, isn't it?"

"It is," my sister confirms.

"And for when she found the butt cheek prints on my workstation and called everyone to find out if they were theirs," Payton adds.

"That was funny," I retort.

"Or how about when she gave me a sex swing and you thought it was the funniest thing in the entire world?" Abby asks.

I shrug, fighting the smile, as everyone snickers at the memory.

"And when she thought Linkin was a stripper and had him dance for me while I was blindfolded and tied to a chair? You laughed."

I did. I laughed then, and I'm laughing now. Turning to the man sitting next to me, I plead, "We're completely crazy. You should run away screaming, quick. No one would think less of you if you did," I tell him, not even close to joking.

"Are you kidding? I'm kinda digging your brand of crazy," he says with that smile that makes my heart flutter and my panties wet.

"Then that must make you a little crazy, too," I say with a matching smile.

"That I am, AJ. That I am."

Sawyer

Two things I've discovered in my brief time here is that this group may be the closest family I've ever met, and at the same time, they're probably the dirtiest. And considering I've spend the past ten years on the road, traveling with guys who have perfected the art of the hook-up, that's fucking saying something.

The grandparents are… well, they're a hoot. I couldn't even tell you when the last time my face hurt this much from smiling. Not much in life has given me reason to smile lately, so it feels awesome just to sit in a lawn chair with a beer in my hand, laughing at the inappropriate banter of the Summer clan.

Listening to their stories and their teasing makes me miss my family.

I end up staying to the end of the party. Partly because the company is so easy and comfortable that I feel like I have real friends for the first time since I don't even know when. For the last decade, everyone wanted something and friendships felt... off. Forced. I'm not saying I didn't find valuable friendships with certain teammates along the way, but nothing like I feel right now. I can see myself having a beer with these guys on a Friday night after a long week, sure, but it's more than that.

It's more than a few guys sitting around, bragging about who they bagged the night before or the new luxury car they bought their wife to keep her happy. It's an instant camaraderie that I felt that first night at the bar and sense it even further now that we're all together in a family setting.

I didn't realize I was missing it until it practically slapped me upside the head.

The other reason I find myself tearing down tables and stacking them in the back of Levi's truck is because of AJ. I crave more time, more moments with her. She's helping pick up her sister's backyard and put it back together after this shindig, so that's what I do too. Plus, I can keep snacking on these bacon-wrapped scallops that Levi made. They're fucking delicious.

"Thanks for your help," she comes up beside me after the final dish has been taken inside.

"It was no problem," I reply casually, shoving my hands into my pockets to keep from taking her into my arms and kissing the shit out of her.

"Hey, AJ, you about ready?" Jaime hollers from the back door, her purse tucked under her arm.

It's late, the breeze off the Bay cool, even for late August. I see goose bumps pepper her arms as she gazes up at me, eyes hooded under long, dark eyelashes. Her eyes fill with confliction, and I know it's time to make my move. Stepping closer, I'm rewarded with the scent of her lotion and sweet perfume. She smells like sunshine, all fresh and intoxicating.

I want to be the one to take her home. I want her in my car, just like she was that night many weeks ago. I want a chance to find out if this indescribable chemistry is as undeniable as it feels. And fuck yes, I'd love to finish what we started that night in July.

But not tonight.

Tonight, I want the chance to spend more time with her, even if it's just a trip across town, because I can't seem to get enough of her.

She feels it. Her eyes shine with resolve, and maybe a little question too, as she turns her head a bit to answer her sister. "Actually, go ahead. I'm gonna catch a ride with Sawyer." Her eyes never leave mine.

Jaime snickers from the doorway. "You're gonna get a *ride,* all right." The insinuation is there and makes me smile.

AJ rolls her eyes. "Knock it off, *Grandma*. Some people can demonstrate self-control."

"Whatever," she replies before throwing a smile my way. "Nice to meet you, Sawyer."

"Nice to meet you, as well."

"Drive safely. Remember to keep the horse in the barn until you're safely at home," she adds, giggling like a little girl.

"Says the girl who's about to give road-head," AJ retorts, earning another laugh from her sister.

"I heard road-head! Let's go," Ryan's voice boosts through the night, as he comes up behind his wife and slaps her on the ass.

After quick goodbyes, we're left alone again. The air becomes electrically charged and I suddenly can't get to my car quick enough. I'm silent as I watch the breeze lightly blow her brown hair across her forehead. My fingers twitch as I bring them to her face and brush back the strands.

"Are you ready?" I ask, not really sure what I'm referring to. Ready to go? Ready to indulge in another mind-blowing kiss? Ready to see where this chemistry takes us?

Yes. All of that.

I lead her around the house and toward my car. My hand rests comfortably on her lower back, the hem of her top riding up and revealing just a sliver of warm flesh. She's silent as I open the door and she slips inside. Her toned legs look six feet long as she sits in the seat, her tanned limbs looking delicious against the black leather. My heart pounds like a snare drum in my chest as an all too familiar sense of déjà vu washes over me.

I wonder if she's thinking the same thing.

We're both quiet as I pull away from the street and start driving. I have no idea where I'm going, but I keep moving. At some point, she's going to have to tell me where she lives, right? Otherwise, my only option is to head to my place, which doesn't sound like a bad idea in the least. Or I could just ask her where she lives.

That's probably the better idea.

Fuck knows if I take her back to my place, I'm going to strip her naked and lick every square inch of her sexy little body.

Adjusting the sudden discomfort in my pants, I turn to my passenger. "Are you gonna tell me where you live?"

"Oh, ummm, yeah. Turn right at the next stoplight."

Following her directions, I pull in front of a small yellow house with a little white picket fence around the front walk. It's cute and quaint and seems perfect for my favorite math teacher. With my car in park, I hop out and meet her around the passenger side of the car.

"You don't have to walk me up," she says as she grips my hand and stands beside my car.

"I want to."

I don't comment on the fact that she doesn't let go of my hand as I walk her up the concrete steps that lead to her front door. "Thank you for the ride," she says, pulling her keys from her purse.

"You're welcome." My eyes are glued to hers and I can see everything swirling around within those green orbs. Excitement, hesitation, and maybe even a little resolution mix together in a tornado of emotions. "Go out with me."

I blurt the words without giving a single consideration, and frankly, there's nothing for me to think about. I want to date her. I want to take her to dinner and maybe a movie. I want to work for her affection in a way I haven't had to in years. The prospect of wooing her, not knowing if a second date is a guarantee just because of my fucking name or occupation, is thrilling.

Almost as thrilling as the thought of stealing a kiss at the end of that date.

"But we work together," she says softly.

"We do," I confirm, reaching up and slipping a loose strand of hair behind her ear. "It's not forbidden, and to be completely transparent, I wouldn't care if it was. I'd love to take you out, AJ. A real date, where I pick you up and we go have dinner. I'll probably hold your hand as we walk to the car, and if I'm a really good boy, maybe you'll reward me with a goodnight kiss."

AJ raises a single eyebrow, the faintest smirk playing on her full, kissable lips. "Well, I don't know about that. Maybe I'm not the kiss-on-the-first-date kinda girl."

I can't help but smile at the memory of her sexy little body wrapped around mine, as we started toward my hotel room, flashes through my mind. I knew nothing more about her than her first name, but neither of us cared. Of course, that night didn't end the way either of us anticipated, but it was still quite memorable.

Stepping into her personal space, I slide my hand up her jaw and thread my fingers into her hair. Her eyes dilate dark, filling with need and anticipation. "That's all right, sweetheart. Something tells me you'll be worth the wait." Leaning forward, my lips connect with the warm, soft skin on her forehead. The slightest little gasp slips from her lips, causing all the blood in my body to rush just south of my belt and my lips to linger just a bit longer than probably deemed appropriate.

"Go out with me. Next Saturday."

Glancing down, I'm rewarded with a genuine smile and sparkling eyes. "Okay."

And now I'm the one smiling. Big. Like a fool.

"I'll see you Monday at school," I say, taking a step back and severing the contact I crave with her. Something flashes across her face. Disappointment, maybe? Like she needs the same contact I do.

"Monday," she confirms with a nod.

I watch as she unlocks her door and pushes it open, about to step inside. "Oh, AJ?" She quickly turns around. "How do you take your coffee?"

Her eyebrows bunch together in confusion, but she answers. "As much cream and sugar as possible. I prefer caramel lattes so I have to doctor up the nasty, weak coffee in the teachers' lounge to get it as close as possible," she says with a shrug.

I nod in confirmation and shove my hands into my pockets. AJ lets herself into her house, turning and facing me once more before shutting the door. Neither of us says a word, but a whole conversation is had with our eyes.

Something is brewing between us. Hell, something has been cooking since that night we left that bar together. It's been simmering, slowly building the most electric charge I've ever experienced. There's no telling what'll happen when I finally get my hands on her naked body, my mouth against that delicate skin.

My cock throbs in my shorts just thinking about it.

"Good night," she whispers before slowly closing the door. I listen for the latch to secure before returning to my car. I'm picturing all of the glorious things I want to do to her body when we finally get to finish what we started. We'll start with a date, but ultimately, I want so much more from AJ Summer.

Sure, her body.

But more importantly, I want her time.

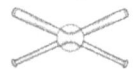

"Randall! How's it goin', man?" my former teammate and probably closest friend Joel Cougar hollers into the phone.

"It's going, Joel. How's it hanging?" I ask in return, waiting for his familiar reply.

"Hangin' to my knees, but the ladies don't complain," he quips before a bark of laughter booms from the cell phone in my hand, making me smile.

"Same ol' Joel."

"And same ol' Sawyer," he replies over the sound of muffled voices.

"What's up, man?"

"Just finishing up practice. Headin' to DC in a few weeks. Thought maybe you'd consider makin' the drive. That Podunk seaside town is only about three hours away from Nationals Park, ya know?"

Yeah, I'm well aware that the Rangers are heading to Washington DC in a few weeks. I know their damn schedule probably better than most of the guys on the roster. "Yeah, I could probably make it up. I'll check into getting tickets for the Sunday game."

"Let me. I'll get you a seat right behind the dugout so we can give ya shit the whole time," Joel says with a chuckle.

"Actually," I start, clearing my throat, "if you'd get me two tickets, I'd appreciate it."

Silence follows my request. "No shit? You seeing someone?"

I shift in my chair on the back deck, the blazing sun not the only thing causing me to feel like I'm in the hot seat. "Kinda," I say, not really wanting to get into it any further. "It's new."

"But, you're wanting to bring her to a game? With all the guys there? With you-know-who there?" I don't need to ask who he's referring to. The weight of his words can only implicate my ex.

"It's not likely I'd see her. It's a big park."

"True. And Carrie wouldn't be caught anywhere outside of the air-conditioned WAG box," he adds, referring to the wives and girlfriends box that is set up at every ballpark. By the end of the game, Carrie had no clue how I played or what my stats were, but she could tell you all about who was screwing who and who's shiny new diamond was bigger than everyone else's.

I snort at his comment because it's true. Carrie loved being married to a baseball player for status, not because she cared for the game.

Or me.

"Anyway, I'll get ya two tickets, man. They'll be at will-call."

"Thanks." A mixture of anxiety at returning to a ballpark for the first time since my injury and excitement to smell the grass and hear the sound of the bat cracking against the ball. Hell, maybe they'd let me wipe some chalk on my hands for old times' sake. It has always been one of my favorite scents.

Well, that and AJ's perfume.

I wonder what she'd say if I took her to Washington to watch a game. Will she bitch and whine like Carrie, or would she scream at the shit calls the umps make and trash-talk the batters? Something tells me she's more of the latter than the former. AJ doesn't scream high maintenance, but she doesn't exactly say bleacher babe either.

I guess time will tell. I'll have a date or two under my belt to get to know her better. Maybe I won't say anything about the game until after our date on Saturday. This way, if it isn't her thing or we don't hit it off the way I envision, there's no weirdness or hard feelings. But something tells me AJ will be the surprising change I need in my life. No, I wasn't expecting to find a woman I'm interested in so closely after my divorce or relocation to Jupiter Bay, but I'm not about to question it.

"Tell me about the hottie, man. I mean she's hot, right?"

Laughing, I decide to indulge my friend just a bit. "She's gorgeous."

"Tell me more," he grunts before I hear a door slam before the background noise is completely gone.

"Why is it suddenly quiet? You're not locked in the bathroom, about to stroke one out, are you?"

"Not in the locker room. I'll wait until I'm home alone tonight to spank it to mental images of your new girl," he teases. Even with the humor in his words, I still see red.

"I'd kill you," I growl, not even caring that I'm giving him the exact response he wanted.

"You didn't give a shit that everyone and their brothers saw your wife practically naked in a magazine, but you're getting all bent out of shape now?" He pauses for dramatic effect. "You really like her."

No point in denying it. "I do."

"Good for you, dude. I can't wait to meet her."

"Never mind. I'm not bringing her now."

"You better! I want to meet this chick who has your dick in knots and your balls in her hand."

"I don't know about that, but I enjoy spending time with her. We'll see if it goes anywhere," I add casually, taking another pull from my beer bottle.

"Anyway, I need to get off here. We're in the weight room after practice this afternoon before catching a flight to Chicago tomorrow morning." The guys are getting ready to start a three-game series tomorrow night against the Sox.

"I don't miss those Sunday practices." The words are spoken aloud, but are mostly for myself.

"I bet not," Joel groans as someone pounds on the door. "Gotta go, man. Griffin's itchin' to get in the john before practice starts."

"I'll see you in a few weeks," I tell him.

"Awesome. I'll email Shelly as soon as I hang up and get those tickets for ya."

"Thanks, man."

"Later," he says before signing off, leaving me alone in silence.

The waves gently crash against the shore as the Sunday afternoon sun blazes high in the sky. I can't get over how much has changed in the last several months. Injured. Let go from my contract, ending my career. Divorced. Relocated to another state. My first teaching and coaching gig. It's a lot to take in, that's for sure, but nothing that I can't handle.

Especially when I think about having someone like AJ by my side.

Smiling, I finish off my beer and head inside. There are still a few boxes to unpack and my home office to set up. Plus, with every tick of the clock, I'm that much closer to seeing a certain brown-haired math teacher who makes my dick hard and my dirty fantasies flare to life.

Five days of AJ before next Saturday.

Date night.

AJ

I juggle my satchel bag, my purse, and my travel coffee mug as I try to slip my key into the knob of my classroom. Inside, the air is cooler than the hallway, but has that stale I-just-sat-here-for-two-days smell. It reminds me that I haven't bought any of those Glade Plugins yet, which helps keep the smell of teenage hormones and sweat from taking over my classroom. Even after PE, the girls aren't so bad, but some of the boys reek of sweaty gym socks and deodorant-less adolescence.

Of course, thinking of the way the boys require extra deodorant after gym class reminds me of their teacher, who was the sole reason I tossed and turned half the night and woke up wet. He'd also be the star of the dirty movie my mind conjured up while I was showering and having to take care of that pesky little problem I seem to have woken up with. If I were a guy, I would have had serious morning wood.

And that just gets me thinking of Sawyer's morning wood. Recalling how hard and thick it was pressed against my stomach, while his mouth devoured me, definitely didn't help matters much this morning, and it appears to not be helping much now.

Fanning my suddenly flushed face, I turn on the lights and enter my room. Locking my purse in my desk drawer, I pull out my grade book and the papers I took home to work on this past weekend. With the celebration of my grandparents' anniversary on Saturday, I ended up spending much of my Sunday afternoon sunning on my back porch and grading the papers. Well, until memories of Sawyer's lips pressed against my forehead and the way his eyes lit up when I said yes to his date offer, crept back into my mind.

And those silly little reminiscences are what keeps my heart fluttering and my cheeks slightly pinked even now, two days later.

"Holy cheese and rice, did you see the way that man fills out those nylon basketball shorts? I think I had an orgasm in the teachers' lounge," Brandy coos as she waltzes into my classroom, our coworker Natalie Johnson hot on her heels.

"She practically groaned when he slid in beside her to put something in the fridge," Natalie says, a wide grin on her pretty face.

"He smells yummy. Like drop-your-panties yummy. We could bottle it up, you know? I'd call it 'Essence of Delicious PE Teacher' and would make millions."

I can't help but snort at the truth in her statement. The man smells incredible, even when he was outside and in the sun half the day. Can you imagine what would happen to hormones everywhere when you add in sweat? Like after one of his baseball games or something? Panties everywhere would combust. It would be an epidemic, I'm sure.

I make a mental note to Google search his games.

"What happened there? You just whimpered," Natalie asks, giving me a knowing smile.

"Nothing," I squeak out over my suddenly parched throat. "How was your weekend?" I ask.

Natalie proceeds to tell me all about their boat trip up the coast, and how her husband, Stuart, caught some of his biggest fish while she read. Natalie and Stuart got married earlier in the year and are definitely still in that honeymoon phase. He often sends her bouquets of her favorite flowers or shows up and surprises her with lunch. Natalie was a year older than me in school, but I've known her most of my life. Her brother, Nick, is well-known, also, even though he was a few more years older than me in school. Everyone knows him as Dr. Adams, one of the dentists in town and Meghan's boss.

"Oh, shoot, AJ, I brought that book you wanted to read. It's in my classroom," Natalie says.

Checking my watch, I reply, "We've got a few minutes before class starts. Why don't we run down and get it?"

"I better get back to the front office. Principal Stewart will be wondering where the hell I am. Maybe he'll even want to punish me," says Brandy, waggling her eyebrows suggestively, before turning and practically skipping in the opposite direction.

I follow Natalie down to her classroom and retrieve the book. It's a smutty romance novel about a bad boy prince, who must take over the throne after his father's death. He leaves behind a trail of broken hearts until he runs into a maid, knocking her on her ass. It's one of those forbidden, taboo novels that I can't help but devour. Abby started me on them a few years back after one that she edited released, and I've been hooked on sexy romances ever since.

When I step back into my classroom, I instantly notice the change in my room. There's a familiar scent in the air. Something masculine and woodsy, mixed with a bit of sweet. On my desk, I see a cup. Not just any cup, but a very tall coffee cup with the logo of my favorite corner coffee house on the front. My heart somersaults in my chest as I approach the gift, noting the Post-It attached to the top.

Good morning.

That was all it said, but I knew who it was from. A smile wide enough to back up traffic on the freeway sweeps across my face as I bring the cup to my lips. Warm, rich caramel sends my taste buds soaring, the aroma of rich caffeine perking my slow brain like those cheesy coffee commercials from my childhood.

A caramel latte.

And it's wonderful.

Well played, Mr. Randall. Very well played.

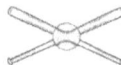

Each morning throughout the week, I return to my classroom with my crappy cup of stale lounge coffee to find some sort of treat alongside my mouthwatering caramel latte. On Tuesday, it was an apple with a note that said *For my favorite teacher*. Wednesday, I discovered a homemade cinnamon roll, the cream cheese frosting still warm. The note read *This smells almost as good as you*. I practically swooned as I reached for the fork and took my first bite. On Thursday, I found a raspberry Danish. The butter crust was flaky and melted in my mouth as I took my first bite. *Sweet, decadent, and mouthwatering. Just like you*. My knees grew a little weak as his words stirred up every desire I had.

Now, as I head back to my classroom, gross cup of nasty coffee in hand, I can't help but wonder what kind of surprise Sawyer has left today. I know I won't be drinking this stuff, but it's part of the song and dance we've been doing all week. I leave my room and he leaves a treat and yummy coffee on my desk for when I return.

Only this time, when I return to my classroom, there's no coffee on my desk. No sweet treat. No note.

Nothing.

Disappointment settles in as I slowly make my way to my desk. Reflexively, I take a drink from the cup in my hand and make a face at the nasty, lukewarm stuff they call coffee. My heart drops in my chest, like my butt does to my chair.

I should have known he was too good to be true. After years of finding nothing but toads, it's not likely my luck will change soon, right? I mean, Sawyer was great on the outside (really, really great), but everyone knows I only attract the cocky assholes who end up leaving before the sheets start to cool.

'But Sawyer didn't feel like an asshole,' I reason with myself. And that's true. He felt different from the moment I laid eyes on him.

"You look a little sad." His voice startles me from the pity party I'm lost in.

"Hey," I chirp as I glance toward the door. My voice is all pitchy and high.

Sawyer is leaning against the doorframe, a drink holder in one hand and a white paper sack in the other. "Why are you sad?"

"I'm not," I mumble, my eyes watching as he makes his way to me. From my position in my chair, he towers over me like a giant, all hard muscles and powerful limbs. I can't help that my eyes feast on the man in front of me. They make their way down his not-too-tight t-shirt and to those fabulous shorts Brandy was talking about. What is it about an athletic man in nylon shorts?

But it's his legs that now hold my attention. Sprinkled with dark hair, his thighs and calves are thick and... hard. Oh, dear Lord in Heaven, they're so hard and rippled with waves of taut muscles, and... am I drooling? Ehh, who cares! I have the sudden desire to caress every inch of his thighs and his calves and his...

"Earth to AJ," he says, pulling me from my fantasy. I was mere seconds away from dropping to my knees and worshipping this man's thighs.

My face burns with mortification.

Worse, I could hear the humor in his voice, as if he was thoroughly enjoying the fact that I was ogling him. And I'm sure he was. I mean, this man is obviously used to being ogled.

"I'm sorry, what?" I ask, forcing myself to look up and meet his eyes.

Oh, bad idea! They're sparkling like aquamarines under the sun and full of hilarity. "I asked why you were sad. You said you weren't. Then you started checking me out and drooling on your chin."

"I was not!" I declare, unable to stop the bubble of laughter that slips from my lips as I jump to my feet. He smiles back at me, easing away the embarrassment and replacing it with desire.

"I brought you a gift," he says. Sawyer steps up beside me and sets the white bag down on my desk, along with the coffees.

I turn my head slightly, catching an intoxicating whiff of his soap. He doesn't move, though, and we remain dangerously close together. It would be nothing for me to reach forward and place my hand on his chest or for him to wrap his arm around my lower back and pull me into his towering body.

"Thank you," I whisper, caught in the spell of his eyes.

"My pleasure." Something about the way he says it triggers every dirty memory I have of this man and makes me shiver. They all replay, in glorious bright Technicolor, and it doesn't take me long to realize I'm practically panting.

But so is he.

"I'm sorry it wasn't here when you walked in this morning. I decided that I needed to see you before I started my day." His words are heady and hold a powerful punch to my lady parts.

"I'm glad you waited a few minutes."

"Yeah?"

I offer a quick nod. We're still standing way too close to deem appropriate for a school setting, but neither of us seem to care. The room fills with a sexual charge that even I can see. Well, that is if I could see past my Sawyer-induced sex fog.

"So I was thinking about tomorrow night," he starts, his hand sliding slowly up my arm, leaving a trail of goose bumps in its wake. "Can I pick you up at six?"

"Sex is fine with me." He smirks and realization sets in. "Six! Six is fine with me! Oh my God," I mumble, dropping my head into my hands.

Warm fingers wrap around my wrists and gently pull them away from my face. "Sex just so happens to be fine with me too, but not yet. I will show you a proper first date, AJ." Before I can reply, he places a kiss on my forehead, causing my body to involuntarily sway toward him.

"Bagel and cream cheese today," he says as he grabs the second coffee and walks towards the doorway.

Glancing down, I take in the white bag on my desk. There's a note written on it, but before I can read it, he speaks again. "Oh, and AJ? All bets are off following the second date."

With that, he winks and strolls out the door like he didn't just render me absolutely speechless and completely turned on with that one statement. I'm so out of whack by his bluntness that I completely miss the view of watching him walk away.

Dammit.

I take a drink of coffee before grabbing the bag. In his now-familiar handwriting, I see his message written across the front of the bag. *To the best first date ever.*

Smiling like a loon, I reach into the bag and pull out the still-warm, fresh cinnamon swirl bagel and container of strawberry cream cheese. Oh, this man is dangerous. He's quickly worming his way into the deep, dark recesses of my heart. A place no man has ever gone before.

And I think I like it.

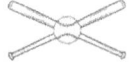

"Hello?"

"What do I wear on a first date when I don't want to appear easy?" I ask in one big rushed breath of air.

"As opposed to all of your other first dates where you wanted to appear easy?" my sister Meghan quips through the phone line.

"Yes."

"Well, where are you going?" she asks logically.

"I don't know."

"What do you know?"

"I know he'll be here in like two hours," I groan, taking in the mess. My bedroom looks like my closet exploded, raining every article of clothing I own all over the room.

"Okay, well, this one's a little tricky since you have two wardrobes. School teacher AJ and party AJ."

"Exactly." I feel so defeated. "I have my clothes that I wear to work, which doesn't scream sophisticated with a touch of fun and flirty. Or I have my weekend attire, which is all belly shirts and shorty shorts. I'm so screwed."

"Well, not yet, but if you play your cards right I'm willing to bet that stallion baseball player is more than willing to do the job for you."

"Not tonight," I tell her. "He said no sex on the first date."

Silence follows my statement. "Did you say no sex?" she whispers as if saying the words out loud is a huge sin.

"Yeah, he said he wanted to do this right. Maybe a goodnight kiss at the end of the night, but no nookie."

"Ohhhh, you are so in trouble with this one, AJ."

"Tell me about it. Now what the hell am I supposed to wear? Three quarters of my clothes are too school-teacher-y so those are out. I want to wear something worthy of a date with a former pro ball player, who, according to Google, was married to a freaking Victoria's Secret model."

"You didn't know that?"

"I didn't read the articles, Meg. I was too busy staring at the pictures."

She snorts a laugh. "You sound like Grandma. Does it bother you that he was married?"

"Married? No, because it's over. And I'm not talking over like it was with that Joe guy. This guy is at least divorced, which makes him already several steps ahead of Joe the Schmoe."

Just thinking about my brief time with Joe Crabtree raises my blood pressure. Joe lived a few towns over and was often in

Jupiter Bay for "work." And apparently, work meant "affair." We met pumping gas and before I knew it, I found myself back at his hotel room, tangled up in his sheets. We stayed up all night talking, him telling me all about leaving his wife and filing for divorce.

After a few weeks of him driving over and meeting up at my place, I got the call. From his wife. Who was five months pregnant with their third child.

There was no work in Jupiter Bay, no leaving his wife, no divorce.

He was a cheater, a user, and a liar.

And I had fallen for it, hook, line, and sinker.

That was the last time I had ever invited a man to my house. There have been a few following the Joe mess, but we'd never meet at my place. It was always his, which might be why the thought of Sawyer picking me up tonight for a real date makes me so anxious. Normally, I'd meet the guy at the restaurant or bar.

Just another reason why Mr. Randall is different.

"So how about a dress?" Meghan asks, pulling my attention back to the present.

"I do have that green one that I borrowed from Abby," I agree, glancing at the piles of clothes spread across my bed.

"You borrowed it from me, but who's keeping track," Meghan replies dryly.

"Oh, sorry. I'll get it back to you."

"Ehh, it's been like two years, AJ. It's not like I'm beating down your door to get it back now." My heart stops beating as realization sets in. When Meghan lost her fiancé Josh, she lost a piece of her soul. Until she's ready to put herself out there again, she doesn't have a reason to dress up for dates. Maybe someday, but she's not ready.

Not that I blame her at all.

"Yeah, well, maybe someday you'll have a reason to wear it." I swallow over the lump in my throat.

"Maybe," she says sadly. "I think the green dress is a great choice. It's simple and classy, yet sexy, and if you pair it with those cute gold flats or those lace-up sandals, I think it's casual enough for just about anything he suggests."

She's right. The dress is all of that and fits the bill. It's the perfect outfit to wear tonight for my date.

"I've never seen you like this. You're all worked up," Meghan prods, waiting me out.

"Maybe I am. He's just… I don't know, Meggy. He's the first guy who makes my heart flutter with excitement. I turn into a babbling idiot half the time, but he doesn't seem to mind."

"Then he's a keeper for sure," she giggles.

"We'll see," I deflect, trying to keep it light, breezy, and not get my hopes up. "How are things going with you?" I ask, pushing aside a pile of jeans to make room for my butt on the bed.

"Fine, I guess. Dad still comes over a couple nights a week just to say hi and make sure I'm still a functioning member of society."

That damn lump in my throat returns, making it hard to breathe. "Dad understands, better than anyone." My voice drops to a whisper with each word I speak.

"I know."

We all know. Dad has been single since Mom passed away from ovarian cancer when I was twelve. I don't recall him ever dating, nor has he indicated that he has. Instantly, I wonder if he's ever gone out with someone. I know how much he loved Mom–I grew up watching them giggle and steal kisses whenever they could–so it begs the question: Was he able to move on with his life or has he been stuck in some sort of foreign land of loss and loneliness?

"Meggy, can I ask you something?"

"Always," my sister replies instantly.

"Has Dad ever dated?" I feel silly asking the question and immediately want to retract it.

Meghan is quiet for so long, I glance down at my cell phone to make sure we're still connected. "You know, I don't think he has," she says softly.

"Do you think he should?" I ask.

"Should? Probably. Will he? Doubt it. I think he feels guilty, you know? Like he's moving on and leaving her behind."

Suddenly feeling braver than I was before, I say, "It's okay to move on. Eventually, when the time is right, there's nothing wrong with dating."

Again, I'm greeted with silence. "I agree. Maybe he will. When he's ready."

"When he's ready," I mimic.

"The green dress, right?" she asks, changing the subject away from the sticky topic of dating after losing your soul mate. Plus, I think she caught on to the fact I was talking to her with my statement more than I was talking hypothetically about our dad.

"The green one," I confirm.

"I don't want it back if you have sex in it, though."

That makes me laugh. "I'll make sure to take it off before we commence with *the sex.*"

"Please do. Anyway, I should go. I told Nick I would meet him uptown to help him pick out a couch and chair."

"Redecorating, is he?" I ask.

"He still hasn't bought anything since he and Collette split. She took everything they bought together, which is funny considering he paid for it to begin with." You can hear the slight annoyance and disdain in her voice as she speaks of her boss's ex-girlfriend.

"What a twatwaffle," I offer, feeling the need to defend Dr. Nick.

"That she is. Anyway, I'll let you get ready. Good luck tonight," Meghan says warmly.

"Thanks. I just hope I don't make a complete idiot of myself."

"You probably will," Meghan instigates in true little sister fashion, which makes me laugh again.

"Bye, brat."

"Love you," she answers with a smile.

"Love you, too."

After hanging up, I set out to get ready for my date. Even though Sawyer took sex off the table, I still jump in the shower and wash and shave all of my bits and pieces, making sure everything from my armpits to my legs (and even my bikini area) is completely hairless and velvety smooth.

I spend extra time on my hair, adding some loose curls to my long, brown mane. Deciding to go a little sexier on my eyes, I opt for the smoky look with charcoal shadows and slate liner. When it's flawless, I declare myself done with hair and makeup and slip back into my room to get my dress.

The hem of the sleeveless green satin dress hits right at my knee and molds seductively to the subtle curves of my waist. I'm fortunate enough to get my figure from my mom, complete with larger chest and understated hourglass figure.

I slip my feet into my gold ballet flats and grab my black wristlet, making sure it has my house key, identification, and cash secured inside. After a quick spritz of perfume on my neck and wrists, I head to the living room to wait for my date. My nerves are at an all-time high as I watch the clock slowly drag its way to six o'clock.

Two minutes before, I hear a car pull into my driveway. My pacing stalls as realization sets in. I'm about to go on a date with Sawyer Randall. *The* Sawyer Randall. My hands tremble a little, a combination of anxiety and excitement.

A knock sounds on my door, and I head in that direction.

This is it.

Taking several deep breaths to calm myself, I grip the doorknob and give it a turn.

It's go time.

Sawyer

When she opens the door, I forget to breathe.

It's crazy how she has the uncanny ability to calm my nerves and render me completely fucking speechless with her beauty at the same time. Her hair is down, falling in big, long curls around her shoulders begging for my touch. They actually tingle with anticipation at the prospect of running my fingers and tangling them in her hair. Her glossy lips are painted a natural color, all plump and inviting. I wonder if they'll taste as good as they look.

And don't get me started on that dress. It's the color of her eyes with a V that dives dangerously low in front, revealing a sexy sliver of silky cleavage. It's not a provocative cut, but grants flashes of the gems it contains within. My cock is already stirring to life, threatening to make all of my decisions from here on out.

"Wow," I say, scrambling to find a word worthy of how amazing she looks. "You look incredible."

"Thanks," she replies softly, the faintest hint of a blush tinting her cheeks. "You look pretty great yourself, Mr. Randall."

Stepping forward, I slip my hand around her waist, resting it on her lower back. "I like it when you call me that."

"Oh yeah?" she asks, stepping out on the porch and securing the front door. "Do you have a teacher/student fantasy?"

"Not at all. I've had a teacher/teacher fantasy since the moment I realized it was you sitting next to me in the teachers' lounge."

She stops in her tracks, halting our progression to my car. Her green eyes twinkle, even during daylight, and the faintest hint of a smile plays on her kissable lips. "Smooth, Mr. Randall. Very smooth."

"I can be when necessary," I tell her, offering my own smile.

AJ continues to my car, the scent of her perfume flirting with the light breeze. "Something tells me you're that way more often than not."

"Smooth?" I ask, making no move to open the door.

"Yes."

"When the situation warrants it, then yes, I've been known to be a bit charming." Her eyebrows pull together and her nose scrunches up as she waits me out. "Fine. Back in the day I was a known ladies' man."

"A player. Flirt."

"I see reading those old articles on me isn't helping any."

"They're not that old. I think the one that called you a playboy was last month's *Cosmo*."

"Chick stories. They always want to angle toward the bad boy."

"And are you?"

"A bad boy?" I take a step closer until I've invaded her personal space. "Oh, sweet AJ, I'm definitely a bad boy, but not in the way you think."

"Define bad boy," she taunts, her nose lifting high as she gazes up at me with a playful glint in her eyes.

"I'm only a bad boy in the bedroom, sweetheart, and never like those stories indicate. I'm not a cheater, a liar, or a womanizer. I've been the focus of those rags since the day I stepped into the majors, for one reason or another, but I promise you most of that crap they print is just that. Crap."

She swallows hard, the gears inside that beautiful head of hers spinning. Hell, she's probably judging my sincerity, and I wouldn't blame her one bit. For some crazy reason, the paparazzi hounded me from day one. They were always nearby, eager to snap a pic of me kissing the cheek of a teammate's wife (completely cropping out the fact that her husband, my teammate, was standing two feet away). Or they'd catch the right angle to make it appear as if I had my hand on some barely-legal stadium bunny, with her triple Ds and painted-on jersey (always with my number) front and center in the image.

"Okay," she whispers, offering me more than just a smile. She offers me a chance. AJ is willing to overlook the pages and pages of garbage she probably binge-read on me this past week, and is giving me the opportunity to show her that I'm not that man.

And I'm not about to fuck this up.

I want her too much to let this opportunity slip through my fingers.

She's willing to trust me, even though she doesn't know me, and I'm not going to let her down.

Brushing my lips across her forehead, I inhale the scent of her shampoo as her hair tickles my nose. My fingers start to burn again, itching to slide into those silky strands, but I keep myself from moving. It's not an easy feat, not with her practically pressed against me. My body is on fire for her, and we haven't even made it inside the car.

Hell, this is going to be a long night.

Especially since I vowed to do this right and not take her to bed.

"Ready to go?" I ask, taking a step back and putting a little distance between her body and my own.

"Yes," she says softly. "Where are we going?"

"It's a surprise," I tell her, smiling inwardly at the plan for this evening. Everything I need is already in the trunk, including some entertainment for after dinner.

Opening the door, I wait until AJ is seated in the passenger seat before I close her door and slip around to the driver's side. She's already buckled in, her eyes readily following my every move. Eagerness buzzes through the air like bees at a picnic, which I suppose is an appropriate analogy, since that's where we're headed.

We're quiet as we head to the location I chose for tonight's outing. Okay, so we're heading back to my place–she just doesn't know it. My plan is to stay out on the beach, not at the house. I just didn't know of any other place available, besides a public beach, where I could make this evening's plans work. A public beach just wasn't what I was shooting for on my first date with AJ.

"So why education?" I ask as I turn onto the highway that runs up the coast.

She slightly angles herself in the seat toward me, my eyes dropping to the smooth flesh where her dress rests a few inches above her knees. "Well, it was an easy decision for me. I love kids and excelled in math. When the math department at the junior high had an opening as soon as I completed my student teaching, I figured I should jump on the opportunity instead of searching other districts or waiting for a position at the high school to open up."

"You want to teach high school?"

"Well, I thought I did, but I'm actually pretty content at this level. Maybe if a high school position opens up, I'll look into it, but I don't really see myself making the move anymore."

"I'm kinda diggin' the junior high right now too, even though I've only been at this new gig for about two weeks. I always thought I'd coach high school, but after giving it more consideration, I like working with the younger kids. You know, help them grow into the athletes they'll be in high school."

"I get it. That's why I want to stick with junior high math," she says with a shrug.

We're quiet as we make our way to our destination. AJ seems content watching the scenery pass by, and she seems especially enthralled as we get closer to the water.

"Where are we going? I didn't think there was anything but residential houses out here," she says as I pull off the highway and worm my way down the seaside road that leads to my house.

"You'll see," I say vaguely, as I pull down the private lane beside my house that brings us to the beach. One of the things I love about this place is that the houses are far enough apart that you don't really feel like you have neighbors. And right now, I'm banking on that distance to give us privacy.

In the handful of weeks that I've been living here, a few of my neighbors have had backyard gatherings. Even with dozens of people, music, and laughter, the noise barely made it to my place. It's like the Bay swallowed it up. Since my gathering is just AJ and I, we should have no problem fading into the peace around us.

"Sawyer? Where are we?" she whispers, her eyes bouncing between the side of my house and the view of the Bay as I park along the fence that runs along the south side of my property.

"Come see," I say, leaving my keys in the ignition and hopping out of the car.

I pop open the trunk as she gets out of the car. I can't help but watch as she takes it all in, her long, brown hair gently swaying around her back. There's more of a breeze here than in town, but, fortunately, I prepared for that.

I grab the small cooler, the picnic basket, blanket, and the bag from the vehicle. When the trunk is secure, I turn my attention back to her and hand her the blanket. "Let's go."

She walks beside me, my arms loaded with our meal, down to the spot I pre-picked on the beach. When we reach the sand, I stop and wait for her to slip her shoes from her feet. I kick off my flip-flops, but make no move to pick them up. I can come back for them later.

When we reach the spot, I set everything down on the sand. AJ seems to understand what's happening and starts to spread the blanket out on the ground. I jump on the opposite end and help finish covering the sand. She smiles as she steps on the blanket and my heart starts hammering in my chest the same way it did when I hit my first grand slam in the majors.

AJ sits on her haunches, her hands resting on her knees, and watches me with eager, smiling emerald eyes. From the picnic basket, I retrieve plastic plates, cups, and silverware and set it all in between us. Then I pull out a container with sliced strawberries and grapes.

Her eyes seem to light up with each dish I reveal. After the fruit, I empty the cooler. The glasses are filled with lemonade and plates piled with pasta salad. Then, I go for the gold. Inside the bag is a thermal container with ballpark hotdogs. When I pull them out and set one on each plate, she giggles.

"These are the best hotdogs in the history of the world," I say, handing her a plate. "Okay, confession. These aren't the actual ballpark hotdogs, but they're close. The nice lady at the grocery store helped me secure these bad boys. I'm pretty sure she thought I was hitting on her."

AJ giggles. "Mrs. Hagley went to school with my grandpa. She's eighty-two."

"Well, I'm not sure she knows that."

"Oh, she does. She's just... spunky. That's why she and my grandma are such good friends."

"Now that I can see," I confirm.

I watch as she brings the hotdog up to her lips and takes a bite. "Oh God," she moans, covering her mouth with her hand while she chews.

"Good, right?"

"So good."

She chews slowly, savoring her first bite of imitation ballpark hotdog, and if I must say, risking the chance to sound cheesy as fuck, it's fucking hot as hell watching her eat. Sexy. Alluring. Intoxicating.

Just like her.

We talk while I clean up the remnants of dinner, watch the water sweep across the shore, and the sun begins to drop from the sky behind us. We rarely break conversation, and on those rare moments when we do, it's not uncomfortable or awkward. It's just two people, who seem to enjoy each other's company, taking a few moments to appreciate what's around them.

I never had that with Carrie, not even in the beginning. When things were quiet, it was tense. Though, it wasn't quiet all that much either. My ex-wife was a talker, especially in certain social circles that she could benefit from. She was the epitome of a social ladder climber, always leeching on to whoever could help her next vertical move to the top.

And for a long time, that was me.

At least it was, until there was no more use for me.

The sun drops behind the trees and the breeze has a slight dampness to it, even for the first weekend in September. AJ shivers and wraps her arms around her chest in an attempt to warm herself. Reaching back over for the bag, I retrieve the other blanket I brought. Just in case. This one is smaller and lighter than the one we're sitting on, and may or may not have come from my own chair. You know, the one that hangs on the back so when you start to nod off, you can grab it and cover up?

That blanket.

The one that I hope will now have the added scent of the outdoors... and AJ.

I know.

I'm already gone.

AJ

When he pulls the blanket from the bag, the first thing I notice is the smell.

It smells just like Sawyer.

I wrap it around my shoulders and instantly feel the warmth. And the crazy part is, I'm not one hundred percent sure it's from the actual blanket itself. It's almost like it's him who's wrapped around my shoulders, holding me close and keeping me warm. How crazy is that?

"Better?" he asks.

No, not really. I have this ache between my legs that always seems to creep up whenever I'm around him. Of course, that's not what he means, and there's no way I'd actually say that aloud. Well, not unless I was asking for the man to get into my pants. Not that I'm not asking, it's just that he's not exactly offering. At least not on our first date. So instead of focusing on the fact that I'm suddenly wet, slightly horny, and ready to jump his bones right here on the beach, I decide to answer his question referring to the blanket.

"Much."

"You're blushing," he adds with a sly grin.

"Am not. I don't blush," I retort, blushing further.

"I bet you do when it counts," he replies, that grin turning wolfish. Something tells me he wasn't referring to a blush of embarrassment, but one that is reserved for the bedroom. Naked. Panting.

And now I might be panting.

"I can't wait to make you blush," he whispers, moments before his hand slides up my jaw and slips into my hair. He's playing with the curls, wrapping them around his fingers, and gently tugging them. It doesn't hurt, but still sends fire rushing through my veins.

"I really want to kiss you." His words are breathy and heady.

"I'd be okay with that."

His hands slip farther into my hair until he's cradling my scalp with his big hand. "It's not exactly first date appropriate."

"We almost slept together before we knew each other."

His smile starts slow and gently takes his gorgeous face from handsome to stunning. Breathtaking. "I almost threw up on you," I remind.

"You did throw up on me. My shoes, actually," he adds, his bubble of laughter mixing with my groan of embarrassment.

"Holy shitballs, are you serious?" Cue utter humiliation. If a tsunami could sweep in now and carry me out to sea, that'd be great. My head drops to my hands praying he suddenly gets a strong bout of amnesia and forgets all about me and my horrible gut-purging attempt at seduction.

Sawyer moves closer, placing both hands on my head and raising my chin. His eyes hold a sparkle of humor, but also something else. Something deeper that steals my breath. The man just confessed that I threw up on him and he... wants me?

"Actually, the vomit didn't bother me in the least. I've seen worse in the locker room following a doubleheader. It was after the puking that sent me into a tizzy. It was the fact that I had a beautiful woman in my bed for the first time in months and I didn't want to let her go. And when I came back to my hotel room later, after my job interview, and found her gone, it bothered me more than I should probably admit. Because spending just that brief time with you brought me to life for the first time in so fucking long."

I let his powerful words soak in, absorbing and relishing them. The fact that it's the first time someone spoke so candidly about his feelings for me–even if they are sparked by the sexual chemistry neither of us seems to deny–doesn't go unnoticed.

Instead of speaking, I lean forward and press my lips to his. They're warm as they instantly move against mine. I may have initiated the kiss, but Sawyer quickly takes control. His lips part mine just enough for his tongue to slide inside for a taste. His hands hold me firmly, at just the right angle for him to take what he wants. And holy hell, do I want him to take. More kisses and whatever else comes next.

Instead of moving into that category, however, Sawyer pulls back. "That's against the rules," he groans, releasing his hold on me. The fact that he adjusts his pants, which suddenly seem a bit tight in the crotch area, doesn't go unnoticed.

"I'm not a fan of the rules," I tell him honestly. I wait for him to call me out on the fact that I'm a teacher, and rules are a part of my daily routine, but he doesn't. I think he knows that I wasn't referring to my day job as much as I was meaning with him.

"I like a rebel," he says, offering me a warm smile.

"It's dark." I realize that night has fallen around us, reinforcing the fact that time just seems to fly when I'm with him.

He seems to take notice too, and quickly puts a bag on his lap. Sawyer pulls a long, narrow box from his bag of goodies as well as a lighter. I giggle when I realize what he has. Pulling out one stick, he hands it to me and grabs the lighter. Sparks fly as the sparkler flames to life, bright against the darkened sky.

"I haven't done this in years," I confess, smiling, as my hand moves.

"Me either," he admits as his own sparkler blazes to life.

"Our family used to do this every Fourth of July. I used to love to write my name when I was little," I tell him, moving my hand and spelling AJ.

"That's not fair. Your name is shorter than mine."

"I used to spell my full name," I whisper.

"What's your full name?" His voice dips low to mirror my own.

"Alison. Alison Jane. I stopped going by it when my mom died." I didn't mean to say the words; they just tumbled out before I could stop them. But now that I've admitted it, I somehow feel lighter. It's as if confessing that secret to Sawyer has lifted a weight off my chest.

"I'm sorry you lost your mom," he says as my sparkler dies.

I shrug my shoulders, even though I'm sure he can't see me. "It was a long time ago."

"Maybe, but that doesn't mean the loss hurts any less."

"True." I take a deep breath and keep going. "She used to call me Alison Jane, and somehow, when she died, I just hated the sound of it. My grandparents will still call me by my full name at times, but for the most part, everyone calls me AJ. It's how I prefer it. Even my dad started calling me AJ when I requested it." Again, I shrug my shoulders.

"AJ suits you," he says, as he links his fingers with mine, the wires of our sparklers forgotten in the sand. "But Alison is a beautiful name."

Glancing his way, the moon reflects brightly off his blue eyes turning them into dark sapphires. "I like it when you say my name." I'm already leaning his way and resting my head on his shoulder.

"I'd happily say it again." His words shake me to my very core almost as much as my reply.

"You could call me Alison. If you want."

We sit together, watching the waves crash against the shore, snuggled under a blanket that smells like him. It's funny how content I feel. After years of kissing frogs and dating toads, it's hard to believe that I might have actually found one of the good ones. I was starting to think they were already snatched up. Lord knows my sisters had each found a diamond amongst the pile of turds.

After another twenty minutes, Sawyer starts to gather our things. I grab my shoes and the blankets while he carries the cooler, bag, and picnic basket. The sand feels cool between my toes, which may actually be one of the best feelings in the world.

"So that's your house?" I ask, gazing up at the very large house with massive windows facing the Bay.

"That's it. I'd give you a tour, but I'm not sure I'd let you leave once I got you inside," he says bluntly. "Besides, I think home tours are reserved for the second date."

When we reach his car, he sets all of the items he's carrying down beside the garage door and takes the blankets from my arms. "So, you're saying there's going to be a second date?" I ask.

Sawyer stops in front of me. He's so much taller and broader than my smaller five-foot, seven-inch body. "Well, I'm hoping," he answers, leading me to the passenger side of his car. "And it's not just a second date I'm hoping for, Alison, but a third and fourth and fifth, too. In fact, I plan to have all of your dates booked up until you get tired of me."

"I'm not sure that's possible. I'm positive this comes as no surprise to you, Mr. Randall, but you're pretty charming and irresistible."

"I am?" he asks, his white teeth shining brightly in the night.

"You know you are. Women swallow their tongues when you walk by. I've witnessed no less than three married teachers, as well as every single hormonal teenaged female student in the school practically lose their minds when you enter the room. I should be embarrassed for the state of the female population."

"Well, not that all of that doesn't sound fascinating, I'm actually only interested in the reaction of one particular woman."

"That's easy. She turns into a teenage girl when you're near too."

That makes him laugh. "I'm not sure if that's supposed to be a compliment or not, but I prefer women over teenage girls. In fact, I have a type," he tells me as he holds open the door and I slide in.

When he slips into the driver's seat, I ask, "And this type. Do I want to know? Wait. Let me guess. Blonde, blue eyes, double Ds and an IQ two points higher than her bust size?"

"Wow, you just described my ex-wife," he grumbles, starting the car and backing down the lane. "Though, I wouldn't exactly say that's my type. Before I entered The Big Show, I dated a woman in college who was going to school to be an archeologist. She had the big glasses and everything."

"Well, if perky double Ds and bleach-bottle blonde hair isn't your type, what is?" I ask as we pull out onto the road.

"Funny you should ask," he says, reaching over and taking my hand with his. "I prefer brunette, over blonde. Green eyes, sassy tongue, about yay-high," he says, indicating with his hand where my head hits on his chest when we stand. "Oh, and someone who vomits on my shoes. I really dig that," he sasses and squeezes my hand.

Groaning, I reply, "You're not going to let me live that down, are you?"

"Of course, I am. Just not tonight," he quips with a grin.

"That's horrible first date etiquette," I remind him as he pulls into town and heads toward my place.

"You may be right, but I wouldn't change it for anything."

"I would. Maybe less alcohol and less vomiting. The end result would have been a lot more... pleasurable."

I can practically hear him swallow as he pulls into my driveway. "I'm sure it would have been. But this isn't so bad either," he adds, putting his car in park. "This way, you get a proper date."

"But less sex," I retort.

"For now," he says, getting out of the car and coming around to my side. Sawyer helps me from the car and immediately sweeps me into his arms.

"Thank you for tonight," I tell him, my voice all low and breathy.

He stares down at me, his eyes intense and almost unreadable. It reminds me of the look on his face in those YouTube videos of his games. Focused. Penetrating. Passionate. And all of that is concentrated directly at me.

Sawyer doesn't reply. Instead, he guides his hands up my jaw and tangles his fingers in my hair, just like he did earlier in the evening when we kissed on the beach. His lips are gentle as they graze against mine in a featherlight kiss. It's like he's testing the waters, dipping his toes in to gauge the temperature. Only I'm the water and the longer he touches me, the higher my temperature keeps climbing.

He coaxes my mouth open with his tongue. Sawyer proves to be an expert kisser as he slowly slides along my tongue with his own. Shivers sweep across my skin as I grip the back of his shirt, holding on for what is proving to be the best kiss of my life. It's slow, tantalizing, and erotic, and honestly, I never knew a kiss could be like this.

"Best first date ever," he whispers as he places open-mouthed kisses on the corners of my lips.

I try to answer, but I'm pretty sure my reply comes out a lusty squeak.

Before I can beg for more kisses, he slowly pulls back. His eyes burn fire into me as my half-lidded gaze locks on his. He's so freaking intense, and I can't believe how much it turns me on.

"It was," I agree, still gripping the back of his shirt.

"Can I call you?"

"I'd like that," I answer, hoping it's not just a line and he really does pick up the phone.

"Thank you for saying yes, Alison." He slowly slips his hands from my hair. I feel the loss instantly.

"Thank you for asking me, Sawyer."

"Just make sure you say yes when I ask again," he says, the corner of his mouth turning upward.

"I don't want to predict the future, but I feel a very strong indication that the answer would be yes again."

He offers me a smile before taking a step back. "Good."

Turning and unlocking my door, I let myself into my house. Before I shut the door behind me, he asks, "Alison?" I stand at the threshold and face him. "Is there any breakfast food you don't like?"

"Bran or poppy seed muffins."

That sexy little smile plays on his lips once more. "Good to know. 'Night." He offers a wave before taking a step backward, but he doesn't turn and walk down the steps.

"Good night," I tell him, lifting my hand to wave.

Part of me wants to throw open the door and invite him inside, but the other part, the part that's winning out right now, wants to take this slow and see where it goes. For once, I'm not just jumping into someone's bed or being the only one ready to take the next step. I believe Sawyer is right there with me, eager to see where this budding thing between us goes.

It's exciting.

And terrifying all at the same time.

But any relationship worth having is worth a little fear.

Without inviting him in, I close the door, securing the lock behind me. My house is quiet, which makes it easy to hear him retreat down the stairs, get into his car, and pull from my driveway. Once he's gone, I make my way to my bedroom to get ready for bed.

Lying in the still of the night, the glow of the moon leaking through my bedroom window, I allow myself to replay every moment of the evening. From the picnic with his favorite foods, to the nighttime sparklers, and the delicious kisses that left me wet and needy, the entire date was better than I could have possibly imagined.

"Best first date ever."

Sawyer 12

"What are you doing in here?" I glance up and find the questioning eyes of Bryce Lehman watching me.

"I brought AJ a coffee," I reply, setting the cup and white bag down on her empty desk.

"Huh," he says, crossing his arms across his chest as he casually leans against the doorjamb to AJ's classroom. "Didn't know you two were friends."

I shrug and step away from her desk, my cup of coffee in hand. "It's on my way in," I tell him, not owing him any further explanation.

He continues to stare at me, sizing me up and searching for my motives. I could tell that first time I talked to him in AJ's presence that he had a crush on her. Not that it bothers me, so long as she's only going out with me. "Have a good holiday?" I ask, taking a sip of my own coffee.

"Not too bad. A few friends and I hung out and played basketball yesterday and grilled out. I love extended weekends," Bryce says, referring to yesterday's Labor Day holiday. "What about you? Big weekend?"

"It wasn't bad." I'm not about to tell him what I did or who I may have spent part of it with.

"Me and a few friends get together often. You want to come sometime, just let me know."

"Maybe," I reply, not committing to anything.

"AJ, is it true you went out with –" Brandy, the school secretary, says as she rounds the corner and comes face-to-face with Bryce and me. "Oh. Hi!" she exclaims, a wide smile spreading across her pretty face. Her eyes sparkle as she zeros in on me, and something tells me, by the way her eyes light up, if she finished that sentence, it would have been my name she mentioned.

Good.

"Oh, hey, Bryce. Sawyer." She practically swoons as she draws out my name and starts twirling her hair around her finger.

"Brandy," I nod as she slips into the room.

"I was just looking for AJ," she says, heading over to her desk and noticing the coffee cup and paper bag. "What's this?"

"Breakfast." I have to fight my smile.

When she glances my way, a Cheshire cat's grin is plastered on her heavily made up face. "Lucky woman," she singsongs. Glancing over my shoulder, she studies Bryce's demeanor. He's standing totally straight, like someone rammed a rod up his ass, and he's making a face of annoyance. "Hey, Bryce. Good weekend?"

"It was okay," he stammers behind me.

"Yeah? I hear AJ had a date. Did you hear that, Sawyer?"

"Nope, didn't hear that," I reply to her eager question.

"Huh, too bad. Then I guess you probably haven't heard who it was with then, hmmmm?" she asks, her eyes shining with mischief.

My armor starts to crack, right along with the threatening smile, because I'm definitely ready to stake my claim. Oh, this woman is evil. I see what she's doing here, trying to get me to confess that I was the mystery man who took AJ out on a date. And while I'm in no way trying to hide that fact, I'm not about to blab to all of our coworkers without AJ knowing first.

"No clue." I stand my ground.

"Interesting," she says, drawing out the word and grinning broadly. "I could have sworn that I heard the guy she was out with was –"

"What are you all doing in here?" AJ asks with a smile, but not missing the questioning look on her beautiful face.

"Breakfast!" Brandy exclaims, holding up the bag I set on her desk.

She glances over at Bryce, who barely moves aside as she slips into her classroom, and then her attention turns to me. Her eyes brighten and she offers me a private, knowing smile. "Hi."

"Good morning, Miss Summer. I just happened to be at that bakery you recommended and noticed they had those blueberry muffins you mentioned. So I grabbed you one and a latte," I say casually.

"Oh, well, thank you so much," she replies, and if I'm not mistaken, blushes a little in the process.

"Holy sheetballs, AJ! Is it true? Did you go out with –" Natalie Johnson, a science teacher, blows into the classroom like the devil is nipping at her heels.

"Hi!" AJ squeaks, her eyes wide with surprise.

"Oh. Sorry, didn't realize you had company." Natalie glances between the others in the room, from Brandy, Bryce, and then me. When she sees me standing there, all casual and with a grin on my face, she gets all giggly and her face practically splits in half by her smile.

That's when things get weird. Everyone just stands there, waiting for someone to confirm what they already know, smiles plastered on their faces. Okay, so Brandy and Natalie have smiles.

AJ looks like she's about to crawl out of her skin with nerves and Bryce appears to be completely clueless as ever.

"Well, if you'll all excuse me, I have to get the ball field ready for first period," I say, heading to the door. I'd prefer to detour towards AJ and maybe steal a good morning kiss, but know that it's not the right time or place. Definitely not with an audience.

"Have a great one, Mr. Randall," Brandy coos, waving and watching my backside as I leave.

"You all too."

I smile as soon as I hit the hall, knowing that as soon as Bryce is out of earshot, the Spanish Inquisition will begin for poor AJ. But I can't focus on that. Right now, I'd like to find out how half the school seems to know about our private dinner date from Saturday night.

Small towns.

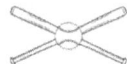

I'm on detention duty today, which is why I'm sitting in the study hall after school on Thursday with two boys who couldn't seem to keep their fists to themselves during lunch period. It was about a girl, of course, because most scuffles usually are, especially with teenagers. The boys have been staring daggers at each other from across the room, which tells me the fight at lunch probably won't be the last.

I dismiss them at four and escort both boys out the front door. They give each other a wide berth, which is good since I'm not really in the mood to deal with teenage hormones and the smart mouths that come with them. Plus, I've learned real quickly that being forced to be the authority figure isn't always fun.

My office door is barely shut when it opens again. When I glance up, I find those sexy green eyes staring down at me. She's wearing a light blue top with black cropped pants and is leaning against the back of my door like some teenage fantasy. AJ Summer is way better than *Playboy* magazine.

"Hi," she says softly, not moving farther into the room.

"Hey."

"Detention duty, huh?"

"That would be correct. It was the most thrilling thirty minutes of my life."

She laughs. "Oh, don't I know it. My turn is coming up."

AJ doesn't say anything else, and I can't help but wonder what brought her down to my corner of the gym well after the school day has ended. Before I can ask, she pushes off the door and walks my way. I'm leaning back in my chair, one tennis shoe clad ankle resting on the opposite knee. Her eyes travel the entire length of my body, landing on the place my now hard cock throbs in my shorts.

"So, I was thinking," she starts, but doesn't finish. She does, however, step closer until her leg is touching mine.

I drop my leg, keeping my knees shoulder-width apart. Mostly because the baseball bat in my pants is restricting my movements. "Me too."

"What were you thinking about?"

"Tomorrow night."

"What about it?" she asks, stepping between my legs and sitting back on the corner of my desk. And suddenly, all I can think about is taking her right there. Seeing her brown hair fanned across my desk while I tower over her from behind, my hands splayed across her lower back as I take her from behind.

"What?" I ask, realizing she asked me a question.

"Tomorrow night. What about it?" she asks with a knowing smile.

Adjusting myself casually, I continue. "I was thinking maybe we should hang out."

"Like a second date?"

"Definitely a second date."

"Can't. Have plans."

Well, I wasn't expecting that. "Plans?"

"Yes. The high school cheerleaders have invited the junior high girls to come and cheer with them for first quarter of the homecoming game."

"So, you're ditching me to hang out at the high school?" I ask.

"Yes," she replies, her knee swinging gently to the side and connecting with my thigh. "But…"

"But?" I ask, holding my leg as still as possible for fear that I'll sever the connection of her contact. It's not the skin-on-skin I'd prefer, but considering I'm sitting at my desk at school, I'll take what I can get.

"But maybe you could come. You know, support the team and all."

"High school football, you say?" I ask, stroking my chin as if considering all options.

"There'll be popcorn," she urges.

"You'll buy me popcorn?" I ask, earning a quick head nod. "With extra cheese seasoning? And a Coke?"

"A Coke might be pushing it a bit," she teases.

Leaning forward, I grab her hand and bring it to my lips. "Fine, so you get the popcorn and I'll get the Cokes?"

"Deal."

"Deal," I agree, pressing my lips firmly to her palm. I feel the shiver sweep through her body like a jolt of lightning.

"Your office is awfully private, Mr. Randall." Her words are all breathy and make me think of sex. Well, think *more* about sex. Specifically, sex with Miss Summer.

"It is," I confirm, running my lips up her wrist, licking and tasting the soft, sensitive skin of her inner forearm.

"That must come in handy," she pants.

"It hasn't yet, but I'm optimistic."

"I bet you are," she chokes, gasping as I swipe my tongue over the crease of her arm.

I slide my other hand up her outer thigh and grip her hip tightly, pulling her body even closer. I can feel the tremble in her legs. Legs that I'd kill to have wrapped around my waist right now. AJ's hands dive into my hair. She tugs and pulls with just enough grip that I almost come in my basketball shorts.

"Does your door lock?" she asks, her question a plea.

"It does," I confirm before standing up. "But we're not locking it."

"We're not?" Confusion is written all over her face.

"Our first time isn't going to be in my stinky office."

"It's not?"

"No way. When I finally get you naked and get to have my way with you, it'll be in a bed and there won't be the prospect of a janitor interrupting us. In fact, I'm pretty sure when you're finally in my bed again, I'll be keeping you there for a long time."

"How long?"

"Hours," I reply, kissing her neck. "Maybe even days." Lick.

"Days?" she gasps.

"Fucking days, Alison," I say just before my lips claim hers in a hard, bruising kiss.

She tastes like magic, like honey and sin, all wrapped in a sexy little package, but as much as it pains me, I have to pull away. Mostly because I'm dangerously close to losing control and we're not in the best location for that to happen. Plus, when I finally get my hands and mouth on her, I'm going to take my time and savor every second of it.

"Tomorrow, I'll meet you at the game. We'll consider it date number two. I'll even buy the hotdogs."

"What is it with you and hotdogs?" she teases, her breath hitting me on the lips and making my brain go haywire.

"They're my favorite," I tell her, slipping my hand back into her hair. "And maybe, if the date goes well, you may consider coming home with me. After." I try to sound casual, but I'm not sure it happens. I'm so fucking worked up right now that I'll probably be beating off to memories of her later tonight.

"You do realize that'll put us both at the football game. Together. In public."

"I'm fine with it if you are."

She seems to really mull it over for a few seconds before nodding her head. "I'm okay with it. I'm also okay with the *after* the game."

"Do you want me to pick you up for the game?"

"I have to be there early. Plus, I think I'd rather have my car. You know, in case you turn all clingy and needy and I need to make a quick getaway."

"Oh, I'm gonna be very clingy and needy," I whisper, running my finger down her jaw and throat until I hit her cleavage.

"You may not be the only one," she murmurs.

"Maybe you can bring a bag with you tomorrow night to the game?"

"Maybe I will."

"Then maybe I'll see you tomorrow night?"

"You will definitely see me tomorrow night," she says, backing away and walking to the door. "Besides, you owe me hotdogs and a Coke," she sasses with a wink before slipping out my office door, the heels of her shoes slapping the floor as she leaves.

Twenty-four hours.

Tomorrow night, I'll join her at the football game, and after that?

She'll be joining me at my place.

Just the two of us.

Alone.

It's gonna be the longest twenty-four hours of my fucking life.

13

AJ

The stands are packed with fans as the Marching Eagles take the field for their halftime routine. I shouldn't be surprised to see my grandparents here, but I am. Rarely do they attend sporting events; at least they haven't much since my sisters and I all graduated.

"That man is pure sin," Grandma bends down and whispers in my ear. And because she's sitting directly behind me, she has a front row seat to our second date. Not that they know that tiny detail. "Have you played bedroom baseball yet, AJ?"

I glance round at the surprised faces of those sitting to my right and in front of me.

Obviously, Grandma's whisper needs a little work.

"This is hardly an appropriate location for this discussion," I mumble, turning to where the girls are conversing on the sideline.

"But look at that ass," Grandma murmurs happily.

When I follow her line of sight, I see Sawyer heading this way, sliding down our row, greeting and chatting with every person who stops him. You can tell he's used to being recognized and goes with the flow. He visits briefly with Mr. Stewart, our principal, his hands full of drinks and snacks from the concession stand.

His back is turned to us, which gives us the perfect view of his deliciously hard derrière. And we're not the only ones appreciating the view. Every female in our section (hell, in the entire bleachers, really) happens to be glancing his way and ogling the fine specimen of man that is the new teacher in town. Not only does that tidbit make him prime gossip material, but throw in the fact that he's *the* Sawyer Randall, and suddenly everyone is buzzing for details.

"If you don't stop staring, your face will freeze that way," Grandpa says from beside his wife.

"What face?" I ask, glancing over my shoulder at one of the two men who raised me.

"That lusty *I want to drop my drawers and do dirty things to the baseball player* face," Grandma chimes in. My jaw drops to my chest in a combination of surprise and embarrassment. Grandpa just nods in agreement. Everyone around me snickers and giggles.

Awesome.

Sawyer slides onto the bleacher beside me, only to jump up right away.

"Oh, I'm sorry, dear. I just set my hand down on the bleacher for a rest," Grandma says, all too familiar smile on her face. She has that guilty I-just-copped-a-feel look.

"Resting your hand?" I mumble as Sawyer takes his seat beside me.

"I had to, AJ. Call it research," she says, happily watching the marching band perform.

Sawyer hands me a bottle of Coke and a bag of popcorn, before turning and offering some to my grandparents. "Sorry it took so long," he says, leaning in to me to be heard over the band.

"It's okay. The price you pay for being famous," I tease.

"Yeah, everyone is my friend," he replies, a slight sarcastic tone bubbling to the surface. I'm sure it's difficult being a professional athlete, not knowing if someone is real or just pretending to be your friend to get what they can out of you.

"I'm your friend," I say under my breath to keep the conversation on the lighter side.

"You are definitely not my friend," he whispers, reaching over and grabbing a handful of popcorn from the bag in my hand.

"I'm not?" I ask, grabbing a few kernels and popping them into my mouth.

Leaning my way, I feel his warm breath against the shell of my ear when he replies, "I don't want to fuck my friends."

My blood swooshes in my ears and I can feel my face heating. Electricity courses through my veins like lightning, wetness pooling between my thighs.

"That was hot," Grandma whispers in my ear, making me groan.

Sawyer glances at me with one eyebrow raised. "They have excellent hearing," I concede and wait for the moment he realizes what I mean. When he gets it, his cheeks turn a cute shade of pink before he cracks a smile.

"Duly noted," he replies, turning his attention to the field.

"Back when AJ was seventeen, Meggy spent the night at a friend's house, so AJ thought she'd sneak her boyfriend into her bedroom after everyone went to bed."

I groan an interruption, knowing what story is coming. "Please stop."

"No, I think I need to hear this," Sawyer begs, laughter laced in his ocean blue eyes.

"Anyway, AJ and her boyfriend had just started to get busy in her bedroom. We could hear them through the walls, you know, so Grandpa waited in the hallway for them to reappear so he could sneak back out. They were so young, so it didn't take long, you know? Anyway, as soon as that young man stepped out of the room, Grandpa asked him if he had another rubber because he was out."

Laughter bursts from Sawyer's throat. "I was mortified," I murmur, trying to focus on anything else around me other than the humiliation happening beside me.

"The best part was that poor young man was so flabbergasted that he actually dug into his wallet and pulled out a peter cover for me to use," Grandpa adds while fighting his own laughter.

"Then we made them come down to the kitchen and eat ice cream with us," Grandma states proudly.

"You shared a drumstick and grossed us both out with your inappropriate groaning and licking," I recall, the popcorn settling like a lead brick in my stomach.

"It was summer and we were hot," Grandma argues. "It's not my fault it was dripping down the side and required extra licking."

"He broke up with me the next day," I remind them.

"Serves him right. He wasn't good enough for my little Alison Jane," Grandpa adds with a decisive head nod.

Grandma's face softens and she gives me a knowing look at the reference to my given name. Hearing it as an adult doesn't hurt as much as it did when I was younger, mostly because, for so long, I could still hear my mom saying it. The authoritative tone mixed with the love in her voice as she called my name.

"Anyway, that's true. He wasn't good enough for AJ. I believe he ended up dropping out of junior college and flipping burgers at that fast food joint uptown," Grandma says as I shovel popcorn into my face like I haven't eaten in a week.

"He was the day manager last time I talked to him," I mumble over the mouthful of popcorn.

"Well, good for him," Grandma says cheerfully. "But he's nothing like our Sawyer here," she adds, patting him on the shoulder, and if I'm not mistaken, gripping and rubbing a little too long on the muscles of his upper back.

"Your Sawyer?" I choke, trying to get the food down my throat.

"Yes, I called dibs after seeing that spread in SI. Sawyer, tell me, how many takes did it take to get the angle of that glove just right?" Grandma coos at the man beside me, a wicked little gleam in her wrinkled eyes. "Did you have a fluffer?"

And now I'm choking on popcorn. It gets lodged in my throat as I sputter and cough, trying to get the food down and the air in. Sawyer leans over and gently beats on my back, his face a horrible shade of red as he tries to hide his own amusement and blushing.

"Uh, no ma'am, no fluffer was required," he sputters, trying not to laugh.

"It wasn't porn, Grandma!" I chastise under my breath as those sitting around me try not to look like they're listening to our conversation, but fail miserably.

"Well, my body still reacted, AJ. And the images I had later that night were definitely more along the lines of pornographic." Grandma smiles wickedly, as if recalling something that would probably require years of therapy for me to overcome.

"I capitalized immensely that night, I believe," Grandpa boasts like a proud peacock.

"And you're gonna capitalize again tonight, Orvie," Grandma coos, reaching over and rubbing my grandpa's thigh.

"I'm going to throw up," I mumble. "See? This is why they all leave. No one sticks around when they meet my grandparents," I whisper to Sawyer.

"Maybe the reason they don't stick around is because they weren't the right guy," Sawyer suggests, his head leans toward me, his lips dangerously close to my own. "Notice I'm not going anywhere."

"You should. You should run away."

He reaches over and links his fingers with mine. "Not happening, Alison." His whispered voice is soft and gravely. It makes my lady parts hum and my heart pirouette in my chest.

Something tells me that this man doesn't scare easily, which is a plus if you're gonna withstand the craziness in this family. My mind turns to Josh, Ryan, Dean, Levi, and now Linkin, all men who weren't frightened off by the loose tongues of my grandparents or their over-the-top gestures and gifts. It's way too soon to make such a statement, so I won't say it aloud, but a part of me (a very big part) wonders if maybe Sawyer *is* one of the few willing to endure the outrageous and stick around after the bedsheets have cooled.

Only time will tell.

The second half starts with the Eagles kicking off to the rival Bobcats. As the minutes wind down in the third quarter, then the fourth, the score remains close. So close, in fact, that as we hit one minute to go in the fourth, the Bobcats score a field goal, giving them a two-point edge.

With fifty seconds on the clock, the Eagles field a kick deep and run to their end zone. Tackles are broken, blocks are made, and yards are gained as our team attempts to score before the clock runs out.

Thirty, twenty, ten yards to go.

He dodges one final defender and dives for the end zone.

Touchdown!

The crowd goes crazy as the Eagles secure a homecoming victory. We all jump up, popcorn flying through the air, screaming and cheering for the home team. Large, warm arms wrap around my waist moments before I'm pulled into a rock hard chest. I don't even care that it's like walking into a brick wall. All I know is that Sawyer's arms are hugging me in celebration.

Or anticipation.

Maybe he realizes that the end of the game means the beginning of the rest of our night. I mean, I pretty much already agreed to go home with him yesterday in his office. Perhaps he's anxious to get to phase two of our second date: the bedroom.

However, when I look up, I don't see the anticipated hunger in his eyes. I see happiness. It's like he's truly ecstatic for the boys on the field. And that would make complete sense because he's an athlete. He appreciates each win and the hard work that goes into achieving them.

"Well, Grandpa promised me naked ring toss, so we're going to head out," she says easily as she gathers up their garbage.

Sawyer glances down at me with so many questions in his eyes, and as much as I'd love to explain it to him, I just can't. It's my grandparents. And I'm pretty sure naked ring toss isn't a round of the traditional ring toss you may have played at birthday parties. So I shake my head and pray that he doesn't bring it up later.

"Be careful going home," I state, offering my hand as we make our way toward the steps on the bleachers.

Grandma links her hand with Grandpa's and together they descend the steps until they reach the bottom. They've always been an overly affectionate couple, but the sight of them tonight, with their warm embrace and adoration for each other in their eyes, makes my heart flutter in my chest. I want what they have; I just haven't been looking for it in the right place.

"Ready?" Sawyer asks, dropping the remnants of our trash into the garbage and placing his hand on my lower back. The butterflies in my stomach take flight as we slowly walk with the masses to the exit.

"Hey, Mr. R," we hear behind us. Turning, there's a small group of boys from our school, all with starry, wide eyes and eager grins.

"Hey, boys. Having fun tonight?" Sawyer asks, giving his full attention to five of his students.

"Awesome! My big brother scored the winning touchdown," Hunter boasts.

"That's great, Hunter. The entire team played well together and stayed focused. Solid win," Sawyer says.

"Yeah. I can't wait to start open gym and weight lifting for baseball," one of the other boys, Connor, adds.

"It'll be baseball season before we know it," Sawyer agrees.

"Well, we gotta catch up with my mom. See ya Monday, Mr. R. You too, Miss S," Hunter declares, turning and heading the opposite direction as us. We both wave at the boys as they walk away, recounting details of tonight's big game.

There's a buzz in the air around us as we walk down the sidewalk to our cars. I'd like the think it's because of the Eagles' win tonight, but something tells me I would be wrong. The air is thick with anticipation and eagerness, and my back starts to tingle where his hand gently rests. It makes me want to push back against his touch, to get even closer.

"This you?" he asks, pointing to the car I was about to walk right by.

See? When he touches me, my brain doesn't function properly.

"Yep," I reply, thankful that it's dark enough that he can't see the blush that's surely creeping up my neck.

"I'm just a few cars down." Sawyer steps closer, but not too close. Residents are still milling around and chatting, making their way to their own vehicles. "Did you bring a bag? I don't want to just assume that we're still on for this evening," he whispers, maintaining eye contact.

"I believe I was told on our first date that sex wasn't appropriate, but that all bets were off on the second date."

"I believe I did say that," he quips, a small smile playing on his lips.

"I believe this is the second date."

"I believe you are correct."

Stepping closer until my chest is pressed against his, I whisper, "Then, I believe you owe me sex."

Sawyer's eyes turn molten as they drop to my lips. To punctuate my point, I lick my lips, making sure they're ready for what happens next. But after several sexually-charged seconds, he still makes no move to kiss me.

"Get in your car and follow me. When we get to my house, pull into the garage beside my car. You won't be needing it this weekend," he states boldly and confidently, a combination that sends my blood swooshing in my ears and wetness flooding my core.

My hands tremble slightly and it takes several tries to get the key in the ignition. I give myself one of those *you got this* pep talks, but as his headlights hit my car, I can't help but wonder if I've bitten off a little more than I can chew where this man is concerned.

He oozes certainty and ability, something I'm not necessarily accustomed to. Sure, the guys I've dated always talked a big game, but when it came time to put the ball into play, most of them fell short. I'm an aggressive girl with tastes that match, and if Sawyer shows me even half of the sexuality he's already displayed in our short time of knowing each other, I'm pretty sure tonight is going to be one to remember.

A shiver slips down my spine, landing squarely between my legs. My body is humming and throbbing and with each block that passes, each mile I put on my car, the closer I am to having the man I've wanted since seeing him in the bar two months ago.

When I pull into his drive, I follow him up the lane and pull into the garage bay beside his car. He's already walking around the hood of his car, meeting me at my driver's door. As I slip out, Sawyer reaches into the back seat and grabs my overnight bag. Taking my hand in his much larger one, he leads me to the entry door.

The house is dark as we enter from a mudroom. I pause to kick off my shoes, but don't get very far when I'm pulled farther into the house. We pass an expansive kitchen, but I don't have time to admire the appliances before we reach the living room. Moonlight filters through the windows along the back wall, giving off just enough light to see.

"Wow, this place is –" I start, but my words are cut off as I spin around and am claimed by his kiss.

His lips are urgent and dominating as his fingers thrust into my hair, gripping and holding my head tightly. He devours. He claims. That's the only way to describe this most epic kiss. The kiss of all kisses. Holy hell, my entire body is alive, a reckless charge of electricity and desire.

Our lips remain locked, our tongues battling for control and as he lifts me with one hand, my legs wrapping around his waist. I can feel every gloriously hard inch of his erection between my legs, rubbing against the one place I need him most. I'm practically panting with need.

Sawyer spins around, pressing me firmly into the wall. Somewhere in the distance something breaks, the sound of glass shattering fills the room. But neither of us stops. We're unable to.

My legs tighten around him as he thrusts upward. The friction between my legs is both heaven and hell. His clothes, my clothes, they all need to disappear. Fast. His hand returns to my head, his callused fingers sliding up my neck and gently gripping my jaw. I gasp huge gulps of sweet oxygen when he rips his lips from my own. Our eyes are locked intently, his breath panting against my lips, our bodies begging for more.

It's right then that I know: this won't be gentle and it won't be enough.

It may never be enough.

Sawyer runs his thumb across my cheek and slides it along the seam of my mouth. My swollen lips tingle from his touch. My tongue darts out and licks his thumb, swirling around it as if it were a delicious strawberry lollipop. His eyes burn with desire as he watches. When I suck his thumb into my mouth, grazing my teeth along the pad, he groans loudly, and I swear I can feel his cock swell even more in his pants. His nostrils flare and his breathing becomes erratic.

I'm witnessing the moment he loses control.

And it's for me.

Because of me.

His mouth claims mine once more as my hands dive for his shirt. My nails catch on the material as I rip and pull, not even caring if I destroy the garment in the process. Sawyer seems to be on the same wavelength. I feel the air kiss my back moments before his big paws sear my skin with his touch. He pushes the offending material up and over my head, his lips only leaving mine for a fraction of a second.

"This needs to go," I beg breathlessly, unable to get his shirt out from under my body.

Somehow, and I have no clue how, without setting me down, he rips his shirt up and over his own head, tossing it somewhere inside the room. My hands dive into his hair as my lips slam against his. His hands grip and knead my ass as he turns. I hear the crash just as his tongue claims my mouth. Whatever he has me pinned against moves under the joint weight of our bodies. It gives way, causing Sawyer to stumble slightly. We both grunt as my back hits something hard and unforgiving.

"Sorry," he mumbles before attacking my neck with his very skillful mouth.

My hand pushes between my legs, searching frantically for his belt. What I encounter leaves me desperate for more. His rock hard erection. It's large and threatening to claw out of his pants, which would be completely A-OK with me.

Sawyer unfastens my bra, pulling it from my arms and whipping it over his head. We're moving again, my chest pressed firmly against his, as he maneuvers us to a more stable surface. As soon as the cool wall hits my back, his mouth descends and his tongue licks one of my nipples.

I moan–or at least I think I moan–as his tongue swirls and licks one hard little bud, then the other. "Sawyer," I whisper a gasp.

His eyes lock on mine. I'm held hostage by the fierceness and drive I see brewing within. His mouth ever so slowly drops down again and he latches on to one nipple. He sucks hard, pleasure mixing with a bit of pain, and I almost come. He soothes the tender nub with his tongue before moving over to the other. I think I'm ready for it, but the moment he sucks, I scream out his name in ecstasy.

"More," he demands as he spins around and drops. Something slams against the floor, but I'm unable to figure out what. Instead, every active brain cell in my head dies a slow death as my aching core meets his throbbing cock.

He's sitting now, probably on the coffee table. Sawyer kisses his way down my neck, to my chest, and lands on my sensitive breasts. He continues to lick, nip, and kiss each breast, all while I'm gyrating in his lap, like a hooker working to get paid. With each movement of my hips, I'm climbing closer and closer to the release I crave.

"I want to taste you so bad, sweet Alison, but I don't think I can wait," he says, kissing the corners of my lips and gripping my hips, halting my movement.

"I don't want to wait. I *can't* wait."

Sawyer kisses me with urgency and moves again. This time, I know I'm on the floor. There's a frantic rush to rid us both of clothing, starting with my shoes, socks, and pants. I gaze up, wild eyed, as he kicks off his own shoes, rips off his socks, and removes his belt. I'm transfixed on every movement of his hands. He grips his button and opens the fly. He shimmies the loose jeans over his hips, revealing one of those drool-worthy Vs that leads straight to his groin. He pushes his tight boxer briefs down his thighs, revealing the most impressive cock in the history of the world. Hard, straight, and thick.

Oh, the baseball bat analogy is spot on.

I whimper.

Grabbing his wallet, Sawyer pulls a condom out and rips it open. I watch every move he makes, transfixed by the sheer beauty of the moment. Yes, it's positively beautiful. The man, his cock, his graceful actions. I can feel his eyes on me, watching me watch him.

When he's sheathed in protection, he moves to cover me, my legs instinctively wrapping around him. His cock is heavy against my stomach as his lips find mine once more. This time, the kiss is slow and tender, yet still packs quite the passionate punch.

"I really want to take it slow for our first time, but I have a feeling once I'm inside you, I won't be able to do slow."

"Don't do slow. I want you to take."

His blue eyes search mine. "You sure?"

"Definitely," I state. To punctuate my point, I tilt my hips, sliding my wetness along the base of his cock.

"Fuck, I can feel how wet you are," he moans.

"Because I want you so bad. You make me so crazy-wet." I'm panting again as anticipation and yearning collide. I'm ready, so very ready for this.

As if to validate my statement, he moves his hand between our bodies and slips a finger into my pussy. "Fuck, Alison," he whispers a raspy breath.

"That's the plan," I retort, knowing I'm pushing the limits on how much of my mouth he'll take. In fact, I'm hoping to shove him straight over his breaking point. Out of control Sawyer is quickly becoming one of my favorite facades.

He growls in my ear before biting my lobe. It sends a shockwave of pleasure straight to my core. He pushes up on his elbow and takes his cock in his other hand. I get a jolt of desire at the prospect of watching him stroke himself off.

I'll have to see if that's on the menu later.

Lining himself up at my entrance, he gently pushes forward. There's a stretch and burning sensation as my body adjusts to allow his girth. His eyes pin me to the floor just as much as his body. He makes small thrusts until he's fully seated inside me. The slight tinge of pain as I accommodate his size is quickly replaced by pure rapture.

Then he pulls almost completely out and stops. Our eyes lock for a heartbeat, and he thrusts forward.

Hard.

And all bets are off.

The pace is set immediately. It's fast and hungry, with slapping skin and guttural grunts. My nails sink into the tender skin of his back, probably hard enough to draw blood, but he doesn't complain. In fact, the pain almost spurs him on. My back burns from the rug, but I ignore it. Instead, I focus on the joy sweeping through my body as it climbs high and higher. So high, the clouds are within my reach.

Sawyer is getting close too. I can feel it in his movements and taste it on his skin. I hang on tight as he takes me straight to the edge. I'm teetering there, hanging on by a thread, and begging for that final push.

"Are you ready to come, Alison?" he asks, pausing when he's buried to the root.

"Yes. God, yes. Please." Each word comes out a gasp, a declaration, and a plea.

Sawyer pulls out and then slams back in. The friction and angle send me flying over the edge, freefalling through encompassing white light. My body bears down on his as my orgasm rips through it like an exorcism. His cock swells one last time as he pumps hard, stilling and spilling my name from his lips with his release. Sawyer moves as shutters wrack his body until he's unable to move any longer.

When exhaustion sets in, he collapses on top of me, a tangled mess of sweaty limbs and labored breathing. There's something incredibly comforting about feeling the weight of his body pressing into me, even if he's pressing me into the uncomfortably hard floor.

Without saying a word, he adjusts his weight to take the brunt of it off me but still keeping me pinned to the floor. My fingers slip into the wet strands of his hair, toying with the ends and savoring the feel of it between my fingers. He cups my jaw tenderly before placing soft kisses along my clammy neck.

"That was," he starts, but doesn't finish.

"Yeah," I confirm, unable to find my own word to describe it.

Incredible? Unforgettable? Epic?

Probably all of those and more.

14

Sawyer

I can't breathe.

I'm not talking about the strenuous exercise that makes you want to hurl your guts up and steals the very breath you breathe. I'm talking about the sheer magnitude of this moment. This woman. She takes my breath and my sanity in a way that has never happened before. Even with my ex.

My lips seem to always want to touch her skin, which is exactly what I'm doing right now. Trailing gentle kisses up and down her neck before I make my way to her lips. My hands caress her hips and outer thighs, her legs are still wrapped firmly around my body. If I could stay right here, just like this with her legs around me and my cock buried inside her sweet pussy, I'd be the happiest motherfucker in the world.

I was rough. Much rougher than I've ever been before, especially with someone I take to bed (or the floor) for the first time. But she didn't seem to mind. In fact, it seemed to light her fire. I think my sexy little math teacher likes it rough and dirty.

Nuzzling my nose along her ear, I slide to my back, landing on something sharp. "Ouch," I bite out, turning to see what I've landed on.

"Holy shit," AJ says, drawing my attention to her face. She's staring wide-eyed at my living room, her mouth hanging open. It makes me want to do naughty things to that sexy little mouth.

I finally glance at what she's looking at.

And that's when I see it.

My living room is trashed.

Like a tornado swept through my house, tearing apart my belongings and discarding them haphazardly.

"What the hell?" I mumble, taking in the upturned coffee table and the scattered magazines.

"Did we do this?" she gasps, her eyes settling on the broken picture that used to be hanging on my wall.

Carefully, I hop up and absorb the full impact of the living room destruction. My television is on the floor, clearly no longer positioned on the entertainment center. The few knick-knacky things I brought from my old house lay smashed and broken in pieces. My lamp won't be shedding light on the room anymore.

It looks like I've been robbed or survived some sort of natural disaster.

Tornado AJ.

Hurricane Ali.

That thought makes me smile.

Sex with this woman was so intense and passionate that we tore apart my fucking living room and didn't even have a clue that it was happening.

Suddenly, I'm laughing. AJ glances at me as if I've lost my mind, and maybe I have. Anyone else would probably freak at the financial loss, but I don't give a shit. It was worth it.

"Looks like I'm calling a cleaning service in the morning," I chuckle, wrapping my arm around her shoulder, pulling her back to my front, and nuzzling her neck.

"I can't believe we did this," she mumbles before leaning back into my embrace.

"I can. I knew our first time would be explosive."

"Explosive, yes. Destructive, no."

"It's kinda funny, actually," I tell her, leaning down and kissing the sensitive skin behind her ear. A shutter sweeps through her naked body, her sweet ass pressing into my cock, causing it to stir to life once more.

"Your TV," she complains, taking in the cracked screen and the odd angle it leans against the stand and the floor.

"I can buy a new one," I insist. In one swift motion, I bend down, slide one arm behind her back and the other beneath her knees, and pick her up. She's in my arms (where she suddenly feels like she has always belonged) as I carefully step out of the room.

"You don't have to carry me," she says as I approach the stairs.

"I like carrying you," I tell her honestly as I make my way into the bathroom.

AJ wraps her arms tighter around my neck, her sweet tits pressing firmly against my chest. "Well, if I'm being honest, I happen to like it when you carry me."

"Duly noted." Depositing her in my large bathroom off my bedroom, I crank on the hot water and turn on the multiple water jets in the shower. I also quickly dispose of the used rubber from earlier.

"Holy shitballs, look at this tub," she coos, walking over and sliding her hand along the rim of the impressive jetted tub. I'll be honest, I didn't buy the house for this thing, but as a former pro athlete, who is accustomed to aches and pains, this baby has already come in very handy after a strenuous workout.

"Nice, isn't it? Maybe we'll use it later," I tell her, running my hands down her sides and cupping her firm little ass.

"I could throw a bath bomb in that thing, grab a book and glass of wine, and not come out for days," she mumbles.

"That could be arranged," I confess, my cock throbbing and moving between her ass cheeks. I'm all too familiar with the sudden desire to be somewhere and not come out for days.

"Do you have bath bombs?" she purrs like a kitten getting her belly rubbed.

"I have Epsom Salt," I offer. "Definitely no bath bombs."

"I'll make you some tomorrow night," she suggests breathlessly. "This way, when you take your next bath, you'll smell like lavender or jasmine."

Leading her to the shower, I confess, "I'd rather smell like AJ," as my hand cups her pussy. "And what's this about making bath bombs tomorrow night?" I ask, grazing my teeth across her shoulder and following it back with my tongue.

"It's sisters' night. We get together the first Saturday of the month, but had to reschedule last week. We always do something together. We've been keeping it close to home since Lexi is getting close to her due date, and she's been on partial bed rest. But she convinced Linkin to let her go out tomorrow night. It's probably going to be her last hoorah before the babies come." AJ's chest is heaving as I slide my fingers through her pussy, pushing two fingers deep inside of her.

"And you're making bath bombs?"

"What?"

"Bath bombs. You're making bath bombs?" I wrap my arm around her abdomen and tease her hard little nipples.

"Yes. God, yes. That."

"Are you still talking about the bath bombs?"

"What?"

"Never mind," I say, wide smile on my face, as I lead her into the big tile and glass shower.

The water is hot as it shoots from jets on three sides of the shower. I use my larger body and pin AJ to the wall. She gasps when her body hits the cool tile, a sound that shoots straight to my dick.

Water glistens as it slides down her curves, my hands following as I drop to my knees. "Turn around," I instruct hoarsely.

Her eyes are already half-lidded as she spins and faces me. She looks like a fucking angel, wet hair hanging in her face and water cascading over her body. This vision of her is so much better than the one I conjured up in my dirty mind. That image has kept me comfy many nights since we first met. This view, however, will replace every dirty fantasy I've ever had.

Lifting her leg, I set it on my shoulder. "What are you doing?" she asks, her wide green eyes following my every move.

"Something I've been wanting to do since I met you in July." Her pussy is on full display right in front of my face, trimmed brown curls atop bare lips. My mouth waters.

"I want you inside me again."

"I didn't bring any protection in here." Even though I want that too, I'm determined to have my fill—a taste—of her.

Gripping her ass, I pull her forward, meeting her halfway. The moment my tongue touches her sweetness, we both moan in pleasure. Her scent and her taste wrap around me, holding me hostage and demanding more. I lick and suck on her clit, savoring her as I slowly work her into a heated frenzy.

Only when I can hear her breathing becoming labored do I slide my fingers in to play. I keep my tongue moving, flicking and sucking on her hard clit, as I maneuver two fingers into her pussy. She grips me tightly with each thrust of my hand. I glance up to see one hand flush against the tiled wall above her head, as if grasping for a lifeline to keep her upright, while the other hand drops to my head. When she pulls my hair, I growl and feast even more.

My pace quickens, my fingers working faster as her inner muscles grip me so fucking tight I swear they numb from blood loss. "Sawyer," she begs repeatedly, my scalp burning beneath her fingers.

She flies over the edge, her body convulsing around my fingers, my tongue not slowing its assault. I feel her weight start to drop as she rides out her release. Quickly pulling my fingers from her body, I wrap my arms around her, bringing her body against mine. Her eyes are half-lidded and hazy as she tries to focus on my cocky grin.

"That was fucking incredible," I tell her before claiming her lips with my own. Her fingers tighten around my shoulders, the slight bite of her nails a welcomed pain.

"I want more," she whispers against my mouth.

I move quickly. The shower is off and she's in my arms as we head to the vanity. Surely it's sturdy enough for what I have planned, right? I guess we're about to find out because my need for her is too great to ignore. It's too great to cart her off to an actual bed, like she deserves. Instead, every animal instinct I have takes control as I reach into the cabinet and pull out a condom. It's secured on my aching cock as I take my place between her legs. And yeah, it's probably wrong and makes me sound like a caveman, but whatever; between her legs feels like *my* place. No one else's.

Mine.

So I go ahead and tell her that as I claim her, pushing myself inside her warm and welcoming body. That one word comes out a growl as I bury myself balls deep.

"Yes. Yours," she huffs, greedily taking everything I give her.

My hands find her ass once more as I help hold her in position. She leans back against the mirror, opening her body up even more for me. The sight of her is my undoing. The passion and trust I see swirling in those deep green eyes completely shatters me like those glass decorative things in the living room.

I know, in this moment, I'll never be the same.

It's more than great sex. I can already tell. I've had enough sex in my life to know the difference. Great sex is around every corner, on every block. But this? This is magic.

It's also not exactly the right time to start dissecting what this means. Instead, I focus on the look of passion written on her beautiful face–a look that I put there, and will continue to put there for as long as she'll let me.

"I'm going to come," she whispers, hanging on to my arms for dear life.

"I want you to come on me, Alison. Fuck, I *need* it, baby." I don't even know this man who is talking. He's dominating and possessive. He's completely enthralled and consumed. He's smitten. And it feels so fucking amazing right now. These crazy feelings are slamming together in a tsunami of emotions, reminding me that I'm completely at her mercy.

Alison.

When she comes, I feel it rip through my soul and spiral down to my toes. My balls tighten up, almost painfully, as my own release grabs hold, refusing to let go. We come together, wild and alive, until we're both boneless and spent.

After a few moments of getting our breathing under control, she throws me a bit of that sass I enjoy so much. "Well, at least we didn't break the sink."

Her comment makes me laugh, especially in light of the fact I was concerned about the stability of the vanity earlier. Laughter seems to come so easily when I'm with her, which is another pleasant change from my previous relationships.

My lips press against hers, slow and steady, as I wrap my arms around her back. "Let's go to bed," I suggest.

Grabbing a hand towel, I make quick work of getting rid of the condom and cleaning up our bodies as best as I can. Honestly, I should probably suggest another shower, but exhaustion is settling in her droopy green eyes. Right now, I just want to hold her against me while she falls asleep. There'll be time for another shower in the morning.

With her hand in mine, AJ hops off the vanity and follows me back into my bedroom. The large bed is made (something I did this morning because I was pretty sure she was coming home with me tonight) so I pull the covers back and wait for her to slip inside. The sight of her brown hair against my charcoal sheets makes my heartbeat gallop in my chest, so strong I feel it in every limb.

Ignoring the bedside lamp, I climb in and pull her body close. The room is dark as her head settles on my arm, her naked back pressed firmly against my chest. Even with the slight height difference, we fit together like puzzle pieces. She exhales deeply, her body relaxing in my arms.

"Good night, Sawyer," she whispers in the moonlight.

"Night, Alison," I murmur, placing a gentle kiss on her neck, before settling in for the night.

Sleep comes quickly for AJ. With my arms wrapped around her, I relax fully, probably better than I ever have. I'm not tormented with the what-ifs that have plagued my sleep since that fateful game that ruined my career. Visions of those final days with Carrie are nowhere to be found. Instead, I find solace with the sexy little brunette in my arms.

If I'm being brutally honest, it's that contentment that allows my brain to venture into new what-if territory. This one has me looking forward, instead of back.

And for the first time in a long-ass time, I really like that fucking view.

"Rumor has it you took our sister-in-law on a date last night." I recognize the voice instantly as I slide onto the barstool at Lucky's Bar. Looking over, I come face-to-face with the very serious glare of Linkin Stone, though I think the tough-guy routine is just an act.

At least I hope it is.

"Lexi got a text message from Grandma," he confirms, taking a drink of something that resembles water.

"Jaime too," Ryan adds.

"Abby didn't respond to the text quick enough, so Grandma called my phone to make sure she was still alive," Levi contributes.

"Plus, I guess there were pictures," Ryan says before popping some popcorn into his mouth.

"Pictures?"

"Online." This from Linkin.

"Online?" That comment stops me in my tracks.

"Yeah, some trashy rag had pictures. You didn't know?"

"No," I whisper, my mind spinning. Were they quick photos taken with someone's cell phone and posted online or am I being tailed by paparazzi? I haven't felt their all-knowing, far-reaching telephoto lenses following my every move since I relocated to Jupiter Bay.

"I didn't see the pictures, but Lexi said they were taken at the football game last night."

"Well, shit," I mumble, glancing over my shoulder for the first time since I arrived at my new town.

"I don't think they were cell phone photos either, if that's what you're thinking. They weren't posted on Facebook or Instagram by some high schooler at the game. According to Lexi, these were professional and taken from across the field with a good lens. I'm guessing they found out where you moved to after leaving Texas," Linkin adds.

"It wasn't a big secret, but I didn't exactly broadcast it either," I mumble, glancing at the guys.

Linkin's completely distracted, glancing repeatedly out the window at the building lit up across the street. It's also the first time I realize Dean is missing. "Aren't you missing someone?"

"Brielle was sick, so Dean stayed home," Ryan says.

"Ahh."

I observe quietly for several moments as Linkin turns back around and watches the building across the street. "You okay?"

Linkin glances my way as the other two guys chuckle. "Fine. Why wouldn't I be fine? It's not like the love of my life has discarded my request to stay home and in bed where she's safe until the babies come."

That makes the guys laugh. "Dude, you can't control that woman," Levi says. "Not when she sets her mind to something."

"No shit," Linkin grumbles. "I'm not trying to control her, but she's supposed to be taking it easy. Making bath bombs isn't at home resting, where I can keep an eye on her."

"Is she supposed to be up and walking around?" Ryan asks.

"Her doc says it's fine, but I think she needs to stay put. Why does she need to get up? I can get her anything she needs."

He sounds a tad overprotective to me, but what the hell do I know about pregnancy and babies? Absolutely nothing, that's what.

Linkin glances over his shoulder once again.

"How long are you waiting until you go over there?" Levi asks with a wide grin.

"Five minutes," he states plainly. "It's been thirty already. How long does it take to make little balls that explode in your bath water anyway?"

"I'm sure she's fine," I add, recalling how excited AJ was earlier today when she told me about tonight's sisters' night. They were meeting at the local homemade bath and body product shop to make their own bath bombs and soap. It sounds a little weird to me, but she was all sorts of thrilled. Maybe it has something to do with the fact that I told her she could use one tonight in my big tub.

Of course, I'd be joining her.

It was also discussed this afternoon that she'd be coming home with me again tonight. We woke up and took a shower, which turned into getting each other dirty again before we could wash each other up. I made eggs and toast while she fixed herself a big mug of coffee with some fancy coffee creamer I found. It's not a caramel latte, but I think it'll do on the weekends.

After breakfast, I tried to call my cleaning lady, but AJ insisted on helping clean up the mess. It didn't take too long to sweep up the broken glass and throw out the television, but the hole in the wall from where one of the corners of the end tables pierced the drywall will have to be fixed. I thought about asking Ryan tonight, but I'm not sure it'll be worth the razzing.

It was when we went to the electronics store to buy a new TV that we discussed this evening. She explained how her sisters got together every month and how the guys always crash it. She even went as far as to invite me to hang out with the guys while she gathered with her sisters. I didn't want to just assume she would stay afterward. No, I needed to hear that she would come back home with me, and she needed to hear how much I wanted her to. I am not even close to having reached my fill of this woman.

She's under my skin.

And later tonight, she'll be in my bed once again.

"Is the nursery done?" Levi asks the dad-to-be.

"Done. Ryan finished building the shelving system in the closet and everything is pretty much washed and ready to go."

"And you don't know what you're having?" I confirm.

"Nope. This is gonna be the best surprise ever," he boasts proudly.

"How long?" I ask, enjoying getting to know these guys more.

"Doc says they'll take the babies at thirty-five to thirty-six weeks. We have an appointment Monday and they'll book the OR then. She'll be thirty-four weeks Monday."

"Holy shit, you're gonna be a dad in like a week or two," Levi reminds Linkin. There's a weird mix of anxiety and anticipation reflecting in his eyes. It's like he's really excited, yet terrified at the same time.

I imagine that's how any new parent probably feels. Though, I have no firsthand experience with any of that. Carrie didn't want kids for a while because of the impact it would have on her career. She was one of the faces of Victoria's Secret and not showing any signs of slowing down her modeling and traveling.

I knew I wanted kids someday. Even when I was young and wild, fresh out of college and heading to the majors, I saw kids in my future one day. It got bad three years ago when I hit my thirtieth birthday, but every time I'd bring it up to Carrie, I'd get her song and dance about not being ready yet.

At least now I don't have to worry about her promise of *someday*. God knows she can't keep a fucking promise anyway.

"I'm going over there," Linkin says, tossing a few bills on the bar and standing up. "I can't take it."

"You're just gonna bust in there, throw her over your shoulder, and carry her home?" Ryan asks, his voice laced with humor.

"This I gotta see," Levi says, throwing more cash on the bar.

Ryan and I follow suit, leaving healthy tips for the old man who owns the bar, before heading out into the September evening. There's barely any traffic so we only have to wait for a few cars before we cross the street. As soon as we reach the door of the business, the happy sounds of female laughter float outside. I swear I can pick AJ's laugh out of all of them, a thought that makes me wonder if I need to turn in my man card.

Linkin pulls open the door and marches inside like a Stormtrooper ready for battle. We head to the back, the noise of female cackles getting louder with each step we take. I can't decide if AJ is going to be upset or surprised at our intrusion, and there's no time to wage a guess. We're outside the room.

This could get interesting.

15

AJ

"I swear to God, if I didn't love that man so much I would kill him. He's driving me to drink," Lexi says, her belly protruding from her midsection so big, that it almost makes me uncomfortable for her.

"But you can't drink," I prompt.

"Thanks for the reminder," Lexi chastises sarcastically.

"It can't be that bad," Meghan says softly, always the peacemaker.

"Oh, it is! He thinks I'm helpless. It's always *No, Lexi, don't move. Should you be up? Why are you walking? No, Firecracker, we can't have sex. The babies, the babies, the babies!*" Her voice escalates dramatically with each word, not to mention the fact that everyone else in the room turned and started listening when she said sex.

"You're not having *the sex?*" Jaime gasps. "I thought you said pregnancy makes you… horny," she whispers so only us sisters can hear.

"It does! And he knows it!" Lexi hollers, adding the oil to the mixture in her bowl and stirring the ever-loving shit out of it. "But why would he want sex with me, anyway," she adds, her voice sounding completely dejected. "Look at me." Lexi drops her hand to her huge abdomen and gently rubs.

"Why wouldn't he want to have sex with you?" Payton asks, dumbfounded. "You're gorgeous. You're glowing and light up a room."

"That's sweat, Payters. I'm a sweaty pig," she says, a single tear slipping down her cheek.

"You're amazing," I add. "Look at you. You're growing that man's babies in your body."

"And we've all seen the way he looks at you, Lexi. That man can't keep his eyes or his hands off you." This from Abby. We all nod our heads in agreement.

"I know," she whispers. "He's the one who's amazing. He dotes on me, anticipates my next move before I do, and treats me better than anyone ever has. And don't get me started on when he sings to the babies at bedtime," she says with a teary smile on her face.

"Aww," we all coo together.

"He sings?"

"It's the only thing that calms them down. I'm pretty sure we're having boys because they already fight like cats and dogs, and let me tell you, there is absolutely no more room for horseplay in this womb."

"He loves you so much," Meghan says, her own eyes glistening with tears.

"He does," Lexi confirms. "Even when I'm a hormonal psychopath who screams at him for not letting me go to the bathroom alone." She sniffles, completely forgoing her bath bomb mixture in front of her. Hell, we've all pretty much disregarded our bowls. "And I love him too."

"He knows that," I remind her, reaching across the table and patting her hand. "That's why he puts up with your hormonal psychopath side," I add lightheartedly.

She laughs and wipes her tears. "We better get these finished. He's probably chomping at the bit to come over and drag me back to the house."

"How did you convince him to let you out?" Abby asks. It's no secret Linkin has gone to the extreme to make sure our sister is taking it easy.

"Road-head," she says loudly, drawing the attention of the ladies around us once more.

"You're giving him road-head? Atta girl!" Jaime boasts, a proud little gleam in her eye.

"Are you kidding me? I can't give road-head like this! I can't see my feet, Jaime! God, I miss my feet. I haven't seen them in months," she mumbles, grimacing a little as if in pain.

"What was that?" Meghan asks as all of us watch our baby sister adjust her position in her chair.

"Nothing," she waves off. "Just those Braxton Hicks things. I've been having them all day. Totally fine. Why are we not talking about AJ and the fact that she's having sex with a major leaguer?"

"Former major leaguer," I correct.

"But you *are* having *the sex* with him, right?"

I glance around and notice a couple of young ladies at the table next to us are very quiet and they appear to be leaning in our direction. I know I won't be giving them any of the gory details like they're hoping, especially not in a public place with very open ears eager to hear all of the personal details. There's something about hearing about the paparazzi that followed and hounded Sawyer that has me biting my tongue right now.

"Why don't I come over tomorrow and paint your toes," I offer Lexi, changing the subject. I mean I know I'm staying with Sawyer again tonight, but I should be back at my place mid-morning, right? Early afternoon at the latest, I'm sure.

Maybe?

"Thanks, AJ, but Linkin already did it last night when we watched *Sixteen Candles*," she says, making us all abandon our bomb-making and look at her. "What? It was my night to pick."

For the next five minutes, we mix in the rest of our ingredients and start to press out bath bombs. I opt for plain Jane circles, especially since I'm going to leave a few of them at Sawyer's house. I'm not sure if he'll use them or not, or maybe it's just an excuse for me to go over and use his big bathtub. We're just setting them down on the tray to dry, the air a mixture of soothing lavender and tantalizing strawberry, when the door flies open.

"That didn't take long," Jaime mumbles under her breath as Linkin leads the charge into the room, followed by Ryan, Levi, and Sawyer.

"What are you doing here? It's been like thirty-eight minutes," Lexi demands, trying to get up, but failing. Linkin is right there, placing his hand under her arm to help. "I got it!" she chastises, but fails again. "Fine. You can help," she mumbles dejectedly.

"Do you have to use the bathroom?" he asks sweetly as he helps her stand.

"No, I don't have to use the bathroom," she grumbles as she stands. "Crap, now I have to use the bathroom."

We all watch as she waddles toward the restrooms, Linkin hot on her heels, trying to be supportive, but getting his ass chewed the entire way. The best part is when she has her back turned, we can see the small grin on his face. I think he's doing it on purpose, but I'm not about to jump in the middle of their power struggles by asking.

"How's it going?" Sawyer asks, his warm breath tickling my ear.

"Excellent. Lexi was just telling us how much she loves and hates Linkin. It's quite entertaining," I tell him.

"What is this mess?" he asks, turning his attention to the colorful sand-like material scattered all over the table.

"Bath bombs. I may or may not have made a sandalwood one for you," I reply with a wink.

"Is that a manly scent? I only want manly scented bath bombs for my nightly soak, AJ."

"Definitely manly," I confirm as I turn and press my chest into his. "But maybe it would help if you had a bath partner. Then, it wouldn't matter what the scent was," I suggest.

"A bath partner, you say?" He pretends to really think about that idea. "That could work, as long as I can turn on the jets."

"Oh, the jets are mandatory. Who would use a tub like that without the jets?" I ask, feigning disbelief.

"That is true," he says, wrapping his hand around my waist. "So, do you get to take the bombs home with you tonight? I think we should test this sandalwood."

"They're supposed to dry for twenty-four hours," I tell him.

"Let me get this straight. You make them with wet material, have to let them dry, just so you can throw them in the bathtub?" he asks.

I stare at him for several heartbeats, but realize I don't have a logical explanation. "You just singlehandedly wrecked the entire bath bomb industry." That earns me a little chuckle that's deep and sultry. My lady parts stand up and beg.

"Okay, so I've noticed Lexi grimace at least twice since we've been here," Abby says, concern etched on her face.

"She said it was those Braxton thingies."

"Is it?" Lexi's twin asks.

"How would I know? I've never had a baby," I argue.

"No one here has," she reminds me. "Where's Dean?"

Payton overhears the question and walks our way. "He's home with Bri. She wasn't feeling well, so he decided to stay home instead of taking her to spend the night with Dad, Grandma, and Grandpa. Why?"

"He's the only one here who's had a baby. I was wondering about those Braxton thingies."

"They're like practice contractions," Payton says.

"I know, but I could tell by the look on her face that she was really in pain. Plus, she's really uncomfortable. She wouldn't say, but I know. I feel it," Abby whispers, really worried about her sister.

"I'm sure everything's fine, Abs," Payton replies.

Just then, we watch Lexi walk out of the bathroom. Linkin is behind her, trying to help guide her back into the room, when she stops and makes a face. It's one of complete discomfort and maybe a little worry. Linkin doesn't see it, but we all do.

"Everything okay, Lexi?" Jaime asks cautiously as she comes over and joins us.

"Fine. Everything's fine," she confirms.

"You sure?" I ask slowly.

"Why does everyone keep asking me that? It's just a little Braxton Hicks contractions," she assures.

"Braxton Hicks? You're having contractions?" Linkin asks, his eyes wide with panic.

"Braxton. Hicks," she bites out, taking a large pause between the two words for emphasis.

"But when my mom was pregnant with twins, she–"

"Stop right there, Stone. I've heard every detail of your mom's pregnancy with the hellions. I know what I'm talking about here," she insists.

"But she thought–"

"Enough, Linkin! I know what contractions are and these aren't them!" she hollers, but then bends down and grabs her stomach, moaning a little. "Holy shit, that hurts," she pants.

"We're going to the hospital," Linkin demands.

"I'm fine," she whispers, trying to catch her breath. "It's not time yet for the babies."

Linkin seems to transform right before our eyes. He bends down until he's face-to-face with Lexi. "I know you're fine, Firecracker, but humor me, okay? Let's go to the hospital so that they can tell us they're Braxton Hicks and send us home. Then you can tell me I told you so for the rest of the night while I massage your feet," he says softly as he brushes the hair off her forehead. He's so gentle and supportive of her that it brings tears to my own eyes, not to mention the tears that well up in Lexi's eyes.

"Okay, babe. Let's go," she concedes gently, allowing him to lead her toward the door.

"Is she okay?" Sawyer asks as I start to gather up our things.

"He thinks she's in labor. I could tell by the way he completely changed his demeanor. He's not giving her a hard time anymore."

"Is she in labor?" Jaime asks.

"It's not time yet," Payton says, her voice laced with worry.

"Let's go to the hospital just to make sure," Meghan suggests.

Together, we all rush from the building. I jump into the passenger seat of Sawyer's car and we immediately fall in line with the rest of my family, making our way to the hospital. It's the first time this evening I'm glad we weren't drinking.

I know what you're gonna say–a Summer sisters' night without booze? It happens. Well, it happened tonight. No one wanted to drink in front of Lexi, especially since she's so irritable and emotional lately. She's been talking a lot about having a drink when the babies are born, so we didn't want to rub her nose in the fact that we could all drink and she couldn't.

We're both quiet as we race to the hospital. Sawyer reaches over and links his fingers with mine, quietly offering me support. My uneasiness is a palpable creature, living and breathing in the car with me. My foot bounces against the floorboard and sounds like a snare drum during a pep rally.

"I'm sure she's fine. They'll probably send her home, like Linkin said," Sawyer assures me.

"You're probably right. But it still concerns me a little. She's not scheduled to have them for a couple more weeks."

"Let's just get to the hospital and see what's going on, okay?"

"Yeah." It's hard to swallow over the huge lump in my throat.

Sawyer parks in the lot next to Ryan's truck. We make sure everyone is accounted for and then all head into the hospital together. Our group bypasses the front counter and heads to Labor and Delivery.

"Should we call Dad?" Abby asks.

"Let's wait until we know something. We don't want to worry him and have him get here to find out they're sending her home," Payton reasons.

"True," Abby mumbles.

When we reach the Labor and Delivery hall, Payton gives Lexi's name to the little box on the wall that connects the outside hallway to the L&D unit on the opposite side. We're buzzed in and pointed to a small waiting area. The place is deserted, even though it's only a little after eight.

After ten minutes or so, a young woman comes to greet us. "You must be Alexis Summer's family. They're hooking her up to the fetal monitor now. Her doctor wants to monitor those contractions for a bit and see what's going on. Once we know more, someone will come back out," she says politely, not giving us any information at all.

"So we wait," Jaime says, sitting down in one of the chairs, her husband joining her.

"I'm going to slip out and call Dean, let him know what's going on," Payton states, cell phone in her hand.

We make small talk as we wait for any word on Lexi, but even then, no one appears very chatty. It's about an hour, and one cup of horrible waiting room coffee later, that Linkin enters the room.

"She's in labor," he confirms. "At first they were thinking Braxton Hicks, but then the contractions started to register. They've been getting closer together over the last hour. The babies' heart rates look good on the monitor and they even did an ultrasound to make sure they're both in the right position. They're gonna let her go naturally." He seems to take a big breath. "We're gonna have babies tonight."

I move first, throwing my arms around his big body. There's a slight tremble in his arms as he wraps them around my back. More arms encompass us as my sisters all join in and turn it into a group hug.

"She's gonna be fine," Payton whispers to him, offering him an encouraging smile.

"She is," he agrees, nodding his head. "She's the strongest woman I know."

"And they don't think it's too early for the babies? I mean, she wasn't scheduled to be induced for another week or two," Abby asks, clearly still worried about her twin sister and our nieces or nephews.

"Yeah, the doc says it should be okay. They gave her steroids to help make sure the babies' lungs are developed, which they say is just a precaution. They also have some antibiotics in her IV as a preventative measure."

"You're about to be a dad," I state, a wide smile spreading across my face.

Linkin seems to take in my heavy words for a few moments before his own grin spreads across his face. "We're gonna be a family," he whispers, and if I'm not mistaken, blinks away wetness in his eyes. "I better get back in there," he adds, nodding toward the hallway.

"Go! Keep us posted," Jaime says happily.

"I gotta call my mom first," Linkin says, pulling out his cell phone. "Wait, your dad." He looks up at Meghan.

"I got it," she says, pulling her cell phone from her purse and following him into the hallway.

"I can't believe we're about to be aunts tonight," Jaime says, an excited grin on her face.

"Me either. It seems like she just told us she was pregnant," I say, walking over and sitting beside Sawyer. He's deep in conversation with Ryan and Levi about baseball.

"Everything okay?" he asks, when I slide into the chair beside him.

"Fine, I guess. They're not stopping her labor. They feel she's far enough along and the babies are strong enough to be born now."

"That's good," he says, pulling me into his chest and kissing my forehead.

"You could probably head home, if you want. You don't need to stay here and wait with me."

"Are you kidding? I'm not going anywhere," he says with conviction.

"It could be a long night," I add, giving him another out. It's not that I want him to go or anything, but I don't want him to feel like he needs to stay.

"I don't mind," he says into my hair. "Unless you want me to go. I would understand if you wanted this to be just your family."

I'm shaking my head before he's even finished saying the words. The truth is I want him here. The comfort and support he has offered tonight has been a welcome reprieve, something I've never had before. It's nice to have a friend to lean on, and know has my back, if something should happen. "No, I kinda want you to stay."

"Then I stay," he says, placing another kiss on the top of my head.

Abby and Levi are cuddled up next to us, sharing a chair, and the guys continue to talk baseball. It amazes me the stats and general knowledge Sawyer has for the game, and not just his team, but all of the others too. You can hear the love for the sport in his voice as he talks about his career and even a little about the injury. I've read many articles that focused on the play, the surgery, the recoup time, and the decision that his shoulder would never be the same, resulting in the termination of his contract. Even now, as he talks to Levi and Ryan, he sounds almost clinical. He states the facts easily, but I can sense the pain. I can hear the sadness buried deep in his words. I can feel his hurt.

Soon, a commotion draws our attention to the doorway. Grandma and Grandpa are there, with Dad hot on their heels. "Where's my granddaughter. I need to see her," Grandma says to the nurse at the counter.

"I can check with the patient to see if she's up for visitors," the kind nurse says, making Grandma scoff.

"I'm Grandma, dear," she says slowly, as if her title alone is equivalent to the Queen of England and earns her a free pass to do or say whatever she wants.

"I'll be right back, ma'am." The nurse hurries down the hallway to a room at the end.

"Good evening, family," she announces happily when she enters the waiting room.

"Hi, Grandma," Abby says, hopping off Levi's lap and giving her a hug.

"Oh, you don't have to stand, Abs. You have one of the best seats in the house. You know, hospital storage rooms are usually locked nowadays, but the bathrooms are fair game. At least you know they're super clean; nothing like bar bathrooms," she says to our sister, who blushes a thousand shades of red.

"This hardly seems like the appropriate time or place," Abby babbles, stumbling over her words.

"It's always the right time for *the sex*, dear. In fact, your father had to interrupt our playtime in the playroom this evening," she says softly, as if she were referring to something as simple as the weather.

"I'm traumatized for life," Dad mumbles, looking at the floor.

"Oh, hush," Grandma says just as the nurse returns to the waiting room.

"Lexi has agreed to a few visitors. Two at a time and for only a few minutes," she says as Grandma barrels to the front of the room, grabbing Abby on her way by, leaving the rest of us to sit.

And wait.

Something none of us does well.

16

Sawyer

The waiting room is silent, which is probably why Orval's next comment feels like it was blasted from a megaphone. "We didn't get to finish," he says quietly to Ryan, who's seated beside him.

And poor Ryan actually glances down. The look on his face is a combination of horror and like he's going to be sick, poor bastard.

"Grandpa!" Jaime chastises as she tries to mask her discomfort with a laugh.

"Oh, it's okay, Jaimers. It'll go down when the pill wears off." Orval leans back in the chair, his arms crossed firmly over his chest as he closes his eyes. He looks like he's trying to nap. Except for the fact that his pants are tented in the front.

And no, it's not like I was trying to look at this point, but that's not exactly something you can miss when your attention is drawn to it.

I'm probably going to have nightmares now.

"It's okay if you want to run screaming from the building," AJ murmurs beside me. "I wouldn't hold it against you."

"Are you kidding? I think they're great. My grandparents died when I was pretty little, so I'd like to think this is just a glimpse at what I've missed," I reply with a casual shrug.

"Oh, I happen to know for a fact that my grandparents are nothing like anyone else's."

I chuckle. "Maybe."

"Tell me more about your family," she asks. I reach over and touch the soft skin on the inside of her forearm, running the side of my finger up and down her arm. She shutters under my graze, reminding me of how much I really enjoy touching her.

"Well, I was born and raised in Charlotteville. My mom and dad have been married for almost forty years. I have an older sister, Courtney, who works in admissions at the college there, and a younger goofball brother, Dylan, who's married and works for an advertising agency. I went to college there at University of Virginia before being drafted by the Rangers, and was fortunate enough to play my entire career for the same club."

"And where does Carrie Doherty fall in all of this?" she asks. No, I don't really want to talk about my ex-wife, but it's going to keep coming up until she knows all the details.

I exhale slowly and look her way. "I met her during my fifth year with the Rangers. I went to a New Year's Eve gala for one of my sponsors in New York and she was there. My agent introduced us, and I guess, as they say, the rest is history."

She seems to absorb my words, and by the look on her face, is contemplating asking for more details. I mean there are a lot of details. She probably knows what the rag magazines said about my cheating and womanizing for the duration of my marriage, but I hope she also takes the source into consideration.

She opens her mouth to talk, probably to ask me some of the burning questions I know she wants to ask, when Emma and Abby come back into the room. "You're up, Grandpa. Linkin's in the hallway outside of the room while they give her the epidural," Emma tells her son-in-law with a wide smile on her face.

Without saying a word, Brian jumps up from his chair and heads down the hallway.

"Everything okay?" Payton asks through a yawn. I glance at my watch and notice it's nearing eleven o'clock.

"Fine, fine, Payters. She's progressing beautifully, though she still has a ways to go. Plus, the focus right now is on Linkin's hand," she replies with a bubble of excitement.

"What happened to his hand?" Levi asks.

"Lexi tried to rip it off during one of her contractions," Abby informs him with a big smile.

"I've never seen such a petite little thing bring a big strong hunk of a man to his knees like that," Emma chimes in.

"Literally," Abby whispers to Levi.

"The doctor had to check it out and make sure it wasn't broken," Emma continues.

"There were tears," Abby gushes.

"Lexi's?" AJ asks.

"No, Linkin's," Emma finishes. "Anyway, the anesthesiologist just arrived to do her epidural. She'll be feeling no pain any moment."

"Good," Jaime says.

"I don't know how Linkin was able to sit there and watch her be in pain," Ryan adds, rubbing Jaime's shoulders affectionately. The look on his face speaks volumes that it won't sit well with him when he's in Linkin's shoes.

"That man was amazing. Besides the hand incident and the fact the anesthesiologist cleared the room for her epidural, he never left her side. He's feeding her ice chips and rubbing her back and shoulders. I teared up a little," Abby says.

"I hope she's finally able to rest now. That's why we left," Emma adds.

"We left because they asked us to go," Abby clarifies.

"Who asked you to leave?" Meghan asks.

"No one," Grandma says at the same time Abby responds, "The doctor and nurses."

"Wait, why did they ask you to leave?" Payton asks her grandma.

"I offered one tiny little suggestion and he got all bent out of shape," Emma declares.

"One tiny suggestion? You insinuated that he go clean his pipes so he had a clear head," Abby huffed.

"It's a proven medical fact, Abs. Men think clearer when they've unloaded the gun. Ask Sawyer! He used to perform professionally. Did you have to flog the log before your games so you could achieve peak performance?" This ornery ol' woman has a wicked gleam in her eyes as she waits to see how I reply.

And cue the very manly blush. I can feel it creep up my neck and tinge my cheeks, especially since all eyes in the waiting room are trained directly on me. Most of the faces have smiles on them as they anxiously await my response. I feel like this is a test, so I make a quick decision in hopes that Emma would appreciate a little humor. "Every game. The more hand to gland combat you engage in, the better you… play." I throw the old lady a wink just to seal the deal.

"Keeps you from going blind! That's what my dad used to say," Orval confirms. "Why do you think I still have twenty-twenty eyesight?"

The guys bust up laughing, while the girls try to decide if we're kidding or not.

"Hand to gland combat?" AJ asks, fighting her own laughter.

"It was all I could come up with on the fly."

"I think you did pretty well. They'll probably adopt you as their long lost grandson at this point. Did you really do that before every game?" she asks, her eyes darkening with desire.

"What if I did?" I whisper against her ear.

"I'd probably want to watch." Her words shock me, yet don't, since my little kitten seems to like to walk on the wild side. I feel the warmth of her fingers through the material as she grips my shirt, sending my blood just below my belt. If I'm not careful, Orval won't be the only one sporting a trouser bat in the waiting room.

But then she drives the nail in my coffin when she leans up on her tiptoes and licks the shell of my ear. "Or maybe even help."

Fuck. Me.

Oh, she could help all right. I think I wouldn't mind having both her hands on my–

"Settle down there, boy, or your officer's gonna be at attention like mine," Orval says, stepping up behind me.

Well, there goes any boner I'm probably going to have from now until eternity.

We all settle into the room in what is probably going to be a long wait. Over the next hour, everyone speaks casually, but it's more of an idle chitchat than real conversation. Somewhere around midnight, Linkin came out to call his mom with an update, as well as keep us all posted. Brian never returned to the waiting room, however. He stayed where he was needed most.

At three a.m., with AJ curled up on my chest and softly dozing, Linkin comes in with another update. We wake up the sisters, who are all catching a few winks too, and give him our full attention.

"Everything looks good. She's almost to eight centimeters and nearly effaced. The doc says it's almost time," he looks exhausted, there are bags forming under the big guy's eyes, but just saying the words seems to give him a second wind.

"How is she?" Meghan asks.

"She's a fucking rock star," he replies with a chuckle. "My little Firecracker is... well, she's simply amazing. Now that they got some drugs in her, she's powering through like a fucking champ, and she says she's ready to push."

"I can't believe it's almost time," Jaime says.

"I promised her I wouldn't be gone too long," he says with a smile. "Better get back," he adds, pointing to her room and heading back down the hallway. "Oh, uh, they do have a helicopter and neonatal team at the children's hospital in Richmond on standby, just in case. They don't anticipate anything major, but they're still being born early. They want to be prepared." It's the first time I really see a chink in his armor. The big guy is afraid, yet keeps his own fears hidden from the rest.

I know that look and feeling all too well. When I woke up in the hospital, I did everything I could to not show fear. My parents arrived the morning after the injury and had enough worry and anxiety for all of us. So I kept my cool and composure, even though I was slowly dying inside.

Linkin runs back down the hallway to join the mother of his babies. Grandpa gets up and makes a fresh pot of coffee, pouring cups to anyone who wants one. My body is starting to ache from sitting on these hard plastic chairs, but I'm not complaining. I'm here, with AJ, during a major family moment, and I'll be honest, it feels good. It's been a long-damn time since I've felt this needed and wanted. Even with Carrie, she had so many *people* surrounding her, caring for her every whim and need, that she rarely asked me for anything. And if I ever just wanted to hang out and be with her on a random day, she had someplace to be or something to do. Or I was breathing wrong and she found it distracting.

Looking back now, it's easy to see our marriage wasn't anything to write books about. Even though we were two people in the public eye, that was about the extent of what we had in common. They say you learn from your mistakes. Ain't that the truth. I'd never say I regret marrying her, but I definitely wish things would've been different.

"You okay?" AJ asks, sliding onto my lap and snuggling in close.

"Perfect," I tell her honestly, wrapping my arms tightly around her.

"I'm so tired. I can't wait to go home and stretch out in a real bed."

"My bed?" I ask, still hopeful that she's planning to come back with me.

"Depends. Will you be in that bed?"

"I will be in whatever bed you'll be in," I reply.

Her eyes are bright under the darkened fluorescent lighting in the small waiting room as she gazes up at me with a knowing look. She knows exactly what I'm picturing, which, of course, is many, many different dirty things. I don't care how exhausted I am. I still want her. To touch and taste her, her scent wrapped around me like I imagine her legs. The uncontrollable need I feel for her is quickly consuming my every thought. I'm addicted, for sure. It started the night we met and is showing no signs of slowing down.

In fact, if I sat back and allowed myself to really think about it, I'm not sure I want it to slow down. How easily I could drown in everything AJ Summer.

I'm just not sure if that drowning would be my salvation or my demise.

"Oh, I have something to tell you," I say, adjusting the hold I have on her with my arm.

"Do I want to know?" she quips, though a hint of worry laces her eyes.

"It's about the football game. Apparently, we were photographed."

"Really?"

"Yeah, someone was across the field. There's some photos online that appear to have been taken with a long-range lens."

"Oh." That's all she says. One word.

"I'm sorry I've dragged you into my mess."

AJ turns in my arm and faces me. "It was bound to happen sooner or later, right? I mean, if we're going to hang out, then there's a chance we'll be spotted, and possibly photographed." She shrugs her shoulders, as if it really doesn't bother her much.

I exhale a huge sigh of relief and lean back against the wall. AJ cuddles into my side. "I was worried," I confess quietly.

"About the photos?"

"Yeah. I was afraid you'd run for the hills at the first sign of those damn paparazzi."

"It takes more than a few photos to send me packing," she sasses. "Unless they're bad pictures."

Chuckling, I tighten my hold on her. "You couldn't take a bad picture. You're gorgeous." She turns her head and makes a face. AJ crosses her eyes and sticks out her tongue, making us both laugh. "Nope," I say, leaning down and kissing her nose. "You're still gorgeous."

Just after four, Linkin bursts into the waiting room. "I need help!"

"Oh my God, is it Lexi?" Abby begs.

"The babies?" Payton gasps.

"She wants to get married." We all stop and stare at the man in front of us. "Now."

"Who wants to get married now?" Ryan asks.

"Lexi! She says she's not having the babies until we're married," he tells us tightly, running his hands through his hair.

"Well, that's silly. She can't *stop* having the babies, can she?" Meghan asks, glancing around the room.

"No, but she says she can't bring them into the world if we're not married," Linkin says, sounding defeated. "This is not how I wanted to ask her to marry me."

"But you *are* going to ask her to marry you, right?" AJ asks.

Instead of answering her question with words, he pulls a ring box from his pocket and hands it to her. AJ glances at him, as if seeking permission to open the box, before she does just that. "Holy shitballs," AJ gasps, glancing down at a pretty impressive rock.

"I've had it for months," Linkin confesses, "but she always said she wanted to wait until after the babies were born before we got married. Now she's freaking out in there and says she won't push until we're hitched. It's like four a.m. What the hell am I supposed to do?"

"Let Grandma handle it," Emma says, stepping forward and patting Linkin on the shoulder.

"What are you going to do?" Payton asks.

"I'm going to marry my granddaughter and the love of her life," she states plainly and proudly.

"Wait, you? How– When– What?" Abby asks, shell-shocked.

"Oh, I've been ordained since I was asked to stand up for Liz and Richard in the seventies," Emma replies, waving her hand.

"Liz and Richard?" Meghan asks.

"You wanna talk about a bridezilla, you should have seen Liz Taylor. What a diva." Emma's matter-of-fact statement makes all of us stop and stare.

"Liz Taylor and… and Richard Burton? You knew Liz Taylor?" Payton seems just as shocked by her question as the rest of us.

"Of course, I did, Payters."

"Oh, Lizzy. Yes, that woman could kiss like a dream," Orval adds, breaking the silence with his big knife-wielding statement.

"What!?" Abby, AJ, Payton, and Meghan all gasp.

Emma just seems to wave their question off. "What happens in Vegas, and all that."

I swear you could hear a pin drop somewhere far off in an entirely different wing of the hospital.

"Anyway, the point is, I can marry you! Of course, it wouldn't be legal because you don't have the license," Emma says happily.

"But we could go through the motions? I could still give her the ring," Linkin says, his face showing his skepticism like a mask.

"Of course! Let's get you two unofficially hitched!" Emma claps her hands before swooping down the hallway, Linkin hot on her heels.

Before he enters the room, he turns toward us all. "You might as well all come in. She wouldn't want to do this without her sisters."

I feel AJ's smaller hand slide into mine as she pulls me eagerly to the delivery room. The happiness surrounding the family wraps around my throat and starts to choke me. I'd be a fucking liar if I said I wasn't affected by the love they all share for each other. Sure, I'm close to my family, but nothing like this. They've already made me feel completely welcome and have accepted me as part of their own.

And for the first time since my life–and marriage–went to shit, I want that.

I fucking want it bad.

AJ

17

It's three in the afternoon before I finally rouse from a very deep sleep. My entire body is fatigued and sore, even after stealing about six hours of sleeping like the dead.

My new nephews came screaming into the world shortly after six this morning. When Linkin came bursting into the waiting room around seven, a proud smile and tearful glint in his eyes, he couldn't contain his excitement to share his news.

Hudson Brian and Hemi James Stone arrived in the same chaotic fashion that preceded their delivery. Hudson arrived first, five whole minutes before his brother. He weighed in at four pounds and seven ounces, started screaming the moment he hit fresh air, and is named after one of his father's favorite classic cars, the Hudson Hornet.

Hemi, however, caused his parents a little more worry. Hemi wasn't breathing the best when he came out and had to be taken right away to the NICU, where he has been on a high-flow nasal cannula to help with his oxygen support. Little Hemi, named after another of his dad's favorite cars, the Hemi Cuda, was a bit smaller than his brother, weighing in at four pounds, one ounce. Both boys are now in the NICU, where they were both given IV fluids for a short time until they are ready to start eating.

It was hard to leave the hospital this morning, mainly because of not meeting them, but it was necessary. We were all equally tired after spending the night in the waiting room, especially after the adrenaline of their quick unofficial nuptials wore off. Lexi and Linkin were both exhausted and needing to rest, and then would be heading to the NICU to be with their sons.

I'll be going to the hospital later this afternoon to meet them, as long as everything is still going well and they're moved to the regular nursery.

I'm tangled up with a very naked, still sleeping Sawyer Randall. I'd love to reach down right now and grab his pretty impressive bat and take it for a few swings, but I'm in need of a little caffeine to get me through the rest of this day.

Gingerly, I slither out of his arms and make my way to my overnight bag. Glancing in the mirror, I'm stunned at my reflection. I look like a hooker after an all-night penthouse party in Vegas. Quietly, I slip into the bathroom for a little damage control. I don't need to look pretty to go get coffee, but I do need to not smell.

I jump in his shower and make quick work of washing all of my bits and pieces, including scrubbing away the raccoon eyes. A smile crests my lips as the scent of Sawyer's shampoo surrounds me. Is it weird that I'm excited to smell like a man? And not just any man, but *this* man, who smells like expensive rich soap and musky shampoo.

After the world's fastest shower, I slip on clean shorts and a fitted tee, pull my hair up in a wet, messy bun, and brush my teeth. That'll do. I don't need makeup, right? Not if it's gonna keep me from getting coffee into my lethargic system.

Opening the door, I tiptoe toward the bedroom door. I don't even make it halfway there when I hear, "Going somewhere?" Sawyer is still lying in bed, his head under his arm, which just gives me the perfect view to ogle his arms and back. I almost have to fan myself. "Stop staring at me from across the room and get back in bed."

"I was going to get coffee."

"I think you should take off your shirt," he refutes.

"What's wrong with my shirt?" I ask, glancing down at the Dierks Bentley concert tee from last summer.

"Nothing," he says, turning and looking over his shoulder at me. His hair is a mess, which just begs for my fingers, and his eyes have a hungry, half-lidded appearance, which reminds me of sex. "It looks great on you, but I think it would look much better on the floor."

"You do, do you?" I ask, crossing my arms over my chest. Sawyer rolls over and is pitching a tent with the sheet, which almost makes me forget about my need for caffeine.

"Definitely," he whispers, hoarsely from sleep. "I think you should get back in bed."

"I will once I get back from the bakery," I reply, throwing him a wink before turning back to the door.

I hear the shifting of the covers and his feet hit the floor as I step from the room. He's right behind me, I can feel it. Before I reach the landing at the top of the stairs, his big, strong arms snake around my waist and pull me back against his hard body.

And his very hard cock.

"Not so fast," he growls against my ear. "You were going to leave without giving me a goodbye kiss." Sawyer licks the shell of my ear before sucking it into his mouth. My entire body sparks to life, my blood pulsing through my veins.

"I would never," I retort, slowly turning in his arms and wrapping my arms around his neck.

"I think you lie. You were going to sneak out of my house without a kiss, and therefore, I think you need to be punished."

"Punished?" I gasp as he grips my ass hard in both hands, warm wetness flooding the apex of my legs.

"Do you like that?" Sawyer squeezes my rear once more before sliding his hands around and dipping one in the front of my shorts. I practically convulse when his warm fingers meet my wet core. "Oh, I think you do like that."

Next thing I know, the offending shirt is being removed from my body, tossed over the banister, while my fingers grip his shaft. "Fuck," he groans as I fist his erection and pump fast and hard.

"That's the plan," I whisper, my inner seductress taking over.

Sawyer lets me lead for a few moments as I drop to my knees. His cock jets from his body like a neon sign, the smooth skin pulled tight. My mouth is watering and I know exactly what I need to do; what I've wanted to do since the moment I first saw him.

Running my tongue along the ridged head, he tastes salty sweet, a taste I know I'll never forget. I look up, my eyes locking on his wild ones as I run my tongue down the vein on the underside. He shivers, and his cock thickens even more.

I keep my eyes focused on his as I lean forward, taking him into my mouth, inch by glorious inch. Sawyer's eyes turn to fire as he watches, one hand grabbing the bun at the back of my head. He guides me over him, but never forces me to take more than I can handle. I set the pace, which starts slow and torturous.

"Oh fuck, Alison," he moans as his hips flex forward. He hits me at the back of the throat, making my eyes water and my hand tighten around him. I alternate between a hard suck and one that's more of a tease with lots of tongue action. He seems to love the hell out of both.

Just when my hand starts to really pick up the pace and his eyes start to glass over, he moves. There's a loud pop as the suction between his cock and my mouth are broken. Sawyer lifts me up and slams his lips down on mine. The kiss is hungry and pure sex as our tongues battle for control.

"Your punishment, remember?" he asks, pulling away from me.

"Punishment?" I ask, feigning innocence as he spins me around to face to wall.

His hands wrap around my stomach and I'm quickly relieved of my shorts. They're followed instantaneously by my panties, which are flung haphazardly over his shoulder. Those things were useless, anyhow. Then he flicks the clasp of my bra, rendering me completely naked. "Yes, punishment," he reminds as he gently places his hands between my shoulder blades, applying just a bit of pressure. The movement presses my chest against the wall and leaves my ass out, as if on display. "Do you recall telling me you weren't going to leave without a goodbye kiss? I believe that was a lie, kitten," he groans, running his big hands up my thighs and across the globes of my ass.

"Oh, that," I pant, anxiously waiting what's next. My inner hussy is fully on board with whatever he has planned.

"Yes, *that*," he bites out, just as the loud smack echoes off the walls. My ass burns from his hand, but the pleasure that mixes with it is intoxicating. My yelp and the sting are followed immediately by his soothing hand as he rubs the burning flesh.

"Are you sorry for lying to me?" he asks as he moves from my sore cheek to the other, where he kneads and grips my ass.

"Yes," I huff, holding my breath as I wait for what's to come.

Smack.

A deep groan rips from my gut, the pain and pleasure crashing together like a tidal wave. His hand continues to massage my smarted flesh, first one cheek and then the other. I can feel the wetness slipping down my thighs as I press my chest farther into the wall, offering my ass up for more.

He delivers two more spankings, one on each ass cheek, before pulling away completely. Instantly, I miss his touch. Sawyer pulls me back from the wall, but presses my palms on the wall. "Don't move," he instructs before disappearing into his bedroom.

The only sound is my own breathing, which is labored and anxious. I maintain my position, not moving a muscle. Though, the prospect of being punished again does hold quite a bit of appeal.

"Good girl," he boasts as he comes back into the foyer. His hands grab just below my butt and slide up, massaging the still tender skin. "Seeing your ass red with my handprint is the biggest fucking turn on."

I try to speak, but the words just don't come.

"Come here," he requests as he grabs one hand from the wall and pulls me to the banister. It extends the entire length of the top foyer, ensuring a splendid view of the living area below.

Grasping the banister tightly, I prepare myself for what's to come next. Fortunately, I don't have to wait long. Sawyer guides my hips, positioning my feet just a bit wider than my shoulders. "Do you like to be spanked, Alison?"

"Yes." My voice doesn't even sound like my own.

"Did it turn you on?"

"Yes."

He guides his hands down to my thighs and then back up. "Christ, you're so fucking wet." He flicks my clit with his fingers, resulting in another loud moan of pleasure. "You ready for my dick, Alison?"

"Yes," I beg.

"Hold on tight, sweetheart. This is gonna be a bumpy ride."

Sawyer takes his place behind me, the coarse hairs of his legs tickling my overly sensitive butt. Hands spread wide, he moves them up my back, his thumbs tracing the bumps of my spine. I feel one hand leave my back as he takes his position. His cock nudges at my pussy, making me whimper with need. "You ready, Alison?"

"Yes."

He pushes into me, torturously slow, coating himself with my wetness. Then, he pulls back, and when he moves, he releases what feels like years of pent-up sexual tension on me. His pace is fast, his movements hard, and I'm embarrassed to admit that it actually takes me no time at all until I'm screaming his name and coming harder than ever before.

Sawyer's right there with me, grunting and howling his own release. His hands grip my ass as he thrusts once more before finally stilling. My body falls limp against the banister, his doing the same and caging me in.

"I'm not sure I'm alive. I think I might have died and gone to heaven," he huffs against my back. His mouth moves gently, placing open-mouthed kisses along my sweaty spine.

"Me either," I wheeze, "but what a way to go."

Sawyer kisses my neck and wraps his arms around my midsection. "That was pretty amazing. I might just decide to keep you here with me all the time, sweetheart." He drags his lips down my back, but my sex-fogged brain is stuck on his comment.

My heart hammers in my chest at the thought of staying. It's way too soon to think like that, but now that the seed is planted, it's starting to take root. It's not like I haven't been caught up in the smoke and mirrors of smooth talkers before. Oh, I've definitely met my fair share of men who talk a big game and can't follow through for shit. I've judged them so wrong before that I wonder if I'm able to actually tell the good ones from the rotten tomatoes.

Sawyer feels like a good one. Besides the fact that the sex is dynamite, there's also the fact that I like spending time with him and talking. It's not just about sex with him, and I don't get the impression that it's that way for him either. He's attentive, supportive, and nothing like those other frogs I've kissed. I think I have a good one.

I just pray that I'm right.

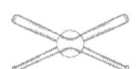

When Sawyer hops in the shower, I head down to the kitchen for food. It's nearly four in the afternoon, so breakfast is out. Hell, lunch is out too. It's nearly dinnertime as I check his fridge for something I could make for a quick meal. I'm meeting everyone at the hospital at five thirty so that gives me just enough time to eat and freshen up before heading out.

Maybe Sawyer will want to go with me.

I'm smiling to myself as I pull chicken breasts and fresh broccoli from the refrigerator, and a pound of whole grain pasta from the pantry. It takes me a few moments to locate a large pan for the noodles and a skillet for the chicken. I'm just grabbing a large kitchen knife when the doorbell rings. I'm not really familiar with what protocol is for answering the guy you're sleeping with's door, but I don't really have time to ask Siri.

The doorbell chimes a second time, which spurs me into action. I round the corner in the dining room and enter the foyer. I glance up and spy my panties hanging from the light–clear up on the second floor.

Awesome.

The doorbell rings a third time. Releasing the deadbolt, I swing open the door and stop dead in my tracks. There, standing on the front porch of the man I'm sleeping with is Carrie Doherty, all five foot ten inch, one-hundred pounds soaking wet, Victoria's Secret model, and actress in the latest Chris Pine movie, Carrie.

And Sawyer's ex-wife.

"Can I help you?" I ask when I find words.

"And you are?" she asks, looking me up and down from behind her designer sunglasses. I'm sure she notices my wrinkled clothes, my makeup-less face, and my recently sexed-up hair, and by the look of disdain pouring from her body, she clearly finds me lacking.

"AJ," I say sweetly, though on the inside my tone is anything but.

"You must be another one of his girls." The way she says it instantly grates on my nerves.

"I'm his only girl," I grind out, probably also grinding down my molars.

She laughs–actually laughs in my face. "Oh, that's cute. I hate to be the one to break it to you, but you'll never be his *only* girl. Believe me, I thought the same thing once upon a time, and I had his ring on my finger." Carrie makes a gesture with her hand, showing me her now-empty ring finger.

"Is there something I can help you with?" I ask.

"I need to speak with Sawyer," she states bluntly.

"I'm sorry, he's not available at the moment. Maybe if you had called first, we could have saved you a trip," I reply, starting to close the door.

Her perfectly manicured eagle talon slams on the door. "Listen, sweetheart, I'm sure it's all wine and roses at this point, but let me give you a piece of free advice. Sawyer Randall is a cheater and a liar. Unless you want to spend your nights at home, alone, while he's out living the highlife with girls younger and much prettier than you, then I suggest you move along, because a man like Sawyer doesn't change. He didn't for me, and he surely won't change for a measly school teacher who wears last year's Target line and doesn't know how to moisturize," she spews, her perfume-laced venom flying in my direction and, sadly, hitting its mark.

I gape at the gorgeous woman in front of me, reeling from her words, and wishing the floor would open up and swallow me whole.

"You don't want to believe those rag magazines, fine. But believe the woman who was married to him for three years. Sawyer Randall will use you until he's had his fill and then walk away without a care in the world. He's completely–"

"Carrie?" His voice is like a salve to my soul and the nail driven straight into it, all at the same time. "What are you doing here?" he asks as he comes down the stairs and approaches the door.

"Sawyer," she gushes, stepping around me and into his house, and straight into his arms. Well, actually, he's just standing there, shocked by her appearance, maybe? Or maybe it's the fact that he wasn't expecting company and he's only wearing a towel?

Fun times.

"What are you doing here?" he asks, stepping back and out of her reach.

"I was in the neighborhood and thought I'd drop by," she coos, touching her chest and smiling her blinding white smile at her ex.

My Sawyer.

"The neighborhood? I find that hard to believe since you don't know anyone from Jupiter Bay," he says, crossing his arms over his chest. The action actually makes that sexy V of his lower abdomen that much more pronounced before it dives into the stark white towel.

"Actually, I'm shooting some photos just up the road. *Sports Illustrated* is shooting their Swimsuit Issue and I'm featured. Isn't that wonderful?" she asks, taking a step closer to him.

My mind is like an ADHD person on speed. I can't seem to focus on anything. Not the fact that she's here and as beautiful as ever, not the fact that he's practically naked and every bit the sexy professional athlete, and definitely not the fact that my panties are swinging from the chandelier above our heads. Okay, maybe I'm able to focus a little on that last one. Sawyer must notice my lack of attention too and follows my line of sight skyward. When he realizes what he's looking at, his face quickly looks back to mine. He wears an amused glimmer in his eyes and a dirty little smirk on his lips.

"... so you see why I had to stop by and say hello, right?" Carrie asks, drawing our attention back to the fact that we're not alone in the house.

"Yeah. No, wait." Sawyer drops his head and takes a deep breath. "Can you stay right here, Carrie? I'll be right back," he says moments before flying up the stairs, taking them two at a time.

"I've seen that look on his face before," Carrie says while checking her nails. "He's probably already screwing the cleaning lady, sweetie." And as if it couldn't get any worse, Carrie finally looks up and sighs. "He's always had... wild tastes."

Before I can say a word, Sawyer reappears at the top of the steps wearing basketball shorts and pulling a clean t-shirt over his head. He tried to tame his out-of-control, wet locks with his hand, but it didn't work. He looks delicious, so very sexy, and recently screwed.

I can't help but smile at that.

"AJ, would you mind waiting for me in the kitchen? I'll be in there in a few minutes," he says casually as he descends the stairs.

I'll be honest; I'm a little stunned at his request. Is it because whatever they need to discuss is a private matter between exes or is there something more to this? If I follow my mind, it's sprinting straight toward the picture Carrie just so beautifully painted of her manwhore ex-husband. That alone has me ready to slip on my running shoes and get the hell out of Dodge. Been there, done that.

Don't even want the fucking t-shirt.

But then there's my heart, and that pesky little organ keeps insisting there's more to the story than meets the eye. And it's that trust I'm instilling in him that has me nodding at his request. "Sure."

I make my way towards the kitchen, leaving Sawyer and his ex-wife in the foyer. With each step I take, I send up a silent prayer that it wasn't a mistake to place blind trust in a man I really don't know that well.

Hopefully, I haven't made the biggest mistake of all.

18

Sawyer

"What do you want, Carrie?" I ask when I'm certain AJ is out of earshot.

"Now, now, now," she starts, walking my way, her high heels crisscrossing in front of her with each step she takes, "is that any way to greet your wife?"

"*Ex*-wife, Carrie. Ex." I stand my ground, trying to keep my distance from her. First off, I don't want her to touch me any more than she already has today, but I'd never want AJ to walk in and see her hands on me.

She tsks and waves her hand. "On paper, maybe, but we'll always be married."

"Not even a little bit," I ground out. She's quickly grating on my nerves and has just about overstayed her welcome. "Why are you here?"

"Is this about the new little tart you have waiting for you in the kitchen? I'm sure she's fun and all," she says, glancing up to where AJ's panties hang above our heads, "but you'll be bored in no time. You always are."

"Do you even hear yourself right now? *I* wasn't the one who couldn't be faithful, Carrie. That was *you*."

"That was a mistake," she retorts. "I was willing to overlook all of your indiscretions, and I would think that you'd be able to do the same."

"Not happening," I state.

"Too bad," she tsks again with her pouty face, a sound that has always been like nails on a chalkboard and a look that usually means she has information she's about to use to her benefit.

"Just spill it. I'm sure you didn't come all the way here on a Sunday just to shoot the shit and catch up. What do you want?"

She seems to stand a little taller. "How much do you know about this woman?" she asks, gently nodding in the direction AJ just headed.

"What does this have to do with her?"

The hairs on the back of my neck stand up, my mind starting to race. Yet, I know Carrie loves to get a rise out of me, so I school my features and pretend whatever she's about to say won't affect me. "I know enough."

"So you know all about the marriage she broke up about two years ago? Your little AJ has a habit of screwing around with married men, Sawyer. In fact, he's not the first Miss Alison Jane Summer has been with who was married to another woman while they were together. I found it a little odd that the man who is so quick to condemn would take a woman like that to his bed," she says stepping into my personal space, the familiar scent of her too-expensive perfume tickling my nose, "but then I wondered… did he really know? Was he aware of the inappropriate behavior of the woman he's sleeping with?"

A ball of something hard swells in my throat, making it hard to breathe. "How do you even know this? What does my love life have to do with you?"

"Besides the fact that we're married and I care for you?" she asks, buffing her nails on the bodice of her dress.

"We're not married. Haven't been since we both signed on the dotted line. So I ask again: why do you care?"

"Because, believe it or not, Sawyer, I still care for you greatly. And I don't want to see you get hurt by some tramp who sleeps around as easily as the sun rises in the morning."

Anger sweeps through me at her words. "Get out!"

"But, Sawyer…"

"No, we're done. Thank you for the information, but I don't need it." Grabbing the doorknob, I hold her exit open and wait for her to get the hint.

As she reaches the threshold, she glances at me over her shoulder. "I just know how much you despise users," she states boldly, the knife of her words twisting deeply in my chest. She knows all my weaknesses, my fears.

Bitch.

But even as I shut the door, cutting off any further chance of looking at her, my gut churns with worry.

I realize I'm still standing behind the closed door, even after I hear a car in the driveway start and pull away. I need to go into the kitchen where AJ is, but my head is buzzing with too many questions. Instead of going where I should, I head up the stairs and into my room. It's quiet there, almost painfully so.

Carrie is a master at playing me, manipulating me as well as the situation, for her betterment. Today is no different. I should say, "Fuck her", return downstairs, take AJ in my arms, and forget about the interruption that was my ex-wife.

But I can't let it go.

How well do I know AJ? Sure, I know how to play her body like a professional athlete, but what about that other shit Carrie spewed? The affairs? I have a hard time imagining AJ being the homewrecker Carrie made her out to be. And how the fuck does she know so much about AJ anyway?

She's knows people, that's how.

When Carrie wants something, Carrie gets it, by any means possible.

I've seen her use PIs to find out details of those in her industry. Hell, I'm certain she was behind half the incriminating photos that were constantly leaked to the media. No, there were never any affairs, on my part, but I always looked like the bad guy.

And Carrie always came out smelling like a fucking rose.

Like now. Best interest at heart? I smell ulterior motives.

A knock sounds at the door behind me. "Hey, everything okay?"

I clear my throat and turn to face AJ. "Uhhh, yeah. Sorry about that interruption."

"It's okay. I made dinner, if you're still hungry," she adds, pointing down the stairs.

"Actually, I'm not hungry anymore."

"Oh, okay. I can put it in the fridge and we can heat it up after we get back tonight," she says breezily, though my own heart feels like it's beating out of my chest.

I realize she's talking about going to the hospital. She's going to meet her new nephews tonight, and asked me to go with her. Of course I fucking said yes. I want to go. Or at least, I *did* want to go before Carrie showed up and fucked with my head again. I should throw on some shoes and head out the door, but my feet are rooted to the hardwood.

"Why don't you go ahead and see your family," I suggest, averting my eyes so I don't have to see the pain I'm sure is there. It hurts me to say it, but I need a little time to just think. I need to run, to clear my mind, and to think.

"Oh, okay," she says.

Even though I don't look, she stands beside me for a few heart-pounding moments before heading to the bathroom to collect her things. I hear her scoop up her toothbrush and whatever other girly things she brought and had on my vanity. I'll completely ignore how good it felt stepping out of my shower earlier to see it there mixed with my shit. It was too nice, too comforting.

She steps out of the bathroom, her bag thrown over her shoulder. She glances around, searching the room to make sure she has everything. I want to tell her to leave it all, to come back later, and stay one more night, but I know I can't. Not right now.

"I guess I'll talk to you later," she says, her sweet voice laced with uncertainty. She's completely leaving her statement open for me to add to, but like the stupid fucker I am, I keep quiet.

"Yeah," I reply, scratching my head. "Have fun at the hospital."

She doesn't reply, which is like a neon sign with a bullhorn blasting how badly I'm messing this up. When I glance up, it's like a punch in the gut. No, I think I'd rather take a straight hit with a two-by-four upside the head than see that look on her beautiful face. And, of course, the fact that I put that look there is another reason I need to step back and think. Because if I go all in with this woman, I'll vow to never witness a look like this ever again.

If you ever get the chance again, dumbass.

She doesn't speak as she turns and slips out of my room. Her footfalls echo down the stairs and into the foyer. I stand right where I am because I'm not strong enough to watch her leave. The fear that I might not ever see her descend my stairs or feel her presence in my house makes my chest feel like someone is carving out my heart (with a butter knife).

The door opens and closes, and my feet finally move. I head down the stairs and to the front door. I pull it open just as her car is turning and driving down the lane. Taillights glowing, I watch her turn onto the road and out of sight.

I just fucked up.

Bad.

I know it, but I'm not sure if I'll be able to fix it.

Tears fill my eyes as I watch Lexi and Linkin though the window. Linkin is skin-to-skin with Hudson, while Lexi sits in the rocker, skin-to-skin with little Hemi. The nasal cannula is there, providing him with a steady stream of oxygen. The NICU nurse, Charissa, said that his oxygen levels are already improving, and that the pediatrician is confident they'll be able to remove the oxygen very soon.

It's a beautiful sight, one I'll never forget.

Longing rears its ugly head, choosing this most inappropriate time to swoop in. Linkin is watching his wife (unofficial, that is) as she talks to their younger son. The smile on his face steals my breath and makes my heart bleed, especially in light of what happened at Sawyer's. No, we're not anywhere close to the same place as my sister and her unofficial husband, but I was under the impression we were in a good place, slowly progressing toward a solid relationship.

Apparently, I was wrong.

"I've never seen anything so beautiful," Grandma says, walking up beside me at the window.

"I agree," I whisper, a soft smile playing on my lips.

"And there's nothing better than admiring a gorgeous, shirtless man, holding a tiny newborn baby. If I still had my ovaries, they would have exploded," she adds with a bit of sass.

"Why must you be so weird?"

"Nothing weird about appreciating a view like that," Grandma flaps.

I opt to move along, steering the conversation away from Linkin's (admittedly) sexy abs and back to them as a family. "They're going to make wonderful parents," I say, unable to take my eyes off the scene.

"How are you?" she asks, waving at Lexi as she throws us a wide, over the moon with happiness, smile.

"Fine."

"I had hoped you'd bring that sexy baseball player with you again tonight so I could ogle him a bit more," she says.

"He had... plans," I stumble, knowing full well that the great Grandma Inquisition of the Year is about to commence.

I wait, trying to figure out if a quick trip to the bathroom fretting a sudden spell of stomach flu would keep her nosiness at bay. Of course, if I go that route, I've pretty much ended any future contact I might have with Hudson and Hemi tonight, and *that* isn't worth a fake bout of puking.

"Plans, huh?"

"Yep. I'll be seeing him tomorrow," I add cheerfully, mostly because it's completely true. We have a Monday morning staff meeting at seven, and therefore I'll be forced to see him.

Not that seeing him will be a hardship. Oh, no. I could gawk at that man all day long and never get tired of it, especially after seeing him naked. Holy hell, God outdid himself when he created Sawyer Randall. But at the same time, things were left… weird and tense. Something happened with his ex-wife, and I'll be damned if I know what.

My siblings all arrive and everyone oohs and aahs over the boys. Dad is exceptionally proud and even tears up a bit when he recounts how amazing his daughter was, and how cool and collected Linkin was in the delivery room. When Lexi had asked him to come in, it was to stay with her for the long haul. She had always pictured Mom being in there with her, but since she wasn't with us anymore, she extended the invitation to Dad.

He's currently standing in front of the window wearing his Proud Grandpa t-shirt and smiling an enormous grin, big enough to see from space.

When Grandma moves on to bug one of my older sisters, Meghan slips in beside me. "Everything all right?" she asks, a concerned look on her face.

"I guess," I mumble, looking around and noticing no one paying us any attention. "Something weird happened tonight."

"Define weird," she encourages.

"We had a really great afternoon after we woke up, but then his ex-wife showed up," I start.

"Wait, you're telling me Carrie Doherty showed up at Sawyer's house? Is that why he's not here?" she asks.

"Honestly, I'm not sure why he's not here. He was in the shower when she arrived and she started in on how much he cheated on her during their relationship, and even went on to insinuate that he's probably already doing it to me."

"Do you believe her?"

"No," I reply instantly, because deep down, I don't feel like Sawyer's a cheater. "I really don't think he's that kinda man, but hey, what do I know? I've judged that book cover wrong before."

"No shit," she grumbles with a humorless chuckle.

"So then he comes down and asks me to go to the kitchen. They were in his foyer for like ten minutes by themselves. I didn't even eavesdrop, Meggy, can you believe it? I stayed put and finished cooking our dinner.

"When I realized it was silent, I went looking for him. He was in his room, a far-off look on his face. I asked him to come down for dinner and he said he wasn't hungry. Then suggested I go to the hospital by myself."

She gives me a questioning look. "That's it? He didn't say why?"

Shaking my head, I confirm, "Not at all. I wanted to push, to ask why he was suddenly distant, but I could tell he didn't want to talk about it. Something happened and maybe he just needs to work it out for himself." I glance back in the room and notice the new parents making their way toward the bassinets.

"Could be. Do you think he'll call you?" she finally asks. Isn't that the million-dollar question?

"I don't know, Meggy. Everything was *fine* before she showed up. Then after she left, he completely shut me out. I hope he calls, but I'm not sure he will. It was like he already checked out."

"Well, give him a little time, and definitely don't give up on him. He seemed great the few times I've been around him, and the guys love him."

"I kinda have a soft spot for him too," I confess.

"I bet. He's pretty easy on the eyes," she adds, bumping my shoulder with her own.

I laugh. "Easy, Grandma, or you'll pop a lady boner in the middle of the NICU."

"Shut up," she laughs, hitting my arm before wrapping her arms around me. "I love you, AJ."

"I love you too, Meggy."

After a few minutes of silence and watching Lexi and Linkin try to tear themselves away from the babies, she finally says, "You know we're the only two single ones left." I nod instead of answering with words. "But do you know what? It's not meant to be, like you seem to think. You may have found some of the duds in this world, but that's not your destiny. You're going to have a wonderful life, filled with love and laughter."

"You think?" I ask, my eyes filling up with tears.

"I know it," she responds, her own eyes glistening with moisture.

"You know, there's love and laughter in your future too, right?"

She sighs and looks back as Linkin wraps his arms around a crying Lexi. She wants to stay with the babies, but it's time for them to go. "Maybe I had my chance, AJ. Maybe my forever has already passed me by."

"I don't believe that for a second and you shouldn't either. I know it's hard now to look too far into the future, but you don't have to look that far. Just take it day by day and when the time is right, you'll have everything you've ever dreamed of. I promise."

Meghan doesn't reply, but I can tell she heard me. The tears welling in her eyes leak down her face and fall onto the floor. I couldn't possibly fathom what she's going through. Since Josh died, she just sort of stopped. She's going through the motions, but she's not living. Oh, she puts on a good show, but I see a lot of the smoke and mirrors she uses to hide her pain.

Someday. She'll get there someday.

I know it.

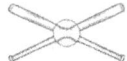

"They look nothing alike. Are you sure they have the same father?" Grandma asks Lexi, stunning the entire room silent.

"Grandma!" Lexi charges, her face turning red.

"What? I'm just asking. This is a no-judge zone, Lexi Lou, so if you have any of those confession time things like Abby and Levi, it's okay to say it. Get it out," she says, waving her hands around encouragingly.

"Woman, you're about to be booted from this room on your ass," Linkin thunders behind her, clearly having heard her comment.

"Oh, don't get all bent out of shape, big guy. I was just asking. I read an article about a woman who had sex with two different men within twenty-four hours. She was pregnant with twins, and when they arrived one was black and the other white." We all just stare, completely stunned by her story.

"Really?" Abby asks, dumbfounded.

"True story. It was on the Internet and you know they don't lie there. Right, Orvie?" Grandma asks her husband.

"Right, sweetums."

"How does that happen?" Meghan asks.

"Well, during her ovulation, she released more than one egg. The woman had *the sex* with one man and his spermies fertilized her waiting egg, where she became pregnant. Therefore, when the hoochie mama slept with the second man right away, he fertilized the second egg. Double *the sex*. Double the babies, Meggy Pie."

"That's... a lot of fertilizing. Thanks," I mumble.

"Well, just to clear up any confusion, both of my sons are Linkin's. Just because they have a bit of size difference doesn't mean anything," Lexi defends, hormonal tears in her eyes.

"I think Hudson looks more like Linkin," I add, trying to smooth over some of the extra tension that has suddenly joined us in the room, like a long lost family member.

"Agreed. He definitely has Linkin's more squared jaw and fuller lips," Payton decides.

"And Hemi looks more like Lexi. His hair is lighter, like hers. His eyes are more almond-shaped, like hers. His nose is small and cute, like hers. And he's a fucking fighter, like her," Linkin says, walking toward his unofficial-wife, who's sitting up in the hospital bed. "I'd be honored to have one, if not both of my boys, look just like their mother." He bends down and plants a firm and possessive kiss on her lips.

"And if you ever suggest there was another man in her life again, I'll have to hide all of your husband's Viagra and lose the key to your little playroom," he adds, standing up to his full height (which seems gigantic when he's in front of Grandma) and crosses his arms over his wide chest. Damn, this man is huge.

"What? You wouldn't dare!" Grandma huffs, crossing her arms over her chest to mirror his stance.

"I will if you ever make your granddaughter cry again by asking something stupid."

The room is quiet as we watch their showdown. They seem to square off, neither wanting to cave first. Grandma has the capacity to go a long damn time when she wants to, but the way Linkin is holding his ground, I'd say he'll outmaneuver Grandma this time.

Her face breaks into a wrinkly smile. "My word in heaven, you sure are swoonworthy when you turn into an aggressive, overprotective husband, Linkin Stone. I think I like you more now than I did before," she says, walking forward and wrapping her thin arms around his waist. Of course, I can tell she gooses him by the way he quickly straightens and blushes a dark shade of red.

Then she goes to Lexi and hugs her. "I'm sorry, dear. You know I didn't mean to upset you. You have two beautiful baby boys, and they are the perfect blend of you and your husband."

"You're just saying that because you don't want Linkin to take your Viagra and lock you out of your weird little room upstairs that we won't be discussing any further," Lexi says.

"But he can't have the Viagra!" Grandma hollers. "We need that! How else will we be able to play cards every afternoon at three?"

"You need Viagra to play cards? What kinda cards are you playing?" Jaime asks.

"The naked kind, Jaimers. With lots of *the sex*."

"Hell yes!" Grandpa bellows from his chair along the wall, causing all further talk of sex to die a quick death.

As I drive home that night, my mind fills with more Sawyer-related questions than I have answers, and as I slip into bed at ten, images of the reason why I have all of these questions accompanies me under the covers.

I just don't understand.

Everything was fine.

Everything was great.

Then suddenly, it wasn't.

Grabbing my phone, I check to make sure I didn't miss any texts. There weren't any earlier and there aren't any now. I set it back down on my nightstand and grab a steamy paperback that Abby lent me. I should be able to submerge myself in the story until I can't keep my eyes open, but once again, I'm only thinking of Sawyer.

Setting the book back down on the table, I reach for my phone.

> **Me:** I met the two most perfect little boys in the world tonight. I hope you had a good evening. 'Night.

Watching, no little bubbles appear to let me know he's read and replying to my message. I continue to stare, willing a return message to pop up, for an embarrassingly long time before I finally take the hint and put my phone away.

Maybe he's busy? Working out? In the shower? In bed already? He didn't get much sleep the night before, so maybe he's already passed out, and he'll see my message and reply tomorrow. Right?

But as I slip farther into my bed and curl up with my pillow, dread starts to overpower my positive outlook.

I guess the only way to know if he'll text in the morning is to wait until morning.

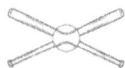

The morning drones on brutally slow, especially in light of checking my phone first thing and not finding a reply. When I arrive at school, unlock my door, and head down to the teachers' lounge, I return to find my desk empty. After the last two weeks of daily yummy treats and deliciously frothy caramel coffee, I'm not sure I'll be able to drink the brown sludge in my cup.

I should start bringing my own coffee.

I head back to the teachers' lounge for our morning staff meeting like I'm heading to the guillotine. Dead man walking. Or woman, I should say. It's like my feet are encased in concrete. The room is already filling quickly, but thankfully, Brandy and Natalie have saved me a seat between them in back. Thank God I don't have to sit by talky Mrs. Porter or stinky Mr. Simpson, or well, any of the chairs in the front row. That's where the ass-kissers and the hard of hearing convene.

Just as Mr. Stewart enters the room, a flash of gorgeous man wearing a Jupiter Bay Hawks t-shirt (a little too deliciously snug in the arms, if you ask me) and pair of black basketball shorts enters the room. My word, that man is pure sex.

"Agreed," Natalie mumbles, causing me to glance her way.

"What?"

"You just whispered that the man was pure sex. I'm assuming you're not talking about Stewart because ewwwww," Natalie replies.

"Stewart is soooo sexy," Brandy coos. "He does this thing when he's reading and looks at me over his glasses. I swear," she shivers visibly. "He's completely doable in that nerdy kinda way."

"Can I have everyone's attention," Mr. Stewart bellows from the front of the room. "There are just a few things we need to go over this morning…"

And that's when I completely lose focus.

Since he was the last one in, he's left with one of the up-front seats by the door, also right next to stinky Mr. Simpson. It gives me the perfect profile view to do a little stalking. Okay, you're right. Stalking is such a harsh word. Maybe intently watching is a better fit. All eyes are on the boss in front, therefore my eyes are on him.

He looks… tired. I mean, not that I care. The man did pretty much boot me from his house yesterday afternoon and completely ignore my text. That alone should be enough reason to not care how worn down he is. The only thing I should care about is when I'm getting my panties back from the chandelier.

Those are expensive panties.

But the more I look at him, I can see more than just fatigue. Sure, there are bags under his eyes big enough to carry my shoes, and worry lines around his mouth that aren't normally there. His hair is a bit askew, which isn't typical of the beginning of his workday. His shoulders are hunched, almost in a defeated manner. His entire appearance is just... so not like him.

I try to pay attention to what the principal is saying, but it's hard. My focus just keeps returning to the weekend and the man I spent it with, which pretty much sucks donkey balls in regards to implementing the new programs our administration has been working on for this school year. New programs? What new programs? I just fantasized about the PE teacher screwing me against the banister and have no idea what you just said.

That'll go over well.

I feel eyes on me. Trying to keep my own eyes trained on Mr. Stewart, the temptation to look is just too great. But when I glance his way, he's not looking at me at all. It's actually Bryce Lehman, who's sitting almost directly in my line of sight of Sawyer. He gives me a warm smile, but it does nothing to my heart or my lady parts.

When the meeting's finally over and the students are starting to arrive, Principal Stewart dismisses us to prepare for our day of teaching the youth of Jupiter Bay. I stand up, my ass already sore from sitting on the hard metal chair, and turn to my friends.

"Educational, as always," I mumble, earning nods from both Natalie and Brandy.

"As always," Natalie agrees.

"Uh oh, ladies. Don't look now, but randy Randall is looking this way," Brandy leans in and whispers.

I can't help it; I turn and glance toward the front of the room. Unfortunately, he's already heading out the door and doesn't turn back around to give me another glance. I feel his exit like one of those polar plunges, jumping into freezing water in the middle of winter. It's heavy, painful, and makes me feel like I can't breathe.

Happy Monday.

Sawyer

20

My feet pound against the sand for the second time today, my calves pulsing and lungs burning as I push past the pain and sprint the last quarter mile. Sweat pours down my forehead, probably from the extra two miles I decided to torture myself with tonight. The pain is welcome. Pain is necessary. Pain is deserved.

I'm gasping for air as I walk from the beach to my back porch. I grab the towel and bottle of water, chugging half of it in one long gulp. My cell phone starts to ring, but I make no movement to retrieve it. Instead, I watch the waves crash against the wet sand and let the warm breeze cool my overheated body.

I wonder how long I'll stay out here tonight. The house has too many memories. Everywhere I look, I see her. The missing knick knacks in the living room, the shower stall, the fucking banister, for Christ's sake, it all haunts me and reminds me of how good it was and how great it could have been.

And damn, was it good. Not just the sex, even though that was the best I've ever had, but everything else too. We talked and laughed, shared stories and memories. I was more open with this woman in one week than in the five years I was with Carrie.

So why did I let her walk out that door?

Damn good question.

After a few minutes of wave watching, my phone starts to ring a second time. I consider letting it go to voicemail again, but I'm afraid whoever the persistent asshole is on the other line will keep calling. Secretly, (like a high school girl with a crush) I hope it's AJ, and it's that thought that adds a little spring to my very tired step as I make my way into the house and retrieve my phone.

Dylan.

"Hey," I say in way of greeting, my breathing still a little labored.

"Jeezus, man, you weren't having sex, were you?"

"I promise you, little brother, that if I were with a lady, taking your call would be the last thing I'd do."

"Good to know," he chuckles. "How come you didn't answer the first time? Busy putting your pants on?"

"Hardly. I actually just got back from a run." I quickly finish off the rest of my water bottle and toss it in the trash.

"Yuck," he grumbles. Dylan is tall, like me, but wiry thin. He was better suited for swimming in high school than baseball.

"To what do I owe the honor?" I ask, grabbing a second water from the fridge.

"Actually, Amber is going to see her grandma this weekend in Indy so I thought I might head your way," Dylan says.

Dylan and I are only two years apart, but despite the closeness in age, we don't have much in common. When I went off to college, and eventually Texas, he stayed back in Charlottesville and married Amber. They met in high school, but didn't start dating until they were in college. She's about halfway through her first pregnancy, and I've been told I'll have a niece arriving at the end of the year.

"I'm not doing much," I tell my brother. "Might go to DC to see the Rangers play on Sunday," I add, my throat constricting and making it difficult to breathe. Lately, it seems thinking about AJ has that effect on me.

"What was that sigh? You know, Sawyer, if it's too hard to watch them play, then maybe you should skip this game." I realize that he must think my sigh and super cheery disposition are the result of not being able to play the game, as opposed to the real reason.

"Actually, it's not about that," I say to my younger brother. "I met a girl."

Silence greets me. In fact, it's quiet for so long, I have to check the phone to make sure I didn't drop the call.

"And?"

"And what? She's pretty cool, but I probably already fucked it up," I find myself saying. I've talked to my brother about things over the years–my desire to finish college and get my teaching degree instead of entering the majors right away, my career over the years, hell even some of the bullshit with the media–but I don't ever recall going to my little brother for love advice.

"Yeah? Wait, she's not some actress or anything, is she? The last famous face you dated you married, and that didn't turn out so great for you."

"No, she's nothing like Carrie. Like, absolutely nothing. AJ is kind and fiery. She makes me laugh and actually listens when I talk, instead of fixing her nails or her hair. She's a teacher at the school I work at."

"So if this thing goes south–or you fuck it up, as you so elegantly stated–the fact that you work with her could be a challenge," Dylan points out.

"No shit. I had a staff meeting yesterday and it took everything I had to keep my focus on the front of the room and not her. But I messed up, man. Carrie showed up at my place Sunday afternoon."

Again, I'm greeted with silence.

"I bet that went over well," he prods.

"You can guess. Carrie said some crap about AJ, and it kinda freaked me out."

"What kinda stuff?"

"That she broke up a marriage and likes to sleep with married guys," I mumble, my shoulders sagging with exhaustion. "She accused her of only being with me for my money and fame."

"Direct hit. How would she know that shit anyway? It's not like Carrie even knows where Virginia is located on the map," he points out. Yeah, my blonde ex-wife brings every blonde joke to life with new meaning.

"She's always had people watching me," I confess. I knew it while we were married, but never let it bother me. It's not like I was ever doing anything wrong or ever actually cheating like the rag mags always proclaimed.

"That's… sick. So she dug into AJ's past?"

"I guess."

"And what happened then?"

Rubbing the back of my neck, I exhale deeply. "I guess I kinda freaked out. Basically sent her away to see her family and then didn't return her messages."

Crickets.

"Dude, you're the dumbest asshole in the world," my dickhead little brother says before laughing. "Let me get this straight, you like her, sleep with her, your supermodel ex-wife shows up at your house, and you send AJ away?"

"Well, I sent Carrie away first, but yeah, I guess that's the gist."

"Man, you are dumb," he adds with another chuckle. "What are you going to do?"

"I don't know, Dr. Phil. I need to talk to her, but I'm not really sure what to say. Plus, the longer I'm silent, the worse it's getting."

"You think?" Dylan clears his throat. "Okay, what you need to do is call her or go to her and ask to talk. You need to tell her all that shit about Carrie and about how she likes to mess with your head. She needs to hear the truth before you can ask for forgiveness for being a dick. Ask her about the married guy thing. If it's true, then you can determine if you can live with that. If you can't, move on."

Hearing him say it just reinforces what I was already thinking. I need to talk to AJ. I need to tell her about Carrie and definitely find out more about what she said about breaking up a marriage. AJ doesn't strike me as that type, but hell, my people-reader has been off before. Case in point: Carrie.

"You're right," I tell him, feeling slightly better after talking to him.

"Of course I'm right. I'm always right," he says with a laugh.

"Whatever, dickhead. You still coming this weekend or what?"

"I can hang back here if you need time to fix the shit you got yourself into," he says.

"No, you're welcome here. Just bring your headphones in case things go well with the talk," I tease, earning a loud groan.

"Please, not that again," he grumbles.

Back when we were both in school, I had an apartment with a couple of teammates off campus. Dylan was in the dorm and came to my building for a party one of the other guys was throwing. He was crashed on my floor when I returned to my room, hot little sorority girl in tow. We fucked right there in my bed, with my brother trying to sleep on the floor. At one point, I tossed him my mp3 player and headphones to drown out the noise. Sorority girl was a moaner.

"No worries, little brother. You'll have your own room this time."

"Thank Christ," he says. "Anyway, I'll call you when I'm on my way. I'll probably head over Friday after work, if that's okay with you."

"Sure. If you get here on time, we can go to the football game," I tell him, feeling surprisingly better about my shit-storm life.

We sign off with plans to meet at my house. I also start to make plans to talk to a certain math teacher who deserves an explanation for my recent radio silence. At this point, I'm pretty sure she thinks I was only looking for a good time and nothing more, but she would be wrong. Sure, I have shit I have to work out in my head, but I've never thought of AJ as a one-weekend-only kinda girl. In fact, the more I think about her, the more I see her as the every-weekend kinda girl.

My girl.

And it's time to man the fuck up and fix the mess I've made.

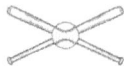

The water turned cold before I finally got out of the shower. My body is bone tired, considering the double run today and the fact that I haven't slept well for the past two nights. My sheets smell of lavender and sex, which makes me painfully hard that I have to jerk off just to get any relief. I've thought about changing the sheets, but every time I go to remove them, the realization that her scent may be gone forever keeps me from replacing them.

How pathetic is that?

Pretty fucking sad, if you ask me.

I'm lying in bed, Sports Center on as background noise, when my phone dings.

My heart rate spikes when I see her name, but then plummets into my stomach when I read her words.

AJ: Thank you for a great weekend. See you around.

She's telling me goodbye. My fingers fly across the letters as I start to reply, but then reality sets in. No one wants or deserves a text apology. She deserves one where she can look into my eyes and see the honesty in my words, because when I finally talk to her, I'm going to be brutally honest.

I delete everything I started to write.

I type a more casual, breezy response, but that won't work either. My feelings for her are neither casual nor breezy.

So I delete that too.

For the life of me, I can't come up with something that's fitting for the moment, considering I have so much to say.

So instead of replying, I set my phone down.

Yeah, I know what you're gonna say and you'd be right. Probably my second biggest fuck-up in as many days.

Grabbing the remote, I turn off the television and get to work on my plan of how I'm going to make this right with the only woman I've wanted since my wife ripped my heart out. AJ Summer may just be the balm I need to finally heal after betrayal.

21

AJ

Tuesday night, more than forty-eight hours of radio silence, I decide to put this baby to rest. It's time to realize it was just a weekend fling and move on. I mean, isn't that how we met anyway? We were supposed to have wild and crazy stranger sex and then move on? It's not like I haven't done that before, but for some reason, the thought of moving on now feels like the air is being choked from my throat.

It needs to happen, though.

With my papers all graded for the night and a half bottle of white wine sitting empty on my counter, I reach for my phone. Even if he dropped me like a sack of week-old potatoes, I still owe him a thank you. I'm not completely rude, even though I'd rather fire off the F-U text.

> **Me:**   Thank you for a great weekend. See you around.

There. Sent.

Before I can put the phone down, bubbles appear.

He's answering!

But then they disappear, with no message popping up.

About ten seconds later, they appear again.

And disappear.

This goes on for the better part of a minute, with no message received.

I drop my phone on my table like it was on fire and let out a loud sigh of frustration. It's fine, really. But he can't just reply with either: You're welcome? It was great? Something? I mean that's just common courtesy to the woman who let you slip a finger into her ass this weekend.

Heading off to bed, my phone still doesn't have a message and my mind is too fuzzy from wine. I leave my cell on the counter in my kitchen so I'm not tempted to tell him off in the middle of the night when the alcohol buzz is in full force. Or worse, cry all over his virtual phone-shoulder while it wears off.

That would be embarrassing.

My bed is as cold as the Artic, even as the calendar slides toward mid-September, but that's what you get after you've spent two nights in bedsheets that were on fire. I toss and turn, unable to relax, unable to find comfort in the lifeless pillow I'm cuddled against. But why should tonight be any different? It's not, in fact. Sleeping alone is just a typical night in the life of AJ Summer.

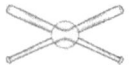

When I reach my classroom door on Wednesday morning, I stop dead in my tracks. I glance down the hallway both directions, waiting for someone to jump out, or waiting for the object to detonate like a bomb.

But no one jumps out and the huge display of red roses doesn't explode.

After unlocking my door, I juggle my latte, work satchel, purse, and the embarrassingly large vase of flowers, since I can't open the door without moving it. The scent instantly hits my nose, a fragrant mix of sweet roses and soothing purple lavender. It's not your typical accent flower for roses, but I'm not normal. It's my favorite, though, and a certain sister who owns a flower shop uptown knows it.

I set the vase on my desk, having to move a tray for students to turn in papers, to accommodate the display. It's huge and at least two dozen dark red blooms. I sip the caramel latte I picked up for myself and stare. There's an envelope, which will surely answer the burning question of *who* brought me flowers. Yet, part of me doesn't really want to know. On one hand, it could be the answer I've been waiting for from a certain hot PE teacher, or it could be the knife that finishes me off if I open the card and don't see his name.

With a semi-shaking hand, I reach for the white packet and pull out the small note. I burst out laughing when the words register.

Nothing sparks a man into action like jealousy.

Love, Gpa

I should have known one of those ornery elders would be behind this.

But I also think he's wrong. There's clearly nothing for Sawyer to be jealous of, if his radio silence is any indication. It's not like he's been beating down my door for the last few days to see me–or even talk to me.

Not like last week.

It's just… over.

A knock sounds on my door and my heart rate kicks up. When I turn in the direction of the sound, I see Bryce standing there, a warm smile on his face. He glances at my desk, noticing the flowers, and that smile falters. "Wow, look at those," he says, walking into my classroom.

"Oh, yeah. A little over the top, right?" I comment with an uncomfortable chuckle, dropping the note into my top desk drawer.

"It depends if you like that sort of thing," he says as he approaches me. It's the first time I notice he's carrying a paper coffee cup and a bag. A white bag. "I stopped at that place you were raving about, and thought I'd grab you one of those fancy coffee drinks and a poppy seed muffin," he adds, extending his hand to me.

My mind instantly recalls Sawyer asking me if there was anything I didn't like. Bran and poppy seed muffins. He was considerate like that.

Pushing thoughts of Sawyer far from my mind, I reach for the bag. "Oh, thank you."

"I see you already have a coffee though. Now you have two," he says with his own uncomfortable chuckle. "And those," he adds, pointing to the vase. "Are they from… Sawyer?"

Shaking my head, I reply, "Oh, no. They're from–" thinking, thinking, I should tell him who they're from, but instead I say quickly, "a friend."

Stupid, right? Now I look like I'm the conductor of the whore train heading straight to Slutsville. One guy warming my bed on the weekend and another apparently sending me flowers just a few short days later.

"Oh, I just assumed. I heard you went to the game with him Friday night."

"He just met me there. He's still meeting people and I offered to introduce him around. What better way to get to know the town than at a Friday night game, right?"

"True." He seems to be really considering his next words carefully. "So, I was hoping I could steal a bit of your time for some help."

"What kinda help?"

"Well, I'm still getting used to all these new regulations on lesson plans, and I really think it would be beneficial to both of us if we worked together. You know, since we teach the same subjects and students go from my class to yours, I think we should make sure our plans match."

"What did you have in mind?"

"Maybe we can meet at that little Mexican joint uptown? They have great tacos and it's usually pretty quiet. We could probably go over quite a bit," he says with eager and hopeful eyes.

I mean it makes sense. Mrs. Cornell, who retired at the end of last year, and I had a great working relationship and often bounced ideas and new techniques off each other. We even would meet for coffee at the café in the evenings. The fact that Bryce is suggesting the same shouldn't surprise me.

Yet, it feels different. Personal. Intimate.

And I can't have that.

"Actually, what if we met at the café right after school? I have plans for dinner with my grandparents." The little white lie flows easily from my mouth. I should feel guilty, but at this moment, I just can't muster it. I know the uncomfortable conversation with him about a date is coming, but I'm just not in the mood to deal with it right now.

"That would be great," he replies eagerly.

Before he can offer to pick me up or drive me there from school, I add, "I can meet you there, if that works. Say four? That gives me a little time to help any students who stop by after school."

"Good idea," he says, nodding quickly. "Four o'clock."

"Great."

"What happens at four o'clock?" The sound of his voice makes my entire body shiver. Dammit.

"We're going to the café," Bryce boasts proudly before I can reply.

When I turn around, I swear this man takes my breath away every single time I see him. And why would it be any different now? Just because I *want* to not feel a damn thing for him doesn't mean my traitorous body doesn't respond anyway. Stupid almost-thirty-year-old body. Here I thought my biggest issue would be saggy boobs and extra weight to my ass when I look at cheese fries.

"To go over our lesson plans," I quickly add when it was left hanging after Bryce's answer. Now, the tension is so thick it feels like a swinging battle-ax wouldn't even slice through the choking haze.

"Ahh," Sawyer says, stepping into my classroom.

He's hypnotizing as he walks toward me. When he's within touching distance, his scent wraps around me like a warm blanket, comforting and familiar. Beautiful blue eyes hold my gaze as he sets something on my desk. Glancing down, I can't help but chuckle.

"I grabbed you a latte on my way in, but I didn't realize you'd already be covered," Sawyer says, nodding at not one, but two coffee cups on my desk. His smile doesn't reach his eyes as he sets the white paper bag on my desk. "Cherry Danish," he answers my unspoken question.

And because my body is traitorous (we've been over this, remember?), my stomach growls. Loudly.

"Oh, I already brought her something. Poppy seed muffin," Bryce brags and indicates the other white bag.

I stand in my place, praying the floor opens up and swallows me whole. Could this get any worse?

"I didn't think you liked poppy seed?" Sawyer asks innocently, but I can see the evil gleam in his eye and hear the underlying tone in his simple statement.

Yep. It could definitely get worse.

"It's fine," I mumble quickly, looking for the exit. "I really should get–"

"Wow, flowers too? Is it a special occasion?" Sawyer asks, his tone stopping my heart like a lethal injection.

He sounds hurt.

He sounds… jealous.

Why is he jealous? He has no right to be when he's the one who hasn't contacted me in three days. I've messaged him, but do I get a return text? Hell no. So why does he have this look in his eyes like someone ran over his family puppy or something?

"Um, no. No special occasion."

"Well, I'll see you later, AJ. I should get back to my classroom before the bell," Bryce says with a smile. "Later, Randall."

Sawyer offers him a head nod and watches him exit.

The silence in the room is deafening. After a couple of tense seconds, our eyes finally collide once more. My God in Heaven, this man can bring me to my knees with just one look. Every dirty thing he did to my body this weekend plays in fast forward through my mind, and if I'm not mistaken, the way his own eyes dilate and turn a deeper shade of sapphire, I'd say he's recalling the same things.

"Am I too late?"

"What?" I ask with a silent gasp.

He steps into my personal space and slides his hand up my arm, leaving a trail of goose bumps in its wake. "Please tell me I'm not too late, Alison. Tell me I haven't fucked this up."

"Fucked what up?" I ask, desperately needing him to clarify.

"This." Again, he touches me. "Us."

"I'm not sure there was an *us* to begin with. It was a fling," I say, trying to find my conviction, but probably coming up short.

"Oh, Alison," he whispers, his words soft, yet seductive. "There is most definitely an *us*. You were never just a fling. Never a one-night stand. You've always been more," he states with so much belief, I feel the righteousness in his voice, feel it in his words.

I open my mouth to reply, but am cut off. "Miss Summer, could you help me–"

Spinning toward the door, I see Kaylee Smith, an eighth grader who I've been helping with her work. I jump back from Sawyer, the connection of his hand to my arm severed.

"Oh, sorry. I didn't mean to interrupt," the young girl says with a blush.

"No, Kaylee, you're fine. Come in and we can go over a few things before the bell rings," I reply, reaching for the first coffee cup I can find. Unfortunately, my hand hits the vase, causing it to wobble. Sawyer's there with his quick hands, diving for the flowers before they can tip over and crash to the floor. "Nice save, Mr. R," the girl coos, completely smitten by the hot PE teacher.

See, even young teenagers aren't immune to his hotness.

Sawyer rights the vase of flowers and turns his head toward me. Quietly, he asks, "Can I see you tonight? I know you have... plans with Bryce, but I'd really like to apologize and hopefully explain a little of what happened Sunday."

His eyes hold mine and don't waiver when he speaks. I have so many questions and there's only one way to get the answers, so I give him a head nod. He seems to visually relax and offers me a relieved smile. Before he heads to the door, he grabs the white bag off my desk. Not the one he brought, but the other one. "Danish," he says softly, pointing to the bag he brought and is sitting in the center of my desk.

With the other bag in hand, he heads to the door. "Oh, hey, Kaylee? Do you like poppy seed muffins?" he asks, flashing the girl one of those smiles that she'll probably dream about for much of her adolescent years.

"Eww, no, Mr. R." Kaylee wrinkles up her nose and giggles. "Those are gross."

"That they are, Kaylee. That they are," he says, dropping the bag into the garbage, throws her a wink, and walks out of the room.

There's nothing but silence left in his wake. "He is so hot," Kaylee mumbles.

"He's your teacher." Sure, I'm stating a fact, but it's not like I can argue with her.

"Mmhmmm. I love PE."

I clear my throat and reach for the teacher's math book. "Let's get started."

Sawyer 22

I've been pacing the floor since I got home from work. I tried to work out, but I was so distracted that I almost killed myself with free weights, so I opted to shower and wait. I'm not sure if she's coming here or if I'm expected there. Hell, if it were up to me, I'd show up at the damn café and third-wheel their little work thing.

But the one thing that kept me from doing just that was the look in her eyes. They're different when she's talking to Bryce versus talking to me. When she communicates with the other math teacher, it's friendly, yet clinical, and the moment her eyes meet mine, it's all fire and desire.

I check my phone again, waiting to see if she's sent a text since I last checked it three minutes ago. I know what you're gonna say: I'm whipped. And ya know what? I don't give a shit. Call me what you want, but I don't care. I don't care because it's true. I'm whipped by a beautiful woman who makes me feel more alive than I ever felt playing baseball.

Now, if I could only get her face-to-face so I can fix my fuckup.

I'm going to find her.

Decision made.

I grab my keys, completely not caring about turning off any lights, and head to the front door. My car is still outside in the driveway, so it's easier to cut out of the house this way than through the garage. Ripping the door open, I almost slam into the woman with her hand raised as if she were about to knock on my door. But it's her scream of surprise that stops me in my tracks.

AJ.

"Shit, I almost ran you over." Yep, stating the obvious. Idiot.

"I'm sorry. I was going to call first, but my car… well, it just drove over here." Her brown hair is pulled into a ponytail high on her head and her clothes are different than what she wore to work. She looks casual and beautiful.

"I'm glad it did." So fucking glad. "Come in." I step aside and wave her in. Her scent sweeps by me as she enters my home.

"I really am sorry for just dropping in on you. I went home after meeting Bryce at the café and was going to call you, but decided to go for a drive."

"It's fine. I'm really glad you're here. Can I get you a drink?" I ask pointing to the living room.

"Actually, do you have any beer?" She wraps her arms around her waist, glancing around as if the place would be different than it was just a few nights ago. Well, everything is completely the same, including the panties hanging from the light in the foyer.

I return from the kitchen with two beers, even though I don't really want one. I need something in my hand. Otherwise, it'll be *her* in my hands and I don't think she's quite ready for that. AJ is standing at the sliding back door that leads to the deck. The sun is setting and the view of the Bay is almost as breathtaking as she is.

"Do you want to sit outside?" I ask.

Glancing over her shoulder, I see the tension and nervousness in her eyes. She nods quickly and opens the door. There's a breeze, but it doesn't bother me any. I'll have to watch her, though, for any sign that she's getting chilly.

"I'm glad you're here," I tell her honestly as she takes a seat in one of the chairs. She curls her legs beneath her body, the casual way she does when she gets comfy on my couch.

"Me too." She takes a long pull from her beer before setting it on the table beside her.

"I owe you an explanation," I start, gazing over at her. She doesn't say anything, which is my only indication to keep going. "I've been labeled as a playboy basically since the moment I stepped into the majors. My PR firm loved the additional exposure, so I was advised to just 'go with it.' I never disputed or argued the claims, even though everything was completely fabricated. Did I have one-night stands? Yes. I'm not about to lie to you and tell you I didn't. Did I have them after I met Carrie? Fuck no. I'm not the man I'm portrayed in the media, AJ."

I take a deep breath and keep going. "When I started dating Carrie, the stories changed. I was the playboy tamed by the beautiful model. Sure, we were still tailed everywhere we went, but at least they were focused more on my relationship than on what they called my extracurriculars. I proposed after we had been dating a year, and we got married a year after that. It was a big, elaborate thing that I really didn't want, but Carrie insisted. We were both in the public eye, and therefore, it was expected of us to let the public in on that part of our lives too. I hated it, to be frank, but went along with it because it was what she wanted.

"About a month after we were married, the first news story hit about me cheating. I was in Chicago, playing a series against the Sox, when I was photographed in a club with a woman. That woman was trashed and stumbling all around. I was sitting on a couch beside my teammate Joel. I reached out and helped steady her, but the damage was done in that fraction of a second. My hand was on her leg and she appeared to be straddling my lap.

The headline read: 'RANDALL OUT FOR A GOOD TIME WITHOUT HIS WIFE'."

I take a deep breath. "At that point, I was labeled, followed, and hounded even more than I already was. My PR agency, again, informed me not to respond. Carrie was pissed, even though she swore she believed me. It was much of the same for years, until my accident."

"Then their focus changed," she confirms.

"Yeah, it changed. And it took three months after being injured before I found her in bed with a teammate."

Her big green eyes widen, a look of shock transforming her beautiful face. "What?" Her words are barely above a whisper.

"I came home from therapy and found her in our bed with my replacement."

"Fucking bitch," she mumbles through her gasp.

"That she was. Is. She told me it was because I wasn't giving her enough attention. I was fucking going to therapy every day. My career was over and I was still trying to come to terms with it. And I wasn't giving her enough attention." I sit back and watch the waves crash against the sand. "Hell, maybe I didn't. It was in that moment that I knew I had to get out. I had to get away. I was certainly not going to stay married to a woman who could cheat so easily to try to get my attention. Especially when she accused me of whoring around our entire marriage."

"I'm sorry, Sawyer." Her apology isn't necessary or needed, but still comforting all the same.

"It's fine. I got over it and am past it. Well, I thought I was until Sunday night," I say, her body tensing in the chair.

"What did she say?" she asks softly.

"She told me things… about you."

"Me?" she asks, sitting up straight.

"Yeah, she said you broke up a marriage not that long ago. More than one, actually," I confess, not at all proud to acknowledge that I chose to let Carrie's words affect me as much as they did.

A look crosses her face, and for a moment I see a touch of guilt mixed with sadness. "Wait, how would she know anything about me?"

I chuckle, but it lacks any humor. "That's the thing about Carrie. She's very… resourceful. In fact, for a long time, I've suspected she was behind some of the photos that showed up in the rag mags. Half the time, I wasn't in a public place that would be accessible for a photog. Yet, they always had a way of finding me, and always in the exact moment some strange woman walked up, posing as a fan, and moments later would plant her lips on mine."

She seems perplexed. "So, you're telling me that Carrie could have been following me?"

"Well, I'm sure it wasn't Carrie personally, but yeah, I think she had someone looking into you. It's the only thing I can come up with as to why she knew… things about you."

AJ seems to be lost in thought for a few moments, so I just let her be. After a few minutes, her eyes meet mine. "I'm sorry you've been caught up in my crazy life. I guess, I just thought when I moved here, I was leaving all the bullshit behind."

"It's not your past that bothers me, Sawyer, it's the fact that you didn't come to me when she told you those things. The fact that you chose to let her words affect you, without allowing me to explain, hurts as much as your silence."

Instantly, I'm on my feet and kneeling before her. "I fucked up, AJ. I'm so used to closing myself off or trying to stay one step ahead of her manipulation."

"I'm not her." Her words are blunt and to the point. The weight carries the force of a thousand knives to my gut.

"I know. Fuck, do I know. You're so much the polar opposite of her that I can't see straight."

"I would have told you, you know. If you had asked about what she said… that marriage thing… I would have told you everything. In fact, I would have anyway because I'm one who believes there shouldn't be secrets between two people in a relationship. And even though we never officially declared anything, it feels like we were headed that way. At least it felt like it to me," she averts her eyes.

"Me too, baby," I answer quickly, bringing my head forward and setting it against hers. "It felt like that because that's exactly where we were headed. Where we *are* headed." My eyes find hers and I see tears brimming.

She takes a deep breath. "Then you need to know about Joe."

Just the sound of the guy's name elevates my blood pressure, but I force myself to school my features and appear calm. I also reach for her hands, linking our fingers together, because if I'm going to hear about my AJ with another man, I need to feel like I'm grounded, and touching her does that for me. "Go on."

"He lived nearby and came to town a time or two a week for work. He told me he was divorced, which it turns out he was not. I found out one night when his pregnant wife called me up and told me."

"Fuck," I groan, knowing where this was going.

"He lied to me for weeks while warming my bed, and then would go home to his wife and kids. I didn't know," she whispers, the tears finally falling and her guilt reflecting in her sad eyes.

"I know, baby," I tell her before kissing her forehead, my lips lingering just a little longer than they should. "He was the ultimate douchebag."

"He was."

"She left him?" I ask, knowing that if the information Carrie was given was accurate, she did.

"I think so, though it's not like she actually called me after that night to chat."

"Of course."

She gives me a sad little smile. "That was the only one," she insists.

"Okay."

"Okay?" she asks, swiping away at her tears angrily.

"I believe you."

AJ stares at me for a few moments, her eyes searching my own. "Thank you."

"Thank you for telling me."

She nods. "And thank you for telling me about Carrie."

"I'm sorry it took so long. You deserved to know the moment she left."

"I did," she states.

"But I want to do better. I want to be better… for you."

She reaches forward and sets her hand on my cheek. Her thumb traces my bottom lip. "You already are, Mr. Randall. I just need you to be real and honest with me, okay? Even though it drove me insane that you were alone with her, I trusted you."

"You have nothing to be jealous about," I say through my first real deep breath in days. My arms wrap around her and pull her into my body, her scent surrounding me.

"I have everything to be jealous about. Have you seen you?" she asks with a giggle, making me pull back to see her.

"I only want you." My words are pure and honest and make her eyes sparkle like emeralds. Then, I pull her flush against me, my body sparking to life the way it only does when I'm with her. "I've missed you," I whisper into her hair.

"I've missed you, too."

"I want to kiss you. I want to kiss my girlfriend and show her just how sorry I am for being an asshole." To punctuate my words, I slide my lips down the long, sexy column of her neck.

"Your girlfriend?" she asks, her lips gently curling upward when my own reach hers.

"Fuck yes, baby. Now that I've had you, I can't let you go. I *won't.*"

"I kinda like the sound of that," she replies, sliding her hand down my chest. All of the blood in my body starts to head toward one concentrated area below my belt.

"You won't mind being seen in public with a former player?" I ask sarcastically.

"As long as the only playing you'll be doing is with me." Her grin is wicked.

"Only you," I declare just before my lips claim hers–finally.

It's a kiss of necessity, like breathing. It's slow and tantalizing as if we're both savoring the taste and feel of each other, a coming together of two halves, like puzzle pieces. All it takes is her rushed exhale of breath, that deep respire of contentment and satisfaction that makes my blood roar in my ears and my libido kick into overdrive.

My hands are in her hair, fingers tangling with the rubber band that's pulling it back. I need that little piece of elastic gone and those locks wild and unrestrained. It's one of my favorite looks, especially when it matches her eyes.

Her nimble fingers grip my shoulders and slide down my arms, squeezing my muscles and making them jump. Soft fingers then move to my chest, where she pushes up my t-shirt and grips my chest. "Fuck, I've missed having your hands on me," I gasp, my breathing harsh.

"I want to touch you. Everywhere." Her words are the accelerant to the already raging fire that's lit within. It flames to life, bright and alive, ready to devour everything in its path. And right now, it's Miss AJ Summer who's there, my body burning for only her.

My Alison.

"Come with me, baby," I whisper, wrapping my arms around her and lifting.

"I can walk," she insists as I lead her into my house, securing all doors before I tote her upstairs. Of course, it takes a hell of a lot longer to complete the task when I pin her against several walls, the entertainment center, and even the refrigerator, to ravish her sweet little mouth, before ascending the stairs.

Her fingers slide into my hair as we enter my bedroom. The sun has set and the moon casts a soft shadow against the dark bedding. It would be the most amazing backdrop, the moon shining off her hair as it's splayed against my pillow. And that thought stops me in my tracks.

"What's wrong?" she asks, when I don't move and stop kissing her.

"I just realized something," I mumble as her mouth trails down my throat.

Her wet tongue slips out, licking and tasting my skin. "What's that?"

"We've never fucked in my bed," I state, the realization a bit comical, yet completely unacceptable.

"Sure we have. We…" she trails off, deep in thought, as if trying to recall that one time we had sex in my bed. But she won't find that time. We've had sex on practically every surface in this joint, tore half of my living room apart by Hurricane Ali, but never in the one place that mattered.

That'll change tonight.

Tonight, we won't have sex or fuck.

Tonight, when I take this woman to my bed, it'll be to make love to her.

No, I'm not declaring anything, but she means more to me than some casual fling or one-night stand. Shit, she's always been more, even when she was passed out in my hotel room and I knew nothing more than her first name. She was under my skin the moment our eyes met, a connection cemented so damn deep, it'll be there until the end of time. She's quickly becoming my everything.

Tonight, I show her.

AJ

23

It's hard to think when his hands are in my hair and he kisses me like I'm oxygen and he's a drowning man.

Sawyer turns and gently lays me down on the mattress. The weight and hard planes of his body are enough to send my already-sensitive skin straight into melting-from-my-body territory. He moves his lips down my neck, his big hands gentle as he cups my breast and massages my nipple through my clothes. They're standing at complete attention, two tight little buds eager for his mouth.

He moves his hand beneath my shirt, gently pushing it upward as he goes. The air is cool against my flushed skin, but it's a welcomed sensation, much like the ones I'm feeling as his rough thumb slips beneath the lace of my bra and teases my nipple.

"Do you know what I missed?" he says, as he continues to expertly play my body like a guitar.

Again, I mewl.

"That. That right there," he says, sliding down my body just a bit. "I missed the sounds you make when my hands and mouth are on your body. The noises you make when I'm filling your sweet pussy kept me awake well into the early morning every night I was without you," he says right before his warm mouth latches on to one nipple. I practically jackknife off the bed. Well, I would have if it weren't for his body covering mine.

"I couldn't sleep either," I confess as his tongue swirls and licks through the lace.

"Did you touch yourself?" he asks before switching to my other breast.

"Yes. So much. Even though I was hurt, I couldn't stop thinking about you," I say, triggering a deep, masculine groan that fills the room. The vibrations against my nipple cause my core to clench.

"Fuck, Alison, I wish I could have been there. I want to watch you pleasure yourself," he declares. Sawyer trails open-mouthed kisses down my stomach. When he reaches my shorts, he swiftly unbuttons the material and opens it wide. My thighs fall open farther, his body positioned between them. "I'm going to taste you."

I try to let him know that I whole-heartedly approve of this plan, but it comes out as a weird series of noises that sound like *E.T.* If Sawyer heard my weirdness, he doesn't comment. Instead, he slips my shorts down my legs, taking my panties with them, and returns to where his mouth is directly above me. My body is pulsing, my core flooded with wetness that's just for him.

The slow swipe of his tongue against my swollen flesh is magical, maniacal, and mesmeric, all at the same time. It's like paradise colliding with a brewing storm. Thunder touches deep in my soul and sets my world on fire, leaving me breathless and yearning for more.

But it doesn't take long before his mouth has me there, ready to fly over the edge of bliss. My body is coiled tight like a rattlesnake, my muscles pulsing. The feel of his tongue swirling around on my clit, flicking it repeatedly with pressure, and then finally sucking it into his mouth, is almost too much. He repeats this process once more, my orgasm barreling down on me with full force. It sweeps through my blood and washes over me as his name spills from my lips.

Giving me no time to recover, he's naked and has a condom in place before I can even open my heavy eyes. But what I see before me wakes my weary body and fuels the feelings I've developed for him. He's gloriously hard (yeah, that too) everywhere, his body a work of art, but it's his eyes that draw my attention. They're a burning blue fire mixed with something softer, something true. Something real. Like I asked him to always be.

Something that looks like love.

But I won't go there, not now. Definitely not now. Not with this gorgeous man ready to pounce, the look in his eyes promising more pleasure than I could ever imagine.

My breath hitches as he comes down on top of me. My legs wrap around his waist, his hands running down the smooth outside of my thigh. His cock nudges at my opening, ready and eager. I link my arms around his neck, my hands sliding into his dark hair as his mouth meets mine in a possessive kiss.

He keeps one hand on my hip and the other holding my hair as he maneuvers enough to slide inside me. It's like heaven, a homecoming of two souls who were lost. Before him, there was sex. With him, there's magic. It's like nothing I've ever felt, but knew existed. It just took me a while to find him.

Sawyer moves my hands above my head, never once breaking his slow pace. His hands trace the insides of my arms before entwining his fingers with mine. Only then do his thrusts become more. Harder, deeper he pushes into me, our hands grasping at each other as if the other was an anchor. My lips are swollen, wet, and eager as he makes love to my mouth with the same tenderness and precision he does to my body.

And that's what this is.

I know it.

My internal muscles start to tighten, gripping around his cock, begging for more. I can tell he's getting close too as he gasps and grunts with each flutter of muscle around him. I feel his eyes on me along with his lips. When I open my eyes, the look he wears leaves me breathless and teary. It's powerful, this connection and the emotions rolling through me, and I can tell it's the same for him.

Sawyer hits that spot deep inside of me that makes my eyes cross and my heart stop beating. He slides his cock against it twice more, each time driving me closer to release. The next time, I let go, flying into the bright white light of bliss, grounded by his lips on mine and our tangled fingers. He goes quickly, following me over the edge, coming hard inside me. It's my name that slips from his lips like a plea and a hymn.

Neither of us moves. His lips trace mine, our breathing twisted together like our bodies. I want to stay here, just like this forever. No one else in the world. Just him and me and the love we make with our bodies. It's crazy, probably too soon by many standards, but I don't care. It's real. It's true.

I'm falling in love with him.

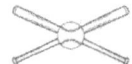

Apparently, there are many opportunities to steal secret kisses throughout the day at a junior high, which should probably concern me a little, considering we deal with horny pubescent teenagers all day long. Nevertheless, Thursday and Friday are filled with random visits between class periods and lunch together in the teachers' lounge. Apparently, when Sawyer Randall calls someone his girlfriend, he goes all in. Well, you know… considering the location.

It's Friday evening and we're at his place, waiting on his brother to arrive. To say I'm nervous to meet someone from his family is an understatement. Outside of high school, I've never met the man I'm seeing's family before, so this is entirely new terrain for me. I think Sawyer has sensed my anxiety too, because he keeps wrapping his arms around me in a tight hug and whispers dirty things in my ear.

A man who takes your mind off your troubles with the promise of oral is a keeper, ladies.

It's near eight when headlights shine through the front windows. I jump up off the couch, Sawyer giving me a look like I've lost my mind, and stand there waiting for him to go to the door. He's smiling as he slowly (my God, how long does it take one man to get up off the couch?) gets up and wraps his arms around me.

"Settle down, baby. He's gonna love you," he whispers before placing a kiss in the middle of my forehead.

"I can't believe how nervous I am. Can you imagine how neurotic I'd be if I ever meet your parents?" I ask, a weird humorless laugh coming from my throat.

"*When*, sweetheart. When you meet my parents, and they'll love you too. They will all see the amazing woman I see every day." Again, I get another kiss, but this one on my lips. "Let's go."

Sawyer pulls me to the front of the house and opens the door. I'm practically dancing in place as a man gets out of his car and gives us a wave. He pulls a small suitcase from the back seat before walking our way.

As he approaches, he completely walks around his brother and pulls me into a big hug. "My God, he didn't mention you were this beautiful. How about we blow this Popsicle stand and you forget all about the has-been baseball player. I'm the better Randall anyway." And then he waggles his eyebrows suggestively and gives me the biggest smile possible.

"Dude, you're fucking married," Sawyer groans, pushing his brother off me.

"Semantics."

"She's pregnant," big brother grumbles to the younger one.

"I'm not even sure it's my kid!" he protests wildly, clearly joking. I'm practically rolling on the ground laughing, and all of the nerves I was feeling before just float away.

"I'm telling her you said that," Sawyer replies, crossing his arms over his chest.

Dylan gasps. "You wouldn't dare! She'll kick my ass all the way to Charlottesville and back."

"Oh, I would, and you know it. Keep your hands to yourself, Sir Grabs-a-Lot," Sawyer directs, wrapping one arm around my shoulders and pulling me in close.

"You're just mad I got the brains *and* the beauty. All you got was some measly ability to swing a bat. It will take you nowhere in life, son."

Sawyer laughs as he pulls his brother into a hug. "Don't forget about my stellar rap skills."

"How could I? For years, you insisted I call you Sir Mix-a-Lot."

"It was a week, and I was nine."

"Nineteen, maybe," Dylan says before turning his attention to me. "Seriously, it's great to finally meet you, AJ. If my brother is ever stupid enough to let you go again, you call me. I'd be happy to slap more sense into him." My eyebrows quirk together and I glance at Sawyer. He called his brother? I'd say by the way he gives me a shy little grin and shrugs his shoulders that his brother's words were true.

"Are you hungry? It's a little late for the football game, so we thought we'd run to town and get a pizza," Sawyer says as he holds the front door open for us.

"Starving. I gotta call my girl first before we head out, though," Dylan says, carrying his bag up the stairs.

"Second door on the left," Sawyer hollers after him.

"Is that as far away from your room as I can get? I forgot earbuds and we don't need any repeats of college," he throws over his shoulder before disappearing into the guest room.

"I think he was adopted," Sawyer grumbles.

"I think he's great," I tell him, wrapping my arms around his waist. "He clearly loves you."

"If you would have seen us back in the day, you may not say that. We fought all the time. It wasn't pretty."

"Don't all siblings? I have two older sisters and three younger ones. Drama and bickering were key ingredients in our household."

Sawyer nuzzles my neck with his nose, his hands sliding dangerously close to the waistband of my shorts. It wouldn't take much to slip his hands into my panties. I mean, if that were appropriate to do while in the presence of your boyfriend's younger brother.

"You sure you don't mind him tagging along Sunday?" he asks a second time. I'm not sure if he thinks I'm going to change my mind or if I don't really want him to go with us. It's neither. I'm actually really excited to go to the Rangers' game in DC on Sunday, and don't have a problem sharing my time with Dylan.

When he invited me along Thursday night, he mentioned that his brother wanted to go. Sawyer's old teammate is getting us tickets, which will be my first professional game. He's also very eager to introduce me to some of the guys he played with, a fact that makes me smile just a little bit more.

"Of course, I don't mind."

"He's interfering with my alone time with you," he whispers against my neck, his hot breath tickling my skin.

"We get plenty of alone time," I inform him.

"There's never enough alone time," he retorts before turning me to face him and claiming my lips with his. This man kisses like his life depends on it. His hands thread into my hair as he holds me in place, devouring my mouth with his. It's one of those kisses that could lead to something else... something very dirty.

"Amber says hi," Dylan interrupts as he starts to descend the stairs.

"Cockblocker," Sawyer mumbles loud enough for his brother to hear.

"Yeah, well, if I can't get any this weekend, neither can you."

"Wanna bet?" Sawyer asks confidently, making my cheeks burn with embarrassment.

"Okay, boys, I'm starving. Pizza is calling," I say as I head to the table to retrieve my purse.

"Can I get mushrooms, Mom?" Dylan asks, giving me the same charming smile his brother possesses.

Something tells me when these boys were young, they were a handful.

"Duh," I sass, heading toward the door in the mudroom that leads to the garage.

"Yes!" he exclaims, his fists poised high in the air. "She likes me better than she likes you," he teases.

"You can get those gross little pieces of fungus on your half of the pizza," Sawyer adds.

"Then the pretty girl is sitting with me at the table," Dylan says in a singsong voice as he slides into the back seat of his brother's car, earning a growl from the man at the driver's door. He actually growls like a possessive animal.

I giggle at the way Dylan seems to so effortless push Sawyer's buttons. "Don't you start," he directs from across the roof of the car. "Or later tonight, I'll have to spank you." The heat reflecting in his eyes matches the fire behind his words. My body ignites, warmth rushing to the apex of my legs.

"Gross, Mom and Dad. Stop talking about sex in front of me. I'm so impressionable at this age," Dylan says, hardly able to keep his laughter at bay.

Sawyer rolls his eyes and slides down into the driver's seat. I'm left with a sudden need so intense that only one man could quench my thirst and the prospect of another spanking on the horizon.

I might just see how far I can push those buttons after all.

Sawyer

24

Dylan is following behind us as we make our way through the streets of DC and toward the ballpark. He'll be heading directly home after the game to see his wife, Amber. Even though he's been a pain in my ass all weekend, I'll admit it's been great having him around. I knew that AJ had nothing to worry about where my goofball brother was concerned, and after seeing their easy interaction these past two days, there's no doubt in my mind that the rest of my family will love her too.

As much as I do.

That's what I was about to say, but I'm trying not to put the cart before the horse here. I know my feelings for her are rounding third and heading toward home, but I'm not sure I'm ready to say it. I just need a little more time, even though that doesn't quite feel right either. I mean, if I'm falling for her, I should tell her, right?

The fact that I already know where this is headed, just a few short weeks of really being together, is telling. I dated Carrie for almost six months before I said those words. I chalked it up to the distance, but looking back now, I know it was because something was missing. Like love.

It's not that I didn't love her, because I did, but it was just different than how I feel right now with AJ. I don't know if that makes me an asshole or what, but whatever. And I bet if you'd ask Carrie, she'd say the same thing. I think feelings were involved, but I don't think it was that all-consuming love you see in the big climax of romance movies. If it were, then would she have cheated?

"You're awfully quiet over there," AJ says, reaching over and setting her hand on top of mine on the shifter.

"Sorry, just thinking," I tell her as I bring her hand up to my mouth and kiss the tender skin at her knuckles. She gives me a look like she might want to ask for details, but she doesn't push. "I was thinking about how relaxed and comfortable this weekend was. With you in it."

I'm rewarded with a bright smile that does things to my heart and my cock. "It was pretty great, wasn't it? Your brother is hilarious. I can't wait to meet Amber."

"She's awesome and doesn't put up with Dyl's shit. He talks a big game, but he's pretty much whipped and knows it."

"Nothing wrong with that," she says, a single eyebrow rising

"I agree. When the right woman comes along, a man doesn't mind at all," I tell her, making sure to hold her eyes for a few extra seconds before returning them to the road.

We pull into a private lot around the back of the stadium and park. I can't help but smile as AJ gets out of the car. Her tan legs look a fucking mile long in her sexy little jean shorts that have frayed edges, but that's not what holds my attention right now. My girl is wearing my number. Apparently she found a jersey online Thursday and had it overnighted. She completely surprised me when she stepped out of my bathroom this morning sporting number fifteen.

My fucking number.

It's fitted in all the right places and makes her tits look fucking amazing. We almost didn't make it out of the damned bedroom.

"Do you have any idea how hot you look today?" I ask her when I reach the passenger side of the car.

"I believe the word you said earlier is scorching," she coos, batting her eyelashes.

"Fucking dynamite. I've been hard since you walked into the room wearing it."

"Boys are so silly," she says with a laugh. "Why aren't you wearing an old jersey?" she asks more seriously.

I give her a shoulder shrug. I'm wearing a team shirt, but not one of the many jerseys hanging in the closet in my workout room. "I'm not part of the team anymore."

She wraps her arms around my shoulders and presses herself against me. "You'll always be a part of the team, even if you're no longer on the roster." Her words strike a chord with me for some reason. She gets it. My love for this game, and this team, runs deep.

I need to kiss her. Now. My mouth sweeps down and claims her lips in a slow, savoring kiss. This may be my only chance to have her lips on mine for the next few hours, so I might as well take advantage of the opportunity while I can, right?

"Enough PDA," Dylan hollers. "You're going to scare the children."

AJ pulls away just as a man and his two boys walk by, both kids giggling and pointing. Then, they just stop in their tracks. "Dad! That's Sawyer Randall!" the older of the two boys yells.

The trio approaches us, big smiles on their faces. "Holy cow, it is! You're my brother's favorite player!" the youngest boy exclaims with a toothless grin, pointing to his brother's shirt. I smile widely when I see my old number.

"What's your name?" I ask the boy wearing my jersey.

"Adam. And my brother's name is Andrew. And my dad's name is Jason, but we call him Dad," Adam says very matter-of-factly, which makes me laugh.

Crouching down so that we're a little closer in size, I ask, "How old are you, Adam?"

"Nine last week."

"Nine, huh? And you like baseball?" I ask, giving all of my attention to this dad and his two boys.

"Love it. I played third base in little league this summer, like you!"

"You must have quite an arm then," I say to Adam, ruffling the hair on his head.

"I have to ask, but would you mind taking a quick picture with the boys?" the dad asks, pulling his cell phone from his pocket.

"I'd love to," I tell him, handing my keys to AJ. She takes them quickly, and goes to put them in her purse. "Trunk," I add quickly, nodding at my car. AJ doesn't ask, but steps around the back of my car. Dylan's there, and I'm sure they can figure out what I'm talking about.

I pose for a picture with each boy individually, and then both of them together. Even though I've taken a few dozen selfies with students at school, it's been a while since I did the full photo and autograph session with a couple of young fans.

"How old are you, Andrew?" I ask the toothless brother.

"Seven. But my favorite player is Joel Cougar! He throws like a rocket!" the young fan proclaims, referring to Joel's cannon of an arm. The man is the best centerfielder in the league and can accurately throw a missile from deep center to home plate–usually without it bouncing.

"He sure does," I confirm to the little guy wearing Joel's number twenty-nine.

Glancing up, I see AJ standing off to the side, a wide smile on her face and her hands full of the items I was hoping she'd get.

"Hey, I've got some stuff for you," I tell the boys, walking over and grabbing the hats and shirts. AJ smiles warmly at me as she hands me a Sharpie marker.

"How about a hat?" I ask the boys, placing one of the new Rangers hats on each of their heads.

"Really?! This is so cool, huh, Dad?"

"Awesome," Jason responds to his oldest son, snapping pictures of the exchange.

"How about I sign those hats for you?" I ask, extending my hand to see if they're interested. I never just assume someone wants my signature on an item of clothing. When both boys practically throw the hats back at me, I sign my name on the bill of each one. Then, I do the same for their dad and hand it to him.

"Thank you so much," he says as he takes the hat. "I've been a Rangers fan since I was born."

"Well, we appreciate the support," I tell him before reaching for the photos AJ has in her other hand. They're last year's team photo and have my old sponsor logos in the corners, but I don't think anyone will care. "Thanks," I say softly to the woman who's standing off to the side, smiling proudly.

"Is that your girlfriend?" Adam asks when I turn back to them.

"It has to be his girlfriend. They were kissing," Andrew replies, giggling in a way that only little kids can do.

"She is my girlfriend." There's no fighting the wide smile on my own face as I gaze over my shoulder at AJ.

After a few more minutes of interacting with the young fans, their dad finally drags them off to the entrance. Both boys were practically floating as they recounted the last ten minutes with their dad–both talking on top of each other.

"You were very good with them," AJ says, sliding her arm around my waist and stepping into my embrace.

"Besides actually playing ball, that was always my favorite part. The exchanges with young fans. The adults I could live without sometimes, but the kids? They made all the drama and bullshit worth it." And that's true. I'd take a young fan with stars in their eyes and baseball dreams in their head over a drunk, rowdy, know-it-all adult any day of the week.

"Can we go in now? I've been dying for a foot long hotdog since we pulled into the lot," Dylan says, starting to walk to the stadium.

Keeping my arm wrapped around AJ's shoulder, we follow behind my brother and head toward the gates. I noticed how she preferred to be just off to the side when I was with the fans. Back when I was married to Carrie, she'd insert herself directly into the middle of any conversation or photo, even those with young kids.

But AJ didn't need to be front and center. She let me do my thing and didn't balk at the interruption or insist she be included in the photos. It wasn't all about her, which is a welcoming change.

And not that I need it to be all about me, but in my line (albeit former) of work, I'm used to fans. I'm used to photos. I'm used to autographs and handshakes and hugs. I've always had to maintain a public persona, and my goal was always to make sure I was as professional as could be.

Even when the rag mags were trashing my reputation.

AJ pulls something from her purse and places it on her head. I stop and stare down at the simply irresistible woman who's wearing my fucking jersey and now my hat. Smiling, I grab the bill of her hat and push it down just a bit more, turning it until it's positioned just right on her head.

There. Fucking adorable.

"Ready?" I ask.

"Ready," she confirms as we turn and head to the gate.

This day is turning out to be pretty fucking great.

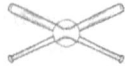

"Are you blind?! What kinda call was that?" AJ hollers at the ump behind home plate while the crowd around us boos and screams their frustration at the horrible call.

"Dude, your girl is vicious. Remind me not to get on her bad side," Dylan mumbles to me as we watch AJ rant at the umpire.

"No shit," I reply, shocked that such harsh words just came from my sweet little schoolteacher's mouth. "It's kinda hot, though."

"Definitely," my brother replies quietly. "Did you see how many hotdogs she ate?"

"More than you."

"More than you and me combined, bro. A woman who looks like that, talks like a sailor, *and* can hold her own in a hotdog eating contest? Marry her, dude."

I snort in reply, merely because I'm afraid if I open up my mouth right now, I might actually propose. If I was falling in love with this woman before today, well, seeing her in my element, trash talking, and burping warm beer has pretty much sealed the deal for me. There's no doubt in my mind that I've fallen head over heels in love with AJ Summer.

"Can you believe that call? What kinda horseshit is that? A blind monkey humping a football could have seen the tag! He was out by a mile," she seethes, her eyes burning with fire and passion.

"I saw," I tell her, wrapping my arm around her shoulders and pulling her into my side. "Horrible call."

"The worst," she grumbles.

"You're scaring the big burly guys behind us, honey," I tease.

She glances over her shoulder at my words. "You mean Bill and Tom? Shit, who do you think taught me those bad words?" she asks, making me laugh. "They really appreciated the autographs, though," she adds. As soon as the Rangers fans sat down behind us before the game started, they recognized me and started chatting. I signed a few autographs for them and a handful for others in the vicinity.

"Want anything to drink?" I ask, needing to stretch my legs. Watching the game is making me twitchy.

"Sprite. Oh, and nachos." Her eyes light up like the Fourth of July.

"How could you still be hungry?" I ask, astonished.

"Well, I do recall a certain baseball player helping me work up an appetite this morning," she whispers against my ear, making my cock jump.

"Ahhh, yes, the workout," I recall happily, thinking back to how she surprised me in my home gym this morning while I was working out. I don't think that weight bench has ever seen so much action.

"I can hear you," Dylan grumbles. "And I could hear you this morning too. Next time, don't put your gym right next to the guest room, dick."

AJ blushes a beautiful shade of pink, very close to the same color of her ass this morning after I spanked it, in fact. I pull her into my chest and press a hard kiss on her lips. "You want anything?" I ask my nuisance of a brother.

"Coke."

"Be right back," I tell them before slipping out of the row and heading up the stairs.

Since it's in the middle of the sixth, the lines aren't too long at the concession stands. After a quick detour to the head, I hop in line at the closest food vendor. My mind wanders back to the moment we entered the stadium this afternoon. AJ could sense my anxiety, could probably feel the tension radiating from my body. But as I rounded the corner and walked out into the seating area, it didn't hurt as bad as I thought it would.

Yeah, I wanted to be out there playing ball with my team, but it felt different being here this time. Like I could sense that it was really over. And more importantly, that I was okay with it.

The guys were warming up on the field as I made my way down to our seats, just to the left of the dugout. My favorite batting coach saw me first, and quickly drew the attention of the rest of the team. Even the douchebag who replaced me at third base (and in my bed by screwing my wife) came over to say hello. He's lucky I didn't punch him in the fucking throat when he tried to extend a hand (which I pretended not to see).

I introduced everyone to AJ and reintroduced them to Dylan, whom most of them have met over the years. A few of the guys asked me about teaching and coaching, wondering if I was ready to make a return to the game like Michael Jordan. I just gave them a smile, not confirming or denying anything. I've gotten pretty damn good at deflection over the years.

And I got to see Joel again. He made sure to hit on AJ and invited her back to his hotel room after the game. Cocksucker. He also pulled me into a hug and told me he was glad to see me smile again. Leave it to Joel to not pull any punches.

"I see you brought the flavor of the week." The voice is all too familiar and makes the hairs on the back of my neck stand up.

Turning to face the woman who legally shared my name (though she never took it publicly because of her image), I let out a long sigh. "Carrie. What brings you down to the bowels of the stadium?" I ask, moving forward a few steps in line.

"I was just passing through and saw you standing here," she says, checking her reflection in a small mirror she pulled from her bag.

"I bet you were. Oh, and how did you know I had someone with me?" I ask, giving her my back as I turn to check out the menu options.

"Are you kidding? You've been flaunting her all over the big screen, Sawyer. The cameras have followed your every move." Figures. I noticed I was on the monitors a few times between innings, but didn't pay too much attention.

"It's hardly flaunting her when I didn't even know you would be here."

"Where else would I be? Shawn is here," she says, referring to the third base replacing douchebag nearly ten years my junior.

I do my best to ignore her, taking a few more steps forward until I'm next in line. I feel her step up beside me, her body close and her perfume assaulting my nostrils. "What do you want?" I ask, unable to keep the irritation out of my voice.

"I miss you." Her words are almost as startling as her hand, which is sliding up my arm and wrapping around my bicep. That earns a humorless laugh.

"Miss me? You have a damn funny way of showing it, sweetheart. You're here cheering on your little boy toy. Why don't you head back up to the WAG suite and watch him play." I turn to the young guy behind the counter and give him my attention. "Nachos with cheese, two Sprites, and a Coke, please."

"It's not like that with us," she says. "We're very casual."

"Good for you," I tell her as I pay the sixteen dollar bill with a twenty and tell the kid to keep the change. "If you'll excuse me," I say, turning and heading toward my seat.

"I'll be back in town in October to wrap up the photo shoot. I want to see you again too, Sawyer," she says behind me, not even bothering to keep her voice low. I can feel the eyes of those around me, but I keep walking. I don't even acknowledge her 'too,' since that probably makes it sound like I wanted to see her first.

Well, I don't.

"Not happening, Carrie," I holler over my shoulder as I take the stairs two at a time down to our seats.

As soon as I see AJ, my body relaxes. She's standing there with her hands thrust high in the air, cheering with the rest of the crowd as Joel rounds second base in a stand-up double.

"Hey, long lines?" she asks, taking the nachos and shoving the first one into her mouth. She chews happily, not even caring that there's a tiny drop of cheese on her bottom lip.

Instead of answering her question, I grab the back of her head and pull her into a deep kiss. She tastes like cheese and every bit the sexy woman she is. My tongue slips into her mouth as the kiss quickly elevates from PG-13 to R-rated.

"Think fast, you're on television." Dylan's words permeate my sex-craved brain.

I turn to see AJ and myself, front and center on the Jumbotron at centerfield. She looks dazed at the camera, appearing very thoroughly kissed, if I do say so myself, before turning and burying her face in my arm. The crowd around us cheers wildly, and I can barely hear the announcers talking about me over the noise.

"Former Rangers third baseman Sawyer Randall is in the crowd, cheering on his former team in today's showdown with the Nationals."

"That's right, Bud. Sawyer played ten years for the Rangers before that devastating play that resulted in torn ligaments and severely injuring his right shoulder."

"And what an injury that was, Davis. Two surgeries were able to repair much of the injury, but the damage was already done. He was cut from the Rangers three months after the initial on-field incident."

"You hate to see any player go out like that, Bud. Especially one who was at the top of his game like Sawyer Randall."

"That he was, Davis. But it seems Randall is doing well," he says with a chuckle. *"He has a guest with him for today's big game, and he appears quite smitten with the young lady."*

Davis laughs. "I do believe you're right, Bud. Sawyer Randall seems to be enjoying his early retirement very much."

I throw the camera a little wave and a smile, then pull AJ into my side as if making a statement.

Damn straight I am.

A big one.

She's mine.

AJ 25

As the warmth of September transforms into a slightly cooler October, Sawyer and I seem to fall into our own comfortable routine. I spend most evenings at his place, curled up at his side while I grade papers. We take turns making dinner, though by the time a meal is finished, we're usually both pitching in and doing it together. We stop at the café every morning to get a coffee and breakfast pastry, which is not going so well for my growing ass.

Turns out though, I really like watching Sawyer while he works out.

I mean, working out with him. Yeah. That's what I meant.

It's Saturday night, and was my night to pick our monthly sisters' night activity. I'm so excited to go! We're headed to the batting cages later, where we'll swing the bats and indulge in too much pizza and cheap beer. Sawyer helped me secure free reign of the facility tonight, which I'm sure cost him a pretty penny, but the manager's son is one of Sawyer's pitchers for the upcoming spring baseball season. I'm pretty sure he just had to make a few calls. Sawyer just dropped us off and is running to get the pizza and beer for tonight's shindig.

Meghan follows me into the building through the back entrance. She's been quiet since we picked her up in Sawyer's car. I asked if everything was okay, to which she said was fine, but I can tell something's wrong. Maybe she just didn't want to say anything in front of Sawyer? I just won't force the issue or make her feel required to talk. When she's ready, she'll spill.

Jaime and Payton arrive next, Ryan and Dean hot on their heels. I expect them to just drop the girls and go, but apparently when there's baseball involved, there is no getting rid of them for even a minute. The guys head over to a side table, but they're chomping at the bit to get into the cages.

Abby and Levi arrive next. They're barely inside the door when it opens again. Everyone turns and then squeals in delight when we see Lexi and Linkin, each carrying a car seat through the door.

"Holy balls, what are you doing here?" Payton yell-whispers as we all gather around the two sleeping infants.

"He insisted I come tonight," Lexi says, pointing to Linkin, as she gently sets Hemi's seat on the table.

"I wanted her to get out of the house for a bit," Linkin adds, starting to remove the restraining buckles from little Hudson.

"There was no way I was leaving them for even a second," Lexi says, carefully removing tiny little Hemi from the seat. We all hold our breath as she maneuvers our youngest nephew into the crook of her arm. "I'm just not ready for that," Lexi adds, tears filling her eyes.

"So we agreed to come for a little bit," Linkin says, running a finger along the top of his son's sleeping head. "It's their first official outing besides seeing the doc."

"Can I hold him?" Payton asks, her eyes misty.

"Of course," Linkin agrees, kissing Hudson's head as he gingerly sets his boy in Payton's waiting arms. God, he's such a good dad.

Payton walks over and sits down beside Dean, her eyes glued to the boy in her arms. There's no missing the way she cries as she holds him close, whispering words that we can't hear. Dean and Payton want a baby, but with her PCOS, it makes it very difficult to conceive. In fact, she was told it may never happen.

"How about it, Aunt AJ. Want a turn with this little one?" Lexi asks, standing beside me. My heart speeds up as it always does when I hold one of my nephews, but my breathing gets all weird too when I hold Hemi. In fact, I've only held him once. He's so small and was in the hospital a few extra days to make sure his own breathing was where it needed to be and he was eating well.

"I'm not sure," I whisper, taking in his itty-bitty little body.

"You got this," she assures me, and nods to the chair beside me.

Sitting down, my hands start to shake as she slowly and gently lowers him into my arms. He's light and I feel like my arm swallows him whole as I gaze down at the perfect little person I'm holding. He yawns big, holding my complete attention. My face starts to hurt from my smile, but I keep it there, along with my eyes, watching every move he makes.

There's movement and talking around me, but my eyes are glued to the baby. I feel his presence before I see him. Sawyer slides onto the chair beside me and leans in to look at Hemi. He reaches over, his pointer finger gigantic compared to my nephew's tiny hand as he gently strokes the soft baby skin of Hemi's knuckles. Gently, I rock him from side to side, not really knowing what more I'm supposed to do with a sleeping baby.

As I stare down at the sweet little face, I feel Sawyer's eyes on me. He's watching me watch the baby. When I glance over, the rawness and tenderness of this moment strikes me like a lightning bolt. His eyes are full of emotions, ones that I'm sure match mine. "Do you want to hold him?" I whisper, afraid of waking him up.

"No way. I'm afraid I'll break him," Sawyer replies quietly with a grin.

"They tell me that's not how it works, but I'm still skeptical. He's so small," I reply, glancing back down again.

"He's perfect. A real fighter."

"He is."

Silence follows, which makes me glance up at the man beside me. I've always known I'd want to be a mother someday, but this is the first time I can really picture it happening. I can see a small little boy with his dad's brown hair and blue eyes or maybe a little girl with dark ringlets and deep blue-green eyes that's the perfect mix of her mother and father. My heart practically leaps from my chest.

Sawyer's blue eyes smile back at me, a reflection of feelings neither of us has spoken aloud. I know where this is heading for me, but is it heading in that direction for Sawyer too? When he looks at me with so much adoration and gentleness, it makes me feel like we're taking major steps toward Lovesville, population two.

He leans forward, his lips warm and soft against mine. It's a tender, closed-mouth kiss, but causes the same butterflies to take flight in my belly as every other kiss he gives me. We're interrupted by the creature in my arms who decides to let a bloodcurdling wail rip from his tiny little body.

I freeze.

Sawyer freezes.

We both stare at each other with fear in our eyes, neither of us too embarrassed to admit it.

"What'd you do?" he whispers, glancing down as small arms start to flail. His small mouth opens in rage, but the sound coming out is clearly that of a very pissed off adult. How can something so tiny be so loud?

"I didn't do anything," I gasp, rocking a little harder, completely afraid to move. "He started that on his own."

"He's probably hungry already," Lexi says, coming over to retrieve the screaming infant from my arms. I miss him the moment he's gone, but that doesn't stop the huge sigh of relief that sweeps through me when he's safely secured in his mom's arms.

"That was terrifying," Sawyer mumbles.

"No shit. I thought I broke him," I say, leaning back in my chair and closing my eyes.

"Are you hungry?" he asks.

"I couldn't possibly eat after that," I confess.

"Okay, but the pizza's getting cold."

Instantly, I perk up. "Well, maybe just a slice or two," I reply, jumping up and heading over to the pizza table.

Abby and Meghan are there, opening up fresh pizza boxes and removing the empties. Thank God I ordered enough to feed the guys too. Actually, thank God Sawyer told me to order two extras because the guys might be hungry too. I think he pretty much knew that our sisters' night was going to be transformed into sisters and significant others night.

While Lexi is across the room, privately feeding Hemi, I offer everyone a beer. Linkin opts for a water (also thank God for Sawyer who grabbed several cold bottles), as does Levi, who has to work later tonight. I grab the case of Michelob Ultra and head over to my sisters. Abby takes one, but makes a face, and Meghan's already on her second. I approach Payton and Jaime next.

"Here," I say, holding a cold can out to Payton.

"Oh, uh…" she says, glancing around the room. "I'm not drinking tonight."

"Oh my God, are you pregnant?" I holler, completely drawing everyone's attention to our oldest sister.

"No!" she exclaims and her cheeks blush. "I'm not," she confirms as Dean, who's now holding Hudson, joins her, placing a comforting hand on her shoulder. He's so natural with the baby in his arms and isn't a big chicken to move around like me. "We're not, but we've started Clomid to stimulate ovulation and possibly increase our chances of fertility, so I'm just taking it easy on the alcohol right now." She shrugs her shoulder, but I can see the nervousness and the excitement in her eyes as they take this step toward conceiving.

"You guys," Abby says, tears filling her eyes. "That's so great."

"Here." I hand the can in my hand to Jaime, who shakes her head.

"Can't. I *am* pregnant." Her words stop me, and everyone else, in our tracks.

"You are?" I squeal, setting the can on the table and wrapping my older sister in a big hug. More arms wrap around us as my sisters all join the hug.

"I can't hug! I have a little feeding machine attached to my boob," Lexi cries from across the room.

"We'll catch you on the next one," I tell our baby sister, not really wanting to be over there while she's feeding her infant son. And no, I'm not against breastfeeding, but it's just… personal.

The guys all congratulate Ryan with guy hugs and back slaps, and there's no missing the proud smile on his face that makes my own face break out in a blinding grin.

"We weren't even trying," Jaime confirms. "It was a total surprise."

"That's because I have super sperm," Ryan hollers, earning an eye roll from his wife.

"They have one job to do, babe. It's not brain surgery," she sasses as he wraps his arms around her and pulls her in for a deep kiss.

"Super sperm," he whispers against her lips, her arms circling his neck.

My eyes find Sawyer, who's watching me intently. He gives me a look that seems indecent and makes me feel naked; it's hunger and desire crashing together like our bodies do at night. Suddenly, I'm ready to leave our sisters' night in favor of bedroom

Olympics with a certain PE teacher who makes me so hot that my sisters could get sunburned if they look too long.

"Let's get these cages warmed up," Linkin says, "before we have to leave."

And that's how we spend the next two hours, eating pizza, drinking beer (well, some of us), and taking cracks at baseballs in the batting cages. Sawyer gives pointers, but only when solicited. Otherwise, he's content to sit back and watch, talking to the guys and even holding Hudson for a few minutes.

When it's my turn, I step inside the netting. Sawyer made sure the ball thrower thingy was turned down as much as possible for the one the girls are using, but I'm still surprised at how fast the ball flies by my face. Ha. Balls. Flying by my face. I can't help the snort that slips from my mouth. Sawyer's eyebrows rise with his smirk, as if he knows my mind was headed someplace dirty.

I take a few more swings, completely missing the ball as it sails into the net behind me. I'm about to throw the bat and give up baseball forever when Sawyer moves into the netted area with me. He steps up beside me just as a ball flies by, hitting the net once more.

"Come 'ere," he says, stepping up behind me. He wraps his arms around me, positioning me the right way. "Spread your legs a little more."

"Is that an invitation?" I sass, moving my legs until they're shoulder width apart.

"I'm already harder than hell watching you take swings, don't tease me," he breathes seductively against my ear. "Keep your eye on the ball. It's coming," he adds, sending dirty images careening through my mind.

And it does come. The ball, that is. I'm watching for it and ready, so when it's in the right spot, I swing the bat. The crack of hard wood meeting the ball is satisfying, instantly putting a smile on my face. Glancing over my shoulder, my eyes collide with his smiling ones. "Great job."

"Thanks," I tell him, getting into position again for the next pitch. "I think it's the teacher," I add, shimmying my ass against the erection he mentioned.

He grunts and grabs my hips to halt my teasing. "Not nice," he growls.

I don't say anything as I swing at the next pitch, sending the ball flying high into the net above the pitching machine. "You could go pro," he tells me, no mistaking the pride in his voice.

Laughing, I reply, "I don't know about that, but this is fun when you actually know what you're doing." I take a few more swings before my arms start to tire. "You're up, Slugger."

Sawyer takes the bat and pulls me in for a kiss. The sounds of my sisters' "awws" behind us makes us both smile against our lips.

"All right, Sosa, step out and watch how it's done," Sawyer says confidently, placing one last lingering kiss on my lips before heading over to the pitching machine. Everyone seems to gather around the protective net as he grabs a longer, heavier bat from the rack and heads over to crank up the pitching machine's speed setting.

Then he takes his place behind the plate, and my entire body hums with desire. His stance is wide, his powerful legs taking up a pretty large piece of real estate at the plate. The corded muscles in his arms flex and jump as he twists his hands around the bat. The look in his eyes intense and completely focused as he stares down the machine, waiting.

And then the ball flies.

He swings with so much power, so much expertise, that when the cracking of the bat fills the room, it steals my breath. I've never seen anything like it as he takes his position for the next ball. When it's released, the same thing happens. We watch it sail into the netting, high above the cage.

That's how it continues as he hits the ten balls he put into the pitching machine. I don't miss how every couple of swings, he stretches his bad shoulder, twisting and moving it around. I wonder if he'll hurt later after this? But I don't think he really cares. Not if the happiness reflecting from his blue eyes or the casual smile on his face is any indication. Sawyer's in his element, plain and simple.

And it's hot as fuck.

Like throw my panties on the ground, wetness running down the inside of my thighs, kinda hot. Now I can completely see the sex appeal that seems to follow pro ball players around from city to city. I'm only witnessing a small piece of his sexual magnetism at work (and not even on a real baseball field), but I totally get it now.

I'm a total bleacher bunny.

When he steps out of the cage, the guys are all over him, complimenting him on his hits and talking baseball. My sisters all look like they're wiping drool off their chins, which causes a small burst of pride to swell in my chest. It also makes me a little thankful that my grandma isn't here to witness Sawyer's uber hotness in action. The poor old woman would probably have a heart attack.

I, however, zone in on how he's favoring his right shoulder. Has he swung the bat like that since his accident? Could he have done a little damage just by hitting a few balls?

He catches my eye and must see the concern on my face. He's approaching me before I can even register that he's moving. "Everything okay?" he whispers, sweeping hair off my forehead.

"I should be asking you that. Did you hurt your shoulder?" I ask, slipping my hand under the sleeve of his t-shirt and gently rubbing the puckered skin left from his incisions.

Sawyer shrugs. "It was a little tight at first, but the more swings I made, the looser it started to get."

I continue to massage the joint, rubbing my fingers around the back of his shoulder and down his arm, then to the front and back down his arm. His eyes become heavy lidded and I can't tell if it's just that relaxing of a massage or if he's getting turned on.

Then he pulls me flush against his front.

Yep, turned on.

He wraps his arms around my shoulders as I inhale the musky, masculine scent that is this man. It might sound a little weird, but I could sniff his clothes and his skin all day long and never tire of it. If I could bottle it up and sell it, I'd be a millionaire for sure.

Before long, Lexi and Linkin take the twins home to get them ready for their bedtime routine. Everyone else takes a few more swings in the batting cages and the rest of the pizza is polished off. Well, everyone but Meghan. She seems… off tonight. More than once, I've found her gazing off at nothing with tears in her eyes. It makes my heart hurt for her, at the pain she's still clearly carrying around.

And then it hits me.

October.

Three years ago, they moved in together. This was when they started mapping out their lives together. If only we'd known that the road would take them so far off course.

When I glance over again, she seems almost angry. Like she's trapped inside her own head, lost in memories she can't seem to forget, and unable to come up for air. I head her way and see the change as soon as she notices my approach.

"Hi," she says, her voice slightly pitchy.

"Hey, you all right?" I ask.

"Yes, of course. Having fun. You?" Her smile is in place, but this isn't Meghan. This is the face of a woman tortured, who's putting on her brave, strong face to keep people from asking questions.

"Meg," I start, grabbing her arm and pulling her a little further away from the crowd. "What's wrong?"

She glances around and her eyes fill with tears. This time, they fall down her soft porcelain skin, unchecked. "He should be here, AJ. Josh should be over there, laughing and talking with the guys. He should be in the batting cages and tossing the ball around with Sawyer. He should be holding my nephews," she chokes out, burying her face in her hands.

I wrap my arms around her shoulders and let her cry. Lord knows that in the last year and a half, we've barely seen her cry. It's like she's had to keep up some sort of Wonder Woman persona for appearances. Well, maybe now she'll let it go. Cry. Yell. Kick. Scream. Let it all out so she can finally take a step forward, instead of being chained to her past.

"I'm sorry," she whispers in my shoulder.

"You have nothing to be sorry for," I tell her honestly.

"I'm messing up sisters' night," she sniffles, pulling back and wiping her eyes and nose on a Kleenex that Jaime has brought over.

"Pfff, are you kidding? Look at all of those guys over there," I say, pointing over my shoulder. "I think they messed up sisters' night long before you did with a few tears. Besides, Lexi cried three times in the two hours they were here," I remind her.

"True," she sniffs. "But she's hormonal. I'm just having a pity party," she adds.

"It's not a pity party when you're still dealing with a lot of emotions for an event that changed the entire course of your life, Meggy."

She nods, but doesn't say anything for a few moments. "I think I'm going to head home."

"Why don't I drive you?" I offer.

"No, I couldn't ask you to leave everyone."

"We're done here anyway. Sawyer told the guy we'd lock up at ten," I say, checking my watch. "In fact, I have an idea. Why don't we have a sleepover tonight? You and me, some ice cream and a total chick flick movie? What do you say?"

"I couldn't possibly pull you away from Sawyer. He did so much to set up tonight for all of us."

This time it's my turn to shrug. "I think he'll be all right without me for one night. And besides, he's coming to brunch tomorrow at the café with everyone. I'll pick him up on my way in the morning."

She doesn't quite seem convinced yet, but I can tell by the way she hasn't completely shot me down that she kinda likes the idea of a sleepover. So I don't let her argue. The decision is already made. "I'll just have to steal some clothes from you in the morning," I tell her with a hip bump.

"Fine, but you better not drool on my pillow," she sasses, hip bumping me back.

"I don't drool! I'm too ladylike for that," I quip, earning a snort from my sister.

With my arm around her shoulders, I pull her back to the crowd. Jaime gives me a knowing smile and Payton squeezes my arm as I walk by. I wouldn't be surprised if we don't have a few more visitors for tonight's sleepover.

Leaving Meghan with our sisters, I head over to talk to Sawyer. "She okay?" he whispers, placing one hand on my hip and giving it a gentle squeeze.

"She will be. She has her ups and downs, and unfortunately, tonight is a down. Listen, I think I'm going to stay with her tonight. She's really–"

"Don't say anymore," he interrupts. "You're needed with her tonight."

I give him a grateful smile before sliding my arms around his waist. "How will I sleep without being next to you?" I ask, resting my cheek against his chest. His arms envelop me, surrounding me in his warmth and scent.

"I could ask you the same thing, Alison Jane," he states simply.

"My car is at your house."

"Take mine. You can drop me off at my place and go to your sister's house."

"Why don't I just grab mine while I'm at your place?"

Sawyer takes my chin in his fingers and raises it until I'm gazing up at his big blue eyes. "I kinda like you taking mine." Then he bends down and kisses me on the lips.

"Fine, but your car is way nicer than mine. I might get used to your fancy butt warmers," I tease, even though there's no need for seat warmers in October.

"You can drive my car anytime you want, but when you need your ass warmed, all you need to do is ask, sweetheart." His eyes turn molten and a wicked little smile plays on his lips. My face heats up at the thought of Sawyer spanking my ass, but that's not the only thing. My entire body seems to respond to his words.

We pull apart and help the rest of the crew pick up the mess we made. Sawyer makes sure the pitching machines are off and the facility is left in the same order it was in when we arrived earlier. When all of the tables are straightened and the trash is taken out back to the dumpster, we all head out into the cooler October night.

"You got her?" Payton asks as she pulls me into a hug.

"Yeah."

"Call me if you need me. I'll come right over," she adds, kissing my cheek.

"Me too," Jaime whispers in my ear when she gives me a hug.

"Levi's working all night. Why don't I join you?" Abby suggests.

"I'm sure she would appreciate that," I tell her.

"I'll run home and grab some clothes. She can ride with us to my place and I'll grab my car," she says and heads to Payton's car, Meghan in tow. Levi drove his truck since he'd be off to work before the party ended, so Abby arranged to grab a ride home with our oldest sister and brother-in-law.

Meeting Sawyer at his car, he helps me into the passenger seat before getting into the car himself. Talk is small as we head back to his house. We both seem to find comfort in the silence, our fingers entwined in each other's on his lap. My mind keeps going to Meghan and what she's dealing with on a daily basis. I couldn't imagine feeling that kinda loss regularly.

The thought of losing Sawyer, even though I've known him a fraction of the time Meghan knew Josh, feels like a knife piercing my gut. It hurts to breathe. Then the thought of our relationship not working out filters through my mind and makes it even worse. Even though we haven't said the words, I know I'm in love with him, and the idea of not having him in my life one day is agony.

"Hey," he says, bringing my hand to his lips. I glance around, realizing we're already in his driveway by the front door. "Everything all right?"

I nod my head, unable to get words past the lump in my throat. As I gaze into his sapphire eyes, I realize that even though I'm terrified of losing him, the prospect of not being with him at all is much worse. Love is scary and most of the time, you're in it blind, but as long as two people are on the same path, it's supposed to be worth it, right?

Are we on the same path?

God, I hope so.

Even without having the answer to that question, I still find myself needing to say it. Speak those three words that I've only ever said one time before, and even then, I'm not sure it was real. But this? This feels real. And right.

"I love you."

If he's surprised by my words, he doesn't show it.

Instead, his eyes soften and a slow smile spreads across his lips. "I love you, too." He says the words moments before his lips plaster to mine and he's practically pulling me across the car and into his lap. "Fuck, I think I fell in love with you that first night I saw you."

My moan is swallowed by his mouth; his lips dominating and consuming me. The slide of his tongue against mine is like gasoline to the already scorching fire that has been slowly burning all evening. "Fuck," he gasps, pulling his lips free from mine. "I want nothing more than to take you upstairs to my bed and make love to you all night long." That makes me whimper. "But you're needed with Meghan tonight," he says as he places gentle kisses along my jaw.

"Maybe I can be a little late," I suggest, gasping as his tongue tastes the sensitive skin under my ear.

"As appealing as that sounds, and believe me, baby, that sounds fucking amazing, we both know you need to get going." He's right. Dammit.

"Fine, but I'm sneaking out early in the morning. This is to be continued."

"I'll be waiting in bed for you," he says, sliding his big hand tenderly along my cheek before kissing me once more. This kiss is closed-mouth, as if he's trying to keep from ravishing me.

"I'll see you in the morning."

"Can't wait," he whispers before placing one last kiss on my lips and exiting the car.

I meet him around at the driver's door and slide inside. Sawyer crouches down and gives me one more kiss. "I love you."

My heart flies out of my chest with each declaration he makes. "I love you, too."

When I pull away, it's with a beaming smile on my face and hope filling my chest. After years of finding every frog in town, I think I finally found my prince. The man who monopolizes my thoughts, dominates my dreams, and makes me happy in between. Our time together is everything I've ever thought a real relationship would be like.

I finally found... the one.

Sawyer 26

She's been gone like five minutes and I'm ready to call her to come back. How sad am I? No, not sad. In love. Fuck yes, I'm in love with her. I have been for a while now, but too afraid to just say it. Tonight when she said those words, I knew it was time. I would have loved to have actually said them first, but I'm not complaining now.

My girl loves me, and it feels pretty fucking awesome.

I grab a beer from the fridge and turn on Sports Center in the living room. The back door is ajar, the cool breeze blowing off the Bay, along with the sound of this weekend's football recap filling the house. There's plenty I could do, now that I have the house to myself. AJ's been here most nights (not that I'm complaining one bit) and I'll admit I've slacked on a few tasks. Laundry, for one. There's a mountain of clothes in my laundry room in desperate need of my attention.

After throwing a load of darks into the washer, I head up and jump in the shower. I'm not going to sleep well tonight, not without her in my bed, that's for sure, but a run might tire me out enough to help me fall asleep. Unfortunately, I'm just not up for a second run today.

The scalding shower water leaves my skin red and tingly. I use the hand towel to wipe the steam from the mirror and place my hands on the vanity. Images of AJ bent over this very unit this morning replay through my mind, making my cock start to stir to life beneath the towel. There's no desire to knock the edge off, though. Instead, I'll keep my hands to myself and wait until my girl comes home in the morning.

Home.

That's what it feels like when she's here.

Throwing on a pair of basketball shorts and a Rangers tee, I head downstairs to grab another beer. When I round the corner, I stop dead in my tracks when my eyes collide with the woman's on the couch. They're all wrong, though. Hers are hazel, her hair blonde.

Carrie.

"What the fuck are you doing in here?" I ask, annoyed at her presence in my living room.

"Your door was open," she says, nodding toward the back door.

"Silly me. I thought being that it's my house and all, and no one opened the door for you and invited you in, meant something."

"Oh, don't be such a fuddy-duddy," she coos. She stands up, her long trench-style coat hitting below her knees. She's wearing those killer heels I used to love so much, but now do nothing for me. Her hair is shiny and tumbles in big waves down her back, and her makeup flawless. She looks like she just stepped off the pages of a magazine.

"Seriously, Carrie. What are you doing here?" I cross my arms at my chest and stare her down.

"I told you I was coming back to town in October," she says, as if that's reason enough for her to be standing in my living room, uninvited.

"What does that have to do with me?" I ask, annoyed that we have to do this whole song and dance.

"I missed you," she whines, taking a step forward. I raise my hand, halting her from stepping into my personal space. "How come you're alone tonight?" she asks, turning and walking over to the mantle above the fireplace.

"None of your business."

"Oh, come on, Sawyer. Don't act like I'm your enemy. I know you. Probably better than you know you," she says matter-of-factly. Christ, could she be any more wrong? She doesn't know the slightest thing about me. Not the real me.

Realizing I'm not getting rid of her until she's ready to either leave or tell me why she's here, I drop down in the chair that AJ likes to sit in and watch the waves crash over the beach. I also realize I didn't grab that second beer, because if I'm going to be stuck dealing with Carrie and her high maintenance drama, I definitely need alcohol.

Getting ready to stand up, she stops my progress. "Here, I hope you don't mind, but I made myself at home and grabbed a drink. I brought you a beer," she says, handing me a fresh beer bottle with the top already popped off.

I take a drink as she grabs a wine glass and sips the sweet white wine that's AJ's favorite. She smiles over the wineglass, a slow and seductive one that heckles my nerves. It makes me drink the beer that much faster. Neither of us speak as I drain the bottle of beer and try to figure out how to get my ex-wife out of my house.

"Spill it," I direct, setting the empty down on the end table beside me. The way her eyes light up, you'd think I just asked for a hell of a lot more than for her to explain her presence in my house.

"I was thinking," she starts, setting the glass down on the coffee table. My mind instantly goes to AJ and watching her set down her wineglass while she's grading papers. "I wanted to apologize for hurting you."

Wait. What?

I blink repeatedly, wondering what alternate universe I fell into. Never does Carrie apologize. In the years I've known her, I could probably count the number of times she's said the words 'I'm sorry' on one hand. Her way of apologizing is to change the subject or give a blowjob. Yeah, I'm not proud to admit my ex could manipulate me through my dick, but it happened.

But not anymore.

"I'm over it," I tell her, my head starting to feel a little heavy.

"Are you?" she asks, getting up and walking to me. Before I realize what's happening, she kneels down between my legs and runs a manicured nail up my thigh. The trench coat splitting open between her legs to reveal nothing.

That's a huge red flag.

Jumping to my feet, I practically knock her on her ass. My head swims and it's hard to focus. What the fuck? I've only had two beers.

"Yes, I've moved on. There's nothing between us but a past, Carrie," I hear myself say, but don't feel my own lips moving. "And that's where we stay. There is no *us* anymore."

"I know," she says, sadness filling her eyes. "I can see how happy she makes you." Carrie crosses her arms over her chest protectively, her store-bought DDs exploding from the top of the coat.

"She does," I confirm, the room starting to spin. "I'm in love with her. I want to spend the rest of my life with her." I take a few deep breaths trying to find my center. When that doesn't happen, I add, "I think you should go."

"You're right," she says, walking over to grab her purse. Carrie returns and stands before me, the coat completely hanging open now and revealing some sort of bra and panty lingerie set. "I'm really sorry it turned out like this, Sawyer. I really am, but this is for the best."

The best? What the fuck is she droning on about? I can't even wrap my head around it anymore. I think I have the flu or something. My head is swimming, my stomach churning, and I'm not sure how much longer I can stand up. Shit, am I still standing up?

"Come on, Sawyer. You'll feel much better in the morning."

Darkness consumes me.

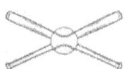

Marching band. There's a marching band practicing somewhere close by, but why? Our school has a band, but why the fuck are they playing in my bedroom?

I reach over for AJ and sigh when my hand connects with smooth, bare skin. I should probably stay away if I'm coming down with something, but I need to feel her against me right now. Shit, I need to be inside of her. But I'm not sure I can without my head exploding from my body. What the hell is wrong with me?

I run my hand down her back, my cock starting to stir to life beneath the sheets. When I reach her ass, I hear her gasp.

But... it's wrong.

It's off.

Something's definitely off.

She sounds... distant.

Cracking open my eyes, I regret it instantly. Soft light filters through the curtains, making my head throb even more. What the hell happened last night? I remember coming home. AJ told me she loved me and I said it in return. She left to go to her sister's. Then, it gets... fuzzy.

"Again? You are insatiable this morning," AJ coos beside me, flexing her ass in my hand.

Only...

It's not AJ.

My eyes fly open and connect with emerald green ones. I know in this moment that those eyes will haunt me for the rest of my life. I'll never forget the way she looks at me, with so much pain and hurt that it slices through my chest and embeds into my soul like a horrible, regrettable tattoo.

I glance to my left and find my ex-wife smiling coyly and brightly at me.

I'm out of bed so fast you'd think my sheets were on fire. And, in a way, they are. The pain in my head makes me stumble as I try to get to her. Trying to push the nausea aside, I sprint across the room until I'm directly in front of the woman I love. A tear slides down her cheek the same as the hurt slides down my chest.

"AJ?" I ask, not understanding what the hell is going on, but imaging how this must look to her. She glances down, her eyes wide with recognition and horror. When I realize what she's looking at, I dive for last night's discarded shorts on the floor. "Wait, this isn't what you think," I start, but the rest of the words get caught in my throat.

Because I, myself, don't even know what to think.

"Oh, then please tell me what this is. Tell me that I didn't just walk in on my boyfriend, in bed–NAKED–with his ex-wife. Tell me that's not what *this* is," her bitter words fly as she waves at the rumpled bed that contains my ex-wife.

"It's not, baby, I swear," I beg, but the crazy thing is… I don't. I don't know what happened last night. I can't remember a motherfucking thing.

"Sawyer," Carrie singsongs behind me. "That's not what you said last night." And then the bitch giggles. She fucking giggles, like nails on a chalkboard, making my stomach convulse and drop to my toes. But what's worse is AJ's reaction. The shock mixed with anger is enough to make me want to put my fist through the wall. Or maybe my head.

"Clearly, I've come at the wrong time," AJ whispers, her wide eyes darting back and forth between my bed and me.

"No, I can explain this," I state again knowing that I can't. But I have to try.

"You know, as much as I'd love to stick around and hear that explanation, I'm going to go," she croaks out, her words slicing and dicing with the precision of an operating physician as she turns and practically runs from my bedroom.

"You can't leave," I beg, reaching out and grabbing her arm when we get to the bottom of the stairs.

She whips around, her eyes full of blazing tears. She looks torn between wanting to tear me apart, limb from limb, and beating me to death with them, and wanting to curl up in a ball and cry. If I had a choice, I'd choose death, because watching her cry is its own brand of torture. It's worse than any death could ever be.

"I love you," I whisper hoarsely, my throat dry and the biggest ball of emotion lodged firmly in place.

"Clearly you and I have two very different ideas of love."

"Alison…" Her name is a plea on my lips and a knife to my heart at the same time.

"Congratulations, Sawyer. You've managed to prove every tabloid right in a single night." She turns and walks to the front door. "But do you know what hurts the most?" She doesn't turn around. She stares straight ahead, her body soldier straight, as she delivers her final blow. "What hurts the most is that you proved me wrong."

The sound of her soft sob, followed quickly by her retreating footsteps, consumes me as I stand, eyes closed, and pray for this to be a bad dream. No way in fuck did this just happen. No way did I take my ex-wife to bed. No way did I just destroy everything AJ and I have been building together over the last couple of months.

I try to remember anything–any shred of memory from last night when Carrie arrived–and come up empty. I know I didn't consume that much alcohol, and no way in fuck would I have willingly invited Carrie into my bed. Not when the only woman I want there just walked out my door.

And who would blame her? I have no recollection of last night's events, no plausible justification. All I have is what looks like a confirmation that I'm the biggest douchebag player ever conceived. This is a nightmare.

My nightmare.

My feet are heavy as I make my way back upstairs. No way in fuck do I want to go back into my room, but I need a damn explanation. Storming into the room, I find Carrie still naked in bed. Her perky tits are on full display, but the sight of them–and her–just makes my stomach repulse that much more than it already is.

"What did you do?" I ask, my hands on my hips and breathing hard.

"Me? I believe it was *you* who did lots of things to me last night," she giggles and slides her hands down her chest.

"What the fuck happened last night, Carrie?" I ask, stomping over to my dresser and grabbing a clean Rangers shirt from the pile.

"I could tell you, but it would be so much more fun to show you." I can hear the sheets moving and the bed dip. I know she's approaching me from behind. I'm not quick enough to get my shirt over my head.

"It's bullshit, Carrie. I know it."

"Do you?" she asks, running her hands up my back. I shudder at her touch, and not in the good way. Not in the way I do when AJ runs her fingers over the puckered scars on my shoulder.

"I didn't sleep with you," I insist, even though I don't know that for a fact and every detail is suggesting I did.

"Oh, there wasn't much sleeping," she giggles once more before kissing my back.

That's it. I can't take it anymore–not her touch, not her voice, not her insinuations. "Get out," I demand.

"What? But last night you said we were together again," she whines.

"I may not remember what the hell happened last night, but I can guarantee that me agreeing to an *us* again, wasn't it."

She stands there, naked, with a knowing smile on her face. "Oh, come on, Sawyer. You got rid of the trash. Now it's just you and me," she coos as she steps forward to press her tits to my chest.

And I see red.

"Get out," I holler, not even caring that I'm raising my voice, something I rarely ever do. In fact, the last time I raised my voice at her was when I found her in bed with my replacement. Even through the divorce, and her constant implications that I couldn't keep it in my pants, I never lost my cool.

"Saw–"

"No! Get out! Get your clothes and get the fuck out of my house, Carrie!"

I don't even wait for her to reply, nor do I wait for her to gather her shit. My feet are moving and they're moving fast. As I race down the stairs, I throw my shirt on over my head. I slip on a pair of running shoes from the closet, grab my keys off the table where AJ discarded them when she arrived earlier, and head out the door to find my car in the driveway next to where hers was once parked.

The sunlight kills my eyes and makes my brain feel like it wants to explode in my head, but I don't stop until I'm in the driver's seat. My knees slam into the steering column, making me curse a blue streak a mile wide, and my brain takes the opportunity to remind me of why my seat was moved forward.

AJ.

I have to find her.

Before it's too late.

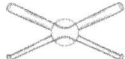

It's been hours.

I've been everywhere.

She's nowhere to be found.

She's gone.

Sawyer

27

"Found him," I hear from a familiar voice over my shoulder as I move the glass to my lips. I've made this move multiple times before, but I can't seem to force myself to swallow the toxin. Instead, I reach for the ice water–the fourth glass I've had since arriving at Lucky's an hour ago.

"What are you guys doing here?" I ask without looking up from the shot of Jack sitting in front of me.

"Came here to kick your ass," Linkin says pointedly.

I realize instantly that I wouldn't fight it. In fact, I'd welcome the physical pain. "Have at it. You can each have a free shot," I tell them, watching out of the corner of my eye as one more sits on the opposite side of Linkin, while two take my other side.

"It's not as much fun if you don't put up a fight," the big guy says, flagging down Lucky and ordering a beer. The others do the same, as I continue to drink water and stare at the whiskey.

I grunt in way of acknowledgement, not really interested in small talk. After several minutes of uncomfortable silence, I finally speak again. "How'd ya find me?"

"Wasn't that hard," Ryan says, taking a drink from his bottle. "You weren't at home or at the ball field. Figured this was the next logical place."

Again, more silence.

"You going to tell us what happened?" Dean asks, casually spinning his bottle on the bar.

"I don't know," I reply, exasperated. That's the hardest part– the biggest pill to swallow.

"You don't know?" Linkin asks.

"Are you telling me *you* don't know?" I ask, turning and looking his way for the first time since they all arrived. Levi is over his shoulder, calmly drinking his beer and watching.

"Nope," Linkin says, taking a drink. "AJ didn't show up for brunch at the café. Meghan got worried and called her, but she didn't pick up. It took several phone calls before she finally did. Said she was sick, or some bullshit like that, but Meghan knew. Said she could hear it in her voice. She was crying."

All over again, it's like someone thrusts a butter knife straight into my gut and twists. "So she didn't tell Meghan that she found me in bed with my ex-wife this morning?" Just saying the words makes it hard to breathe, brings back those visions of her devastated face, and those tears–fuck, those memories are torture.

Linkin stands up. Fast. His barstool falls back and crashes on the floor. "The fuck did you say?" His voice is low and menacing and makes me glad that I've never been on his bad side.

Well, until today.

The others stand too, a show of brotherly solidarity, or some shit. A bond that I thought I was working my way into, but now I'm suddenly pushed to the outside. Hell, I'm so far on the outside, I might as well be in another universe.

"What the hell happened?" Ryan asks, his voice scarily similar to Linkin's.

"I don't know." Fuck, I hate saying that.

"You said that already," Levi reminds me.

"I know!" I bellow, turning in my stool and facing them. There's a little size different between the four, but for the most part they're an intimidating bunch. Even though I have Linkin by an inch or two, throw them together and something tells me I'd probably be on the receiving end of a few hard punches and probably two black eyes.

Taking a deep breath, I keep going. "I really have no clue, all right? AJ dropped me off at my house and everything was fine. I went inside and grabbed a beer, opened the back door to let some of the breeze in. I went upstairs to shower, and when I came down Carrie was there. She came in my back door and was sitting on my couch. That's all I remember until I woke this morning with Carrie in bed with me. You can imagine the rest."

"I should knock your fucking head off," Linkin seethes, clearly getting into his protector of the sisters' role.

"Wait, you don't remember what happened?" Levi asks, a confused look on his face.

I exhale and perch my ass on the barstool. "Listen, if I really made the mistake it looks like I did, I would own up to it. But I fucking can't. I don't know what happened. I remember feeling tired and maybe a little funny. But I have no recollection of what happened."

He keeps staring at me, as if gauging my sincerity. "What did you have to eat and drink?"

"What the hell is this? Are you gonna make sure he did his chores too?" Linkin asks, a smart-aleck smirk on his face as he looks over his shoulder at Levi.

Levi ignores Linkin's comment and keeps staring at me, waiting. "Uhhh, I had the pizza and two beers with you guys at the cages, and then one beer at home. No, wait. Two. Carrie got me one."

"Did you see her open it?" Levi asks, stepping forward and moving in front of Linkin.

"What?" I ask, confused by his question.

"Did. You. See. Her. Open. It. Did she get it from the fridge and you opened it? Or did she go get it and open it?" he urges.

I stare at him, trying to recall. Then it hits me. "She had it on the table. She had a beer for me and a glass of wine for herself."

"You didn't see her open it? It was already there?" Levi confirms.

"Dude, he already said he didn't see her open it," Ryan says.

Again, Levi just stares at me, waiting.

"No, I didn't see her open it," I verify.

A smile spreads across his face. "My man, you were drugged," he says, shaking his head.

"What?" No way. I couldn't have been. I mean, why would anyone want to…

Son of a bitch.

Carrie.

"I'm serious. I bet if we gave you a piss test, it'd come back positive for something. Probably Rohypnol or GHB, and if I had to guess, I'd go with the latter. It would make you lethargic and if given enough, would include gaps in your memory. Man, you were roofied."

All I can do is stare at him. He seems so sure, so confident. I think back to last night, to each detail that I can remember and try to piece it all together. Now, when I look back at it, it shines in a whole new light. Did my ex-wife drug me? It sure as fuck sounds like it. Because if there's one thing I know, I would never, and I mean *never* betray AJ like this. And I sure as hell wouldn't do it with the one woman who cheated on me, essentially ending our short marriage.

"Let me ask you this," Linkin starts. "Do you feel like you had sex?"

My eyebrows raise and I just look at him. "Really?"

"I'm just saying I usually feel… different. Better, I guess you'd say. Know what I mean?" he asks with a smirk.

"We all know what you mean," Dean says, rolling his eyes.

Thinking back again, I try to recall any sense of relief I may have had, especially in light of how worked up I was when AJ left. "No, I didn't feel like I had sex. I mean, the room didn't even smell like it," I add, feeling slightly embarrassed to be talking about AJ with her brothers-in-law.

"I don't think that'll hold up in a court of law, Perry Mason," Levi quips at Linkin. "Without a urine test, we won't know for sure, but I'd bet my next paycheck that she put something in your drink. I mean, it was a little convenient that she was there when this went down, and ended up naked in your bed with you when your girlfriend was expected to arrive."

"How in the hell did she get you naked?" Ryan asks.

"No clue. No way it would have happened had I been sober," I reply.

"We could go to the hospital and do the test, but the drug may be out of your system by now. It usually lasts about twelve to twenty-four hours."

"No, no hospital," I say, shaking my head.

"Then we may never know," Levi adds, grabbing his beer and taking a drink.

He's right. I may never know what actually happened to me, and I hate it. I want to drive to her hotel–or wherever in the hell she's staying–and demand to know what happened. Now that I think about it, the whole thing is definitely fishy, and I'd agree with Levi that she probably drugged me. I just wish there was some way to prove it.

"I need to go see AJ," I demand, trying to push my way through them to get to the door.

"Dude, you're not even wearing the same shoes," Ryan says, making me glance down and notice, for the first time, that I'm wearing two different running shoes. Hell, at least I got the right feet. "But you may want to wait a bit. Have you seen a Summer sister when they get pissed off?" he asks, each of the guys nodding their heads.

"Scary," Dean says.

"Frightening," Levi adds.

"Terrifying," Linkin agrees.

"Certifiable," Ryan affirms.

"But the make-up sex?" Linkin states with a beaming smile.

"The best," Ryan finishes.

"Epic," Levi chimes in.

"Phenomenal," Dean states.

"Earth moving," Linkin proclaims.

"What's worse though, man, is when they all gang up on you. You don't stand a chance," Dean reasons.

"And right now, they're all out for blood. Your blood." This from Levi.

"That's comforting," I mumble, finishing off my water.

"Just go talk to her and try to explain. AJ always seems like the reasonable one," Dean says.

"Are you kidding?" Linkin asks over my shoulder. "I'd say Meghan is the reasonable one. I always pictured AJ as the more... destructive sister," he adds, and my mind instantly goes to the destruction we created in my living room that first time we had sex. Hurricane Ali.

"He's smiling. I think he's picturing her naked," Ryan says, bumping my shoulder.

"And, the good news is that we don't have to kneecap you, Tonya Harding style," Linkin says with that big wolfish grin.

"That is good," I confirm.

And just like that, we're all talking and hanging out like they didn't just threaten to beat me with a metal pipe. It's good to chat, but my mind never strays from AJ. She's out there somewhere, upset and crying, or maybe even breaking shit, because I hurt her.

No, I didn't just hurt her, I decimated her heart.

A heart that she had just fully given me the night before.

I need to make this right. No, I *will* make this right, because there's no way I can just turn my back on our love. No way can I let her go without a fight. I'm probably in for the fight of my life, but you know what?

I'm ready.

_AJ_

28

My eyes still burn. They're swollen and feel gritty, like when you're exfoliating your skin with an expensive face wash, the soothing scents of jasmine and vanilla filling the air. Except these are my eyes. And there's nothing soothing about it. In fact, it's downright painful.

That's why, instead of getting ready for work, I called in sick. I secured a substitute from the approved list and called it in to Mr. Stewart. Honestly, though, it wasn't that hard of a sell. I definitely sound the part. My throat is raw from crying, I sound congested, and I can't stop sniffling.

Though my diagnosis is nothing like a head cold.

This is a case of broken heart-itis.

And it's the most severe case I've ever had.

Dammit, Sawyer.

I start to cry again, only to get pissed at myself for crying again. That's been my cycle since I came home late last night.

I blew off our family brunch, only to be bombarded with worried phone calls. They weren't going to stop calling, so I finally answered one of Meg's calls. I could tell right away that she didn't buy my excuse of being sick. It took a matter of minutes before the calling started up again, this time from Payton. And when I heard the voice of my oldest sister, I finally caved and told her what happened.

Abby:	What can I do? Do you need anything? *crying emoji*
Jaime:	Are you freaking kidding me? *shocked face emoji* *angry face emoji*
Lexi:	I'll fucking kill him. No, I won't. Hemi's hungry. I've sent Linkin to kill him. *knife emoji* *poison syringe emoji* *axe emoji* *squirt gun emoji*
Jaime:	It doesn't have the same effect when it's a little green squirt gun. *sad face emoji*
Lexi:	Screw that and screw him. I'm gonna beat him with a squirt gun... as soon as I get this baby off my boob.
Meghan:	Do we really have to talk about boobs right now?
Me:	Shutting my phone off. Just need some time. I'm fine.

I hope I'll *be* fine eventually is what I should have said. Because right now, I'm not sure I'll ever be *fine* again. That's also when I powered down my phone and dropped it on my passenger seat, ignoring the fifteen texts and seven missed calls from Sawyer in the process.

I drove around for an hour, unable to go home. I couldn't be there, trapped in the silence. What I needed was someplace loud, someplace where there's booze. The bar was probably open by that point in the day, but that didn't exactly sound like a great place to go and drown my sorrows. Instead, I found myself at Brandy's apartment, where I stayed until about ten.

She didn't ask questions, not when she realized what was going on. She let me take up real estate on her couch as though I lived there, brought me wine and ice cream, and listened to me rant about how stupid men were, how they couldn't keep it in their pants, and only tell the truth when they're caught with their pants down and have no way out.

I thought he was different.

That's what hurts the most.

I really thought he was one of the good ones.

Now, Ellen talks in the background from the television I have on just for noise. My ass has been planted on my couch for the last… well, for a while. Since I got home last night, actually. The thought of going to bed–alone–held absolutely no appeal, so I cried myself to sleep on my lumpy old couch that was a hand-me-down when Dad got his new one last year, surrounded by silence and loneliness.

And I'm pretty sure that smell is me.

When a knock sounds on my door just before noon, I consider just lying there (in the divots my body has already made on the couch) and ignoring it. But the knocker is persistent and just keeps at it. "Alison Jane, you open this door before I break a window and let myself in."

Grandma.

I slowly crawl out of the hole I'm in on the couch, my feet shuffling noisily toward the door. "That's called breaking and entering," I say in way of greeting.

"Semantics, AJ. I could spin it as a welfare check," she says, pushing herself right past me and into my living room.

"What's that smell?" she asks, turning and looking at me over her shoulder, horrified.

I don't answer, just shrug. "What are you doing here?" I ask as I plop back down on the couch.

"You're not answering your phone. I came to make sure you weren't pushing up daisies." To that I raise my eyebrows. "Your sisters were ready to storm the castle, so I told them I'd check on you first." She glances around at the dark room, the mess of used Kleenexes thrown on the floor, and the melted and gross ice cream cartons on the coffee table. "Have you eaten real food?"

I shrug, which earns me a sigh. It's one of those sighs I used to get when I was younger and got myself in trouble. Then, she turns and heads into my kitchen, leaving me lying in a heap of nothing on the couch. She bangs around, knocking pans and slamming the fridge, all while singing a happy tune that makes my nausea return… basically making as much noise as humanly possible.

Trying to focus on Ellen proves fruitless, especially with the one-woman rock concert in my kitchen. Shutting off the TV, I head into the kitchen to see what she's doing. My counter is clean, the dishwasher is on, and there's a pot of soup on the stove. She's being total Grandma right now, taking care of everything, and doing it with a smile on her face.

"Aren't you going to ask what happened?" I mumble, dropping onto one of the kitchen chairs.

Grandma shrugs and returns her attention to dishing two bowls of soup. And where did she come up with that? I don't recall having any cream of whatever that is soup in the house, nor did she come in with it. Did she?

Just another Grandma mystery.

"You know, AJ," she starts as she brings the two bowls over to the table and sets one in front of me and the other in front of the empty chair across from me. "Once, I found your grandfather in a compromising position. We were visiting friends and I walked into the room. His arms were around my friend Doris."

I stare at my grandma, not really sure what to say.

"I left the house in a tizzy and went somewhere to be alone. This was before flip phones and those little square thingies that buzzed, so you can imagine how hard it was for your grandfather to find me."

Swallowing hard, I nod. "I bet."

"Turns out, I walked in on a kiss that wasn't initiated by your grandfather. My friend Doris had your grandfather on her hall pass list. He was such a looker back then, AJ. All the ladies wanted him." She gets this dreamy look in her eye.

"Hall pass?" Did she really just say that?

"Oh, sure. Everyone has them, AJ. Sean Connery has been at the top of my list since *Dr. No.* What a gorgeous man he was, my sweet Alison." And just when I think it's safe to have a conversation with Grandma. "I mean talk about wet knickers…"

She smiles again, as if recalling something that I probably don't want to know about. "Anyway, it turns out that Doris was home from working on *Pillow Talk,* and she always thought your grandpa was a stud, which of course, he was, if you know what I mean. So, she approached him and kissed him."

"What did you do?" I ask, my soup all but forgotten.

"Well, I had a choice. I could believe your grandfather that nothing happened and he didn't initiate the kiss, or I could walk away."

"Obviously, I know what decision you made."

"Your mother was conceived that very night, AJ. There's no sex like make-up sex."

My stomach actually twists and I wonder if I'm about to lose my lunch. Well, if I actually had food in my belly, then maybe I would. "Thank you for… sharing that, Grandma, but I don't think my situation is the same. Sawyer was naked in bed with Carrie." And again, I feel like I'm going to vomit.

Grandma just looks at me with a soft smile. "You know, AJ, sometimes a cheater is that. A cheater. But sometimes a cheater isn't a cheater at all. It's a misunderstanding."

I watch as she goes back to eating her soup. I want to reply, but the words just don't come. This isn't a misunderstanding. Is it? I mean he was naked for God's sake, as he scrambled from the bed we had shared just the night before. I may never get the image of

Carrie lying on my pillow, blonde hair fanned out across the dark sheets and a wicked, delighted smile on her face.

Grabbing my spoon, I take a tentative bite. It's still warm. The creamy potato soup tastes amazing and I find myself inhaling the entire bowl as if I hadn't eaten in days. In a way, I guess I haven't. Not real food, anyway.

Silence settles in around us as we both finish eating (I have a second bowl). So much is running through my head and it's hard to distinguish between what my head is saying versus my heart. My head is telling me not to get sucked into the trap. Once a cheater, always a cheater. But my heart is telling me it's Sawyer, and I know him.

I. Know. Him.

My brain is on overload. It just hurts to think now, which is why I push Sawyer out of my mind for the time being and turn my attention back to Grandma. She's definitely met some interesting people in her time. I mean Joe DiMaggio? Elizabeth Taylor?

Doris?

Pillow Talk?

Wait…

"You knew Doris Day?" My voice is definitely a higher pitch as I stare, wide-eyed, at the woman across from me.

"Sure," she says casually. "Who do you think introduced her to Martin Melcher?"

And that, folks, is how my Monday went…

Sawyer 29

"Why are you ignoring my calls?" my brother Dylan asks. It's the first time I've answered his calls or texts, which started yesterday afternoon. Right after it all went down.

"I'm not. Just been busy," I grumble, wishing I had let this one go to voicemail too.

"Bullshit. What's wrong?" he pushes.

I sigh deeply, not really wanting to get into this AJ mess with Dylan. "It's nothing I can't handle. Just an issue with AJ." The issue of her not speaking to me after finding me naked in bed with my ex-wife yesterday morning, nor was I able to talk to her today since she called in sick. You know. That issue.

"What'd you do? Fuck it up already?" His words are like a truth-bomb dropped right in my lap.

"Why'd you call again?"

"Uh uh, you're not changing the subject that easily. What happened? Tell me you didn't push away the only woman who's made you smile in I don't know how long." Dammit, Dylan. I really don't want to get into it right now, but there's no getting around it. He's like a fucking pit bull with a bone when he's on to something.

"Something happened," I confess, rubbing a hand over the back of my neck as that ever-present tightening in my chest grabs hold once more. "Something big."

"What? She's knocked up? She met someone else? She confessed she's not into you because she wants your hotter, younger brother?" Even his brand of humor doesn't get a rise out of me.

"Worse. She found me in bed with Carrie." Just saying those damn words again brings back every ounce of pain.

I'm met with silence for several seconds. Seconds that turn to minutes. "Excuse me? Can you repeat that? Because it sure as hell sounded like she caught you in bed with Carrie. Your *ex*-wife!"

Closing my eyes, I see hers, every heartbreaking tear that rips my soul from my chest and tosses it into a paper shredder. "It's not what you think, man," I start.

"Then what is it?"

Sighing deeply, I drop down onto a chair on my deck. The waves are bigger tonight, slamming into the wet sand with force. "I think she drugged me." Then I tell him the entire story. I start with how we confessed our love before she left to go be with Meghan, and ended with her finding me the next morning.

"And you have no recollection of anything?"

"Not a fucking thing. A few pieces have come back, but not all of it." I take a drink of water, wishing it were something a hell of a lot stronger. But I told myself that I would not get drunk, even though that was my first thought. Instead, I make sure I'm with it in case she returns any of my texts or phone calls.

"Have you talked to either of them?"

"I've called a million times, but she isn't answering. She called in sick from school. And I'm afraid if I'm face-to-face with Carrie that I might do something that lands me behind bars for the rest of my life."

Dylan is quiet for a few minutes, obviously deep in thought. He's always been the reasonable one, the one most levelheaded, so I let him work it out and wait.

"You need Carrie to confess."

"And you think it'll be easy? I mean, it's not like she's going to willingly tell me that she fucking drugged me and set everything up so AJ would find us in bed together."

"True," he replies, but I pick up on the underlying humor in his voice. "That's why you need to scare her."

"What?"

"Hear me out. You remember who is coming to town this weekend, right? That's actually the reason I was calling. Mom was making sure you didn't need any help with setting up," he says.

"What does he have to do with this?" I ask, clearly not following the direction of his plan.

"Who better to scare the crap out of Carrie than him? He always had that intimidation factor going for him when we were growing up. And he's a cop," he points out, the pieces of his plan starting to fall into place. "She doesn't know him, since he wasn't able to go to your wedding, and that game last season in St. Louis, where he brought his family to see you, Carrie was off at that resort having work done–I mean she was sick."

That makes me snort a laugh. I remember that weekend well. She was supposed to accompany me to a game in St. Louis, when she booked a girls' weekend to some exclusive spa that specialized in nipping, tucking, and enhancements. The whole thing burned my ass because she knew part of my family that I never get to see was going to be there. She made me tell everyone she was sick so no one knew she was having work done.

"But how do we get them together?"

"You take care of getting Carrie to your place. Friday night. Six o'clock. I'll make sure the rest of the party is there," Dylan says, his words sounding sinister and mischievous.

"I'm not sure, man," I say, running my hand through my hair.

"Trust me, Sawyer. You get her there at six and I'll take care of the rest."

"Fine," I grumble, not really looking forward to having Carrie in my house once more. "I need to talk to AJ."

"Actually, wait," he says, shocking me.

"What? I can't wait, the longer I leave her hanging, the worse it's getting. I need to fix this–"

"I get that, really I do, but is she going to believe you? Just trust me, Soy. She's not going to believe you until you know for sure, right? You need proof."

I think of her reaction Sunday morning and how much she probably hates me right now. The thought of her hurting, alone, and not holding her is as unbearable as the memories that haunted my fitful dreams last night. But I think he's right. I need to have proof that I was set up.

But avoiding her might actually kill me first.

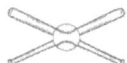

Of course I ignore his suggestion. Wouldn't you?

No, I don't go all crazy ex on her, stalking her every move through a far-reaching telephoto lens. (Admittedly, I consider it.) Instead, I keep doing the little things I've been doing to show her that I care. That I love her.

First off, there's bribery. I'm not above it. I used it to my advantage. I *may* have gotten voucher tickets to next season's Nationals games–six games total–for a coworker (the custodian) to have a copy of her classroom key accidentally left on my desk. Every man has a price, and fortunately for me, his price was baseball tickets.

That key granted me access to her room to leave her lattes and sweet treats. This way, there's no chance of running into each other and upsetting her further. I'd never want to do that at work. It's hard enough just to be in the same building as her without reaching out or dropping by. It's even worse when I'm sitting in my little office, deep in the building, down the long, dark hallway behind the gym, and think about Bryce's classroom being positioned right next to hers. So as much as I want to casually walk by her classroom (five times a day), I don't want to see her upset anymore.

Could the fact that I'm leaving her coffee and goodies on her desk (with a note each day) be construed as hurting her? Quite possibly. But that's not my intention. All week, I make sure to tell her one of the many things I love about her, and each day, I end the note with the same thing. *I love you. Eternally yours, Sawyer.*

So now here we are, Friday, and I've managed to make it through the week with very minimal contact. There was one run-in in the teachers' lounge, resulting in death glares from the school receptionist, Brandy. I also saw her in the gym after school yesterday when she was gearing up for her first cheerleading practice. I sat in my office like a lovesick loser and just soaked in every word she spoke to the girls about teamwork, dedication, and practicing hard.

It was torture.

Like the waiting.

That's what I'm doing now. Waiting for Carrie to come over so Dylan and I can try to expose her deceptive and drugging ways. I heard the door to my garage open a few minutes ago, letting me know that my brother and cousin are here. The plan was for them to go to my downstairs office and wait, while I pace the living room in anticipation of the she-devil who used to wear my ring.

Finally, I see headlights coming up the drive. She parks in front of the garage, clearly expecting to be staying for a while. Little does she know she's already overstayed her welcome.

There's a soft knock on the door. I open it, fake smile plastered on my face, as I let my ex-wife into my home. It literally takes every ounce of patience I have not to unleash six days' worth of anger and frustration on her. It also takes all of my self-control not to pull back when she leans up on her tiptoes and kisses my lips.

"I missed you," she coos, wrapping her arms around my waist and pressing her fake tits into my chest.

I'm tense, and I'm sure she feels it. It's not her arms I want around me, not her lipstick I want smeared on my lips.

"Come in," I tell her, extracting her body from mine. Her bright white teeth shine with her smile as she gazes up at me with those big hazel fuck-me eyes. She has perfected that look over her career, and I'm ashamed to admit she had it down pat with me too.

In the living room, I go to the coffee table, to the chilled bottle of wine and two glasses. Popping the cork, I pour us each a glass, as she gets comfy on the couch, much like she did last Saturday night. "Are we celebrating something?" she asks when I hand her a glass.

"Sure are. I mean we're back together, right?" I choke out over the lump in my throat.

"We are," she coos sweetly, giving me another full wattage smile.

"And I'm glad, too," I lie. "I mean I *am* a little confused about how I went from telling AJ how much I loved her one minute and in bed with you just a few hours later," I add, taking a seat across from her.

"Well, when it's right, it's just right, ya know? We were destined to be together."

"Yeah," I reply dryly. "It still just doesn't add up to me. I mean, last I remember, I was fully prepared to take my relationship with AJ to the next level. Then *bam*," I say loudly, "I'm back together with you."

She visibly swallows hard, her wide eyes transforming into little slits. "What are you saying?" she asks.

"Nothing," I say breezily. "Oh, did I tell you my family's here? I was going to surprise you, since we're back together and all, with a visit with everyone."

"Your family?" she squeaks out.

"Yeah, well, they'll all be here tomorrow, but my cousin is here tonight. I can't wait for you to finally meet him," I say proudly, just as my cousin walks into the room. He's wearing pressed khakis and a button-down shirt with his police force logo, and his badge and gun are both on his hip. He's tall and imposing, and makes me smile to myself as Carrie swallows hard again at his appearance.

"Carrie, this is my cousin, Maddox. He's a cop. An investigator, actually. He's here on vacation with his family, but there has been some weird reports of druggings lately, so it has turned into a working vacation for him."

Maddox doesn't move. Just stands there, his arms crossed firmly over his expansive chest, as he stares down at Carrie. She watches him and seemingly crouches down into the seat cushions a little more. "Druggings?" she chirps, her voice unnaturally high.

"Yeah, druggings. You know, Maddox and I were talking last night and I was telling him all about how I can't remember anything that happened Saturday night after AJ left. You know, when you were here and I was declaring my undying love for you? Anyway, we were talking and he mentioned that my symptoms sounded just like other cases he's worked."

"You were drugged? How horrible!" she declares with a manicured hand to her mouth, her horrified performance clearly securing her an Oscar nomination.

"I know. What's worse is the only thing I can remember eating or drinking was that beer. The one you got me." I let my words sink in and watch a flash of fear sweep across her face.

"I'm going to need to take that beer bottle, Sawyer," Maddox says, keeping his eyes focused solely on my ex-wife.

"Why would I drug you? What if it was AJ? You know, before she left!"

"Could have been," I concede with a nod. "I mean, she had just confessed her love to me. Nothing says 'I love you, baby,' like a roofie."

"That's the only plausible explanation," she gasps, her eyes wide and bouncing back and forth between Maddox and me.

"Actually, I had another scenario in mind," Maddox says, stepping a bit closer to Carrie. "I think *you* were actually the one to put the drug in Sawyer's beer. I think *you* knew that AJ was coming back in the morning. And I think *you* set this whole thing up. When I get that bottle from the trash, I have a feeling I'll find traces of the drug and your fingerprints."

"You won't find it! I took the bottle with me when I left!" Carrie hollers, then seeming to realize what she said and covers her open mouth with her hand. "I… I…" her fearful eyes bounce back and forth between the two of us, and she seems to swallow hard. And then she bursts into tears. "I'm so sorry," she wails, as big crocodile tears slide down her face. "I just thought that if we could spend a little more time together, you'd see that being apart was a mistake."

"The only mistake was marrying you in the first place. I was one hundred percent faithful to you the entire time we were together, and at the first sign of me struggling with my injury, you jump on the first cock to swing your way," I seethe at her. She cries harder. "I should press charges." That gets her attention.

"No, please!" she begs, her wide eyes pleading.

I glare over at her, ready to put this entire scene behind me. "Tell you what, Carrie, you tell us what really happened that night and I won't press charges." She seems relieved instantly, yet reluctant to admit just how far she went. "But… you'll also agree to leave me and AJ alone. No more private investigating, no more showing up in town, and you definitely stay the fuck away from my home."

After a few moments, she swallows again and nods her head. "Fine."

"So what happened?" Maddox asks.

"It was just dumb luck that you left the back door open," she says, nodding at the sliding glass door. "I let myself in when I heard the shower upstairs. I got a beer and slipped some GHB into your drink and waited. I figured AJ was coming back at some point, so I knew I had a small window of opportunity to get you upstairs and in bed."

"How did you get me naked?" I ask, dumbfounded. It's not like she could have carried me.

"Well, that was easy. I told you AJ was on her way to your place. You actually stripped on your own and crawled into bed, mumbling about how much you loved her and missed her while she was gone." Carrie has the decency to look remorseful as she fills in the blanks of Saturday night.

It's silent for several moments as it all sinks in.

"I think it's time to go," Maddox says, taking a step toward Carrie. He pulls his handcuffs out of his utility belt as he motions for her to stand.

"But, wait! You said you wouldn't press charges! You can't arrest me," she begs, crying a fresh wave of tears.

Maddox glances at me, playing the part of bad cop to a T. I stare up at Carrie and watch her squirm. As rewarding as it would be to see her in cuffs and hauled off to jail, that's not what Maddox is really doing here. In fact, he has no jurisdiction in Jupiter Bay. He's here merely as a scare tactic. One that I think is working perfectly.

"Let her go," I tell my cousin, standing up and approaching my ex. "But you'd better hold up your end of the bargain. The first time I see you anywhere near Jupiter Bay or breathe a word about AJ or me, I'll have Maddox all over your ass for assault, you got it?"

She nods profusely, her wide, tear-stained eyes full of fear and relief.

"Get out of my house and don't ever come back," I tell her, turning and giving her my back.

I hear the click of her heels on my floor moments before the door opens and shuts rapidly. A minute later, there's the distinct sound of a car starting and pulling out of the driveway.

"You know, I was sometimes a little envious that you were playing in the MLB and married to a freaking Victoria's Secret model, but that was usually was I was elbows deep in a shitty diaper, or trying to wrangle my kids to bed. Now, I'm just kinda glad she didn't boil your bunny or cut off your balls, man."

I chuckle at my older cousin, feeling relief for the first time since this entire mess started last weekend. I need to find AJ. I need to explain and beg for forgiveness, for another chance, for her salvation. My heart isn't whole without her, and I'll be damned if I'm going to let this second chance at happiness slip through my fingers.

Grabbing my keys, I turn to Maddox, but before I can tell him I'm leaving, movement catches my eye just over his shoulder. Dylan steps out from his hiding place.

With AJ.

She looks like an angel. Her hair is pulled back in a ponytail and her face has very minimal makeup, mostly in an attempt to cover the bags under her eyes and puffy eyelids. She's wearing well-worn jeans, a Hawks cheerleading sweatshirt, and a look that's hard to decipher.

But she's here.

In my living room.

And she's a vision.

30

AJ

Why am I so nervous? When Dylan opens the door the rest of the way and nods for me to follow him, I'm suddenly terrified to step out of the room. After everything I just heard, I want to run into the room and throw my arms around him, vowing to never distrust him again. Never to walk away. Promise to always stay and fight.

Now I understand what my Grandma meant.

Sometimes, a cheater is a cheater.

But sometimes, a cheater is a man with ocean blue eyes and a sexy swagger who leaves my body humming and yearning for just one more touch. Sometimes, a cheater isn't a cheater at all.

Sometimes, he's your forever.

My legs are shaky as I step into the living room. The sun has set and the room is bathed in soft overhead lighting from the vaulted ceiling. It does nothing to camouflage the anguish on

Sawyer's face as he turns from the doorway he was about to exit to face Maddox.

Then his eyes connect with mine.

And it all fades away.

Everything.

I open my mouth to speak, but nothing comes out. What would I say anyway? I'm sorry seems trivial in the grand scheme of things. His eyes transform right before my own into relief, into elation. He's moving before I can even think about heading in his direction. Within seconds, he sweeps me into his arms, his nose buried deep in my neck. My own arms pull tightly on his shoulders and my legs wrap around his waist, as I hang on for dear life. His embrace steals my air, but I don't complain. Not one bit.

"You're here," he states into my neck, his warm breath tickling and calming me at the same time.

"Yeah," I choke on my emotions.

"Did you hear?" he asks, pulling back a little so we're face-to-face.

"Yeah."

Once more, relief washes over his handsome features. "I never want to hurt you, baby. Never ever again," he vows.

Nodding, I give him a gentle smile. "I know. I'm sorry I doubted you."

Shaking his head, he adamantly replies, "No, you don't need to apologize. I know what it looked like, and the fact that I couldn't remember anything that happened," he shakes his head again. "I don't blame you for not trusting me. Hell, when all of the chips were stacked up against me, I didn't really trust myself either."

I take my hands and place them on his cheeks, reveling in the feel of the several days' old stubble on his strong jaw. He's breathing hard, his eyes bouncing around my face, as if drinking every piece of me in.

And then they land on my lips. They're slightly ajar, my own breathing a little shallow. Instinctively, I lick them and watch him watch me. I can also feel a little something stirring to life between my legs, just below his belt. Okay, so it's not little, but it's definitely something.

It's like slow motion as his mouth gradually moves toward mine. Right before our lips connect, his eyes meet mine. It's a look of happiness, of contentment, of love.

And then his lips graze softly across my own. He holds it together just long enough for a taste, one we both long to savor, but then lust takes hold. Sawyer urges my mouth open with his lips and tongue, and devours. He feasts like a man starved. A man possessed. The kiss is bruising and fierce, but does nothing to quench the insatiable burn I feel for him. In fact, it does the exact opposite.

"Wow, this is getting uncomfortable, real quick," Dylan says after clearing his throat.

"Shit," Sawyer mumbles as he pulls his lips from my own. He turns to face his brother and cousin, his hands still firmly gripping my ass and me still attached to his front like a spider monkey.

I practically jump off him like I was burned, but Sawyer isn't interested in letting me go, which means I basically stumble backward as I try to right my askew sweatshirt and turn to face the others in the room.

And holy hell.

Sawyer's cousin is… yowzers! We rode to the house together, but he was in the back seat, so unfortunately, I didn't get too good of a look. But now that I can see him in the light, he's tall, dark, and handsome. Just like his cousin.

"AJ, this is my cousin, Maddox Jackson. He's a cop in Missouri."

"We met in the car, but it's nice to officially finally meet you," Maddox says, stepping forward and extending his hand. His smile is warm, but those eyes. They're like chocolate diamonds, all intense and sexy-like. Grandma would like him. A lot.

"Nice to meet you," I reply, feeling my cheeks burn with a flush.

"Maddox and his family are in the area on vacation," Dylan adds. "We were all supposed to get together this weekend here at Sawyer's house, but when he told me how big of an idiot he was, I thought it might not hurt to get our older cousin involved."

Maddox shrugs. "Glad I could help."

"Oh, you definitely did. I'm pretty sure we won't be seeing Carrie any time soon," Sawyer says, wrapping his arm around my shoulders and pulling me into his chest.

"Good."

Just then, Maddox's phone chimes. When he glances at the screen, a wide smile spreads across his gorgeous face. "That's Avery. Apparently Dax is a little wound for sound, and isn't having any of the bedtime thing."

"How are all the kids?" Sawyer asks as we slowly follow them to the garage door.

Again, he smiles widely. "Awesome. Ryder started baseball this past summer. The kid's a natural, like you. Ellie keeps us busy with dance class, and Dax just keeps us busy. That kid is into anything and everything. And Bean is going to cause me to have a heart attack by the time I'm forty. She's not even a teenager yet and I'm already having sleepless nights." Both Dylan and Sawyer laugh.

"You'll be around this weekend?" Maddox asks me when they head into the garage where Dylan hid his car.

I glance over at Sawyer who gives me a warm, casual smile. "Yeah, I think I will."

"Good deal. You can help keep my wife from assaulting Sawyer. She's a huge fan and says he has an amazing ass," Maddox says, pulling a face, which makes me laugh.

"It is a pretty nice ass," Sawyer teases his older cousin, earning him the middle finger.

"See you tomorrow," Maddox says, throwing us a wave over his shoulder and gets into the passenger seat.

"He seems nice," I say as we watch them back up from the garage and pull away from the house.

Sawyer pushes the button to close the garage door and pulls me into the mudroom. "He is. I think you'll like his wife, Avery."

"Four kids, huh?" I ask, slipping my hands into his.

"Yep. Brooklyn was hers from a previous relationship, but Maddox took to her right away and adopted her as soon as he and Avery were married. They had Ryder and Dax right away, and then were surprised with the arrival of Ellie not too long after that."

"Sounds like a big, boisterous family," I tell him, stepping into his embrace and wrapping my arms around his waist once more. I can't get enough of the feel of him against me, the scent of his skin. God, I've missed him.

"They are," Sawyer confirms. "So tomorrow, everyone is coming over here and having dinner. The Italian restaurant is catering it. I don't want my mom or aunt to have to worry about cooking dinner. It's been a few years since they've seen each other, so I want them to be able to spend as much time together without it being in the kitchen."

"That's very sweet of you."

"It's the least I can do. I have the biggest place for a gathering, and Dad wants to try the fire pit outside," he says.

"I'm sure they're all excited to finally see your place," I tell him, knowing that his parents have been dying to get over here and see him again.

"I think they're excited to finally meet the woman I love," he says, stealing another kiss from my still-tingling lips.

The kiss ends way too quickly, though, and when I open my eyes, his blue ones are fixed entirely on me. "I'm sorry, Alison. I never meant to let my past come down on you like this and hurt you. Fuck," he whispers, closing his eyes to hide his pain. "I'm just so damn sorry." His words hold so much remorse and truth that the honesty in them practically reaches out and touches me.

My need to touch him again is too strong to fight, so I reach up and cup his jaw. "Stop apologizing. You didn't do this. Let's put the blame on the person who's solely responsible for this mess."

He nods in reply, but I can tell he's not convinced. He feels extremely guilty for the events that transpired, which were not in his control. How was he to know his ex-wife would do the things she did to get me out of the picture? He couldn't have.

I guess I'm just going to have to be more convincing...

I thread my fingers into his hair and pull his head toward mine. Sawyer seems a little surprised by my boldness, but he quickly recovers, wrapping his own arms around my waist and lifting, pulling me flush against his hard body. My toes dangle just off the floor as he moves us farther into the house, flipping off light switches and making sure all of the doors are locked.

When he reaches the stairs, he sets me down on my feet, but only long enough to slide his arms behind my back and knees, and picks me up, as if carrying me over the threshold. Wrapping my arms around his neck, our lips collide as he starts to ascend the stairs, heading to his bedroom.

Inside, he peels his lips from my own and stands sideways to the bed. "It's all new," he says softly, his eyes searching my face for a reaction. His words bring a small smile to my face. It's comforting to know he removed every trace of Carrie from his bed, from his house.

Gently, he sets me down on top of the new gray and navy comforter, and stretches out atop me. "I missed you," he whispers as he runs his hand down my cheek.

"I missed you too." God, did I miss him.

"I haven't even slept in here since you left." His confession strikes me straight in the heart like an arrow. "Even with the new bedding, the thought of sleeping without you didn't hold any appeal."

Instead of speaking words, I tell him how much I understand with my lips. It starts gentle and sweet, but quickly turns ravenous and intense. Sawyer slowly strips my clothes from my body, savoring and tasting every part of me as if it had been years, not days. When I'm completely naked, he shimmies out of his clothes and grabs a condom from the nightstand.

He covers himself quickly and rejoins me in bed. I slip beneath the blankets, eager to start new memories in this bed. His hands are in constant motion, sliding along my outer thighs, back, arms, and finally, my chest. His touch ignites that constant burn, that ache that I've had ever since this man came into my life. It's amazing how much I want–no, need–him.

Gently, he thrusts inside me, my body practically convulsing with need and relief at the same time. When he's completely seated within, his eyes meet mine, alive with desire and so much love it makes my heart leap in my chest. His hands are warm and soft and he continues to touch every part of me.

Within minutes, I'm already climbing higher, my body filling with coiled tension on the verge of an epic release. My fingers grip his skin, my legs locking in a death grip around his waist, and my internal muscles squeeze his cock tighter with every thrust. There's no way I'm letting go, and I'm not just referring to the now. I'm talking about tomorrow and the day after that. I'm thinking about years from now, when our home is filled with little footsteps and laughter. To when we're old and gray and sitting on the back deck with a glass of lemonade (probably spiked) and watching the waves of the Bay.

I know, right now in this moment, that I will always fight for him, like he has fought for me. It's not going to be easy, and at times I'm sure one or both of us may question the path we've chosen, but that's love. It's coming to a crossroads and deciding to take the same path–together. It's forgiving him or her, along with yourself, when they make a mistake and do everything they can to make it right.

It's never forgetting all of the million little reasons why you fell in love with that person in the first place.

And as we fly over the edge of bliss, together, each other's names spilling from our lips, I know that I'll always love him, faults and all.

"I love you, Alison Jane," he whispers, his breath a pant against the shell of my ear.

"I love you, Sawyer," I reply a split second before his lips could stop my words with a searing kiss.

A kiss meant to be a declaration, a beginning.

A kiss that is the start of something more.

31

Sawyer

THREE MONTHS LATER

She's mine.

That's all I keep thinking as I move her stuff into my house.

Our home.

Her entire family is helping, some more than others. The guys have been a huge asset, helping with the heavy lifting, while the girls seem more interested in snooping through every drawer and closet in the place, pretending to be looking for a hammer or some other needless object. I know what they're looking for; I'm on to their game, but they won't find it. Not unless one of them checks my pants.

Jeezus, I sound like Grandma. In fact, I better make sure that nugget of info doesn't get out or the crazy ol' woman will have her hands down my pants so fast, I won't know what hit me.

The ring.

It's in my pants. My pocket, to be exact, because I knew her nosy sisters would be all over this place and probably find it too.

"Where are we headed with this desk?" Ryan asks, carrying the other end of the desk AJ had in her home office.

"The room off the living room," I say, walking backward in the direction of the room. Honestly, she probably doesn't even need the desk since she does most of her paper grading on the couch next to me, but I insisted she have her own space, right along with mine. That's why I gave up half of my own unused office for her stuff. Now we can have a fully unused office, complete with his and hers desks and other crap we'll probably rarely need.

Ryan and I set the desk down and Dean follows us into the room with her chair. "There's an awful lot of giggling coming from the upstairs," Dean says as he slides the chair into place.

"They've all been gone a while. No telling what they've gotten themselves into," Ryan adds.

"And we haven't seen Emma in a while either," Levi chimes in when he and Linkin deliver the bookshelf into the room.

"Really?" I ask, feeling a bit more concerned now. Last I knew she was in the kitchen putting something together for dinner. The girls all together and cackling are one thing, but a missing Emma usually spells trouble.

"You locked your bedroom, right? Lexi and I learned that lesson the hard way," Linkin mentions when he sets down his end of the load.

Did I lock the bedroom door? Uh, that answer would be no. Even though AJ had most of her daily personal belongings at my place, she still had a few things for the bathroom and closet to transfer.

"Yeah, last time she had access to our bedroom, I found a fucking cat," Ryan adds, recalling the story he likes to tell every chance he gets.

"Shit," I mumble as I turn toward the doorway and head up the stairs.

When I reach the top, I notice our bedroom door shut, but the guest bedroom wide open. All giggling quickly stops the moment I pop my head in. "What's so funny?" I ask, catching them off guard. Something in AJ's hand is quickly tossed under the bed. They all giggle profusely, some even turning a brilliant shade of pink. "All right, ladies, what's going on?" I ask, crossing my arms over my chest and waiting them out.

"Oh, you know, Sawyer, just checking out AJ's housewarming gift from Grandma," Payton says, a wide smile on her face.

"Gift?" Fuuuuuck. I've heard all about these little *gifts* Emma likes to give, usually sexual in nature. "Let's see," I add, holding my hand out.

"Are you sure?" AJ asks, trying so damn hard not to smile. My interest is definitely piqued now.

"Yep, let's have it," I reply, keeping my hand out, palm up.

I watch as she crouches down and reaches beneath the bed. I'm stunned silent when she pulls out a dildo–a fucking huge-ass dildo–and sets it in my hand. "The fuck?" I ask, resulting in six girls all busting out laughing.

"Isn't it something?" AJ asks, placing a kiss on my cheek as I stare down at the massive black cock in my hand.

"What's wrong with your grandma?" I ask, unable to stop the words before they spill from my lips.

"Too much to list," Lexi says with a big smile, a cooing baby in her arms.

"AJ's not impressed though," Jaime says, fighting a smile and rubbing a hand on her baby belly.

"You're not?" I ask, glancing between my woman and the massive rubber dong in my hand.

Why am I still holding it?

"She says you're bigger," Lexi says, shrugging. "You're gonna have to show us."

My head whips around to the petite brunette with a wicked gleam in her eyes and an ornery smile on her face.

"What?" I gasp.

"It's a rule," she replies loudly.

"It's not a rule," Abby insists.

"Well, it should be," her twin sasses.

"Why do you have a dildo out in front of my children?" Linkin bellows from the open doorway. "And why the fuck are you holding it?" he asks me with a disgusted look.

Of course, I go ahead and toss the thing onto the bed, where it bounces off and hits the floor.

"Don't say fuck in front of my children!" Lexi replies.

"Our children," he says softly before placing a kiss on her lips. "How's my baby doing today?" he asks, reaching around and placing a hand on Lexi's stomach.

Everyone gasps.

"Shit." Linkin closes his eyes before glancing down at Lexi. "Sorry."

"You're pregnant?" Abby asks her twin.

"Apparently," she grumbles.

Linkin has a huge smile on his face and takes the baby from her arms. "My little men are gonna be big brothers, aren't you?" he asks Hudson.

"How? When? What?" Meghan gasps, all attention turning to Lexi.

"Well… Do you know how hard it is to wait six weeks? It's practically a lifetime! It's impossible!" she declares, tears filling her eyes.

"She couldn't keep her hands off me," Linkin chimes in.

"How far along are you?" Jaime asks.

"Ummm… about three months," she whispers.

"Three months?!" all of her sisters holler at the same time.

"I know, I know," she says, dropping her hands to her side and going to Hemi, who's tucked in Jaime's arms. "I was gonna tell you, but…" she glances at Payton and then around the room, wide-eyed. "I was afraid. And there were no condoms since we hadn't used them in a year. Actually, we had never used them. And I just *needed* it. It had been so freaking long." Lexi glances back to Payton. "I'm sorry."

Payton steps forward and wraps her arms around the youngest sister and baby. "You don't ever have to be afraid to tell me anything, Lexi Lou. I love you and am so happy that you're having another baby. And I know when, and if, the time is right, I'll have big news to tell you too. Someday, maybe I'll be the one sharing the excitement." Payton shrugs, but doesn't fight the tears.

Damn those tears. They all have them in their eyes, even AJ.

Clearing my throat, I reach down and grab the big black cock and toss it back on the bed. "I'm just gonna…" I start and point to the escape. AJ's tear-filled eyes glance my way, a big smile on her face, and she mouths, "I love you."

"Love you, too," I tell her as I kiss her forehead and exit the room.

Too much emotions. Too many tears. Too much estrogen.

Needing a quick breather, I slip down the hall to my bedroom. *Our* bedroom. She's slept here every night since that fateful October evening when my world finally felt right again. Inside, it's quiet and somewhat undisrupted, even though there are a few boxes stacked on the far wall and the bathroom light is on.

When I look to my left, I find the life-size cutout of me in my baseball uniform from one of my sponsors. I laugh, not really surprised by its random appearance in our bedroom. AJ loves that thing and regularly molests the cardboard cutout. When we work out, she always grabs my cardboard crotch. Usually that happens before I grab her.

And give her my real crotch.

Something beside the cutout draws my attention. It's sticking out of the wall on the opposite side of the cardboard me. When I reach it, I'm stunned. Shocked. Mortified. And a little turned on.

Attached to my wall is a long, thin red dildo. It's suction cupped in place, and I don't know whether to laugh or cry.

"AJ!" I holler, shell-shocked at the appearance of yet another sex toy in my house.

The love of my life slips into the silent bedroom. "Is everything okay?"

My eyes are still trained on the dick. "Another gift?" I ask, finally glancing over my shoulder and watching as her eyes search, landing on what I'm referencing. Then, she collapses in a fit of laughter.

"Holy shit," she says, holding her stomach and bending forward in amusement. When she gets herself under control, she walks over and slides under my arm, wrapping both of hers around my waist.

Kissing the top of her head, we both gaze at the protruding wall dick. "That might be fun," I concede.

AJ starts to giggle again. "Actually, I don't think that's for me."

Wait. What? "Pardon?" I ask, wide-eyed and shocked.

"Well, look at the position. It's actually lined right up with Mr. Randall's sexy cutout."

"Exactly, it's the perfect height for you."

"No, you're tall. You have to widen your stance when you give it to me from behind," she says, making my dick instantly hard in my jeans.

Before I can reply, I hear a drawer close in the bathroom. Moments later, Grandma appears behind us, happy little grandmotherly smile on her evil face. "Oh, I see you've found it!" she cheers, clapping her hands.

"What is this exactly?" I ask, turning to face the elderly woman, while still keeping AJ in my arms. "And why were you in our bathroom?"

Ignoring the second question, she says, "Your present!"

"Mine?" My throat is instantly dry.

"Sure is. I picked out that big Bubba cock for AJ, and Grandpa chose the slimmer, more flexible model for you."

"Grandpa?" AJ asks, her voice hoarse and quiet.

"Did you notice it suctions to the wall," Grandpa says, exiting our bathroom with a pleased look on his face.

"Oh, hell," I grumble as AJ gasps.

"You're out of rubbers," Grandpa says as he joins us in the bedroom.

"Don't worry, though. We remedied that," Grandma adds.

"Don't use them. Never use condoms from Grandma and Grandpa. I wouldn't put it past them to tamper with them," AJ whispers into my side.

"We'd never do that to you. Abby and Levi? All bets are off with them," Grandma says with a shrug, as if it's no big deal.

"Well, we'd never do that before the wedding. You know, if Sawyer ever gets off the pot," Grandpa adds.

"But Abby and Levi aren't married," AJ refutes.

"Semantics," Grandma waves off.

"When are you gonna get off the pot?" Grandpa asks me with an inquisitive glare, putting me firmly in the hot seat.

"What were you doing in my bathroom?" I ask, giving him my own look.

"Do you really want to know?" he sasses back, crossing his arms at his chest.

"No!" AJ pleads, but my eyes are still firmly locked on the old man. He's challenging me, calling me out, and putting me on the spot.

I swallow hard, staring him down and weighing my options. This isn't what I had planned. There's nothing romantic about this moment. We're not even alone, for fuck's sake. But here I am, getting ready to propose to the woman I love. Oh, I'm gonna do it. I know it, and he knows it.

"Get out," I say to the ornery old man, nodding toward the door. His smile practically splits his face in half as he reaches over for Emma's hand and leads her from the room.

"What just happened?" AJ asks, watching them go.

"They're giving us privacy," I reply, turning so that we're facing each other.

"For?" she asks, the question flashing through her eyes.

That's when I fish out the ring from my pocket and drop to one knee. Her surprised gasp is like music to my ears. The only thing better would be a confirmation for the question I'm about to ask.

"Alison, I knew when I saw you across the room that there was something special about you. Even though you puked on my shoes, I wanted more time with you. When I saw you sitting next to me in the teachers' lounge, it was like fate bringing us back together." I take a deep breath and reach for her shaking hand, not even saying what I had originally planned.

"It hasn't been an easy road," I say, chuckling a little and making her smile. "But it's the only road I want to be on. As long as you're by my side. My coach once told us never to let the fear of striking out keep us from playing ball. So here I am, swinging for the fences, baby." Deep breath. "Will you marry me?"

Tears fill her eyes and I swear time stands still. She gives nothing away as she gazes wide-eyed down at me. Until she finally says the sweetest word. "Yes."

I whoop (very macho-y, I might add) as I jump up to my feet and take her into my arms, my lips eager as they connect with hers in a bruising kiss. She sniffs, grabbing my face with both hands and giving as good as she gets in a no-holds-barred, mind blowing kiss.

"Can we come in now?" Grandma hollers outside the door and knocking gently.

Pulling my lips from hers, I smile down at the woman I love, my fiancée. "You said yes," I smile, pushing some loose hair away from her forehead. It's a tender motion that will always remind me of the night we met.

"There was no other answer," she says, reaching up and wrapping her arms around my neck. "But, didn't you say something about a ring?" she teases.

Shit. I open my hand and show her the two carat round diamond that I chose to slip on her finger. She holds her hand out, a slight tremor visible, as I make it official.

"It's beautiful," she cries, gaping down at her new ring.

"You're beautiful," I tell her as I slide my hands along her jaw. "And I love you."

"I love you," she says before my lips claim hers once more.

I don't even notice that her family bursts through the door. It doesn't bother me that there's a plethora of dildos in my house brought in by an eighty-something year old woman. I only care about the woman in my arms and the fact that she's agreed to spend the rest of her life with me.

Our life.

"You're mine. Forever."

"I was yours the moment you approached me in the bar," she says, giving me a coy grin. "Plus, this means I get to fondle cardboard Mr. Randall for the rest of my days," she adds, making me laugh.

"That's fine, but just promise me you'll get that foot-long red cock off my wall as soon as possible." Now it's her turn to laugh.

"Not interested in playing?" she teases, glancing over at it.

"Oh, I'm interested… I was just thinking maybe I could use it on you," I whisper, nipping at the corner of her mouth.

"Are you asking me to stay after class this afternoon, Mr. Randall?" The look she gives me goes straight to my dick.

"I love it when we get to play teacher/student."

"How quickly can we get rid of my family and start the celebration?" she asks, glancing around at all the people in our bedroom.

"Time to go!" I holler.

And then I proceed to ignore everyone else except the woman in my arms. It's time to start the rest of my life with the woman I love at my side. Miss AJ Summer, eighth grade math teacher.

My fiancée.

My life.

Epilogue

AJ

It's a Summer sister tradition that on the first Saturday of each month, the six of us get together. We take turns picking the location or activity, anything from margaritas and a movie to wine and painting classes at the small gallery uptown. One thing, though, is as certain as the sun rising over the Chesapeake Bay every morning: there will be alcohol involved.

Always.

Well, for most of us.

Tonight, only fifty percent of the Summer girls are drinking. Two are knocked up and one is hoping to be. Me? It's not even on our radar yet, so I volunteer to drink their share. I'm a good sister like that.

Since not everyone can drink and it was Jaime's night to pick, she settled on a chocolate making class at the local bakery. It was offered as a way for couples to enjoy a night out, while making yummy chocolates, but we decided it would be much better to take the class as sisters. Especially since there's only one remaining single sister, and no one wants to make her feel like a third wheel… or an eleventh wheel, if you count us all up.

So we've taken over the entire back table, our group of six, and completely ignore the couples in the room feeding each other chocolate and licking traces off each other's fingers. Our group is loud, even without half of us consuming alcohol we had to bring ourselves.

"I like this one," Lexi says, shoving another sea salt and chocolate covered caramel into her mouth.

"We know. You've told us. You know the object of this class is to take your goodies home with you, right?" Abby asks her twin.

"I'm not sharing with Linkin. He's already back to his overprotective ways. I'm barely four months pregnant and he's already talking about me going on maternity leave."

"That's because he loves you so much," Payton says as she fills chocolate molds with cherries.

"No, I totally get what she's saying. Ryan wants to install bars in the tub and shower in case I slip. What am I? Eighty?" She grumbles, rubbing her swollen belly. She's five months pregnant and has the cutest little ball attached to her midsection.

"How about you, AJ? How are the wedding plans coming along?" Abby asks, pouring dark chocolate into her mold.

"Good. He finally reached out to all of his groomsmen and asked them to stand up for him," I tell them.

"His brother is best man, right?" Jaime asks, concentrating intently on her treat in front of her.

"Yeah, his brother and his two cousins. He asked two of his former teammates to stand up too."

"The hot cousin who was here last October?" Lexi asks, looking so much like Grandma right now.

"Yeah, and Maddox has a younger brother too. Aiden," I share, watching their eyes light up at the thought of seeing the two

Jackson brothers together. I saw them both at Christmas, standing side-by-side, and I have to say… H.O.T.

"There are two?" Lexi gasps.

"You're married," I remind her.

"So! Married doesn't mean I can't ogle the hot cousins!" she declares loudly, drawing the attention of a few couples around us.

"I can't believe you're going to have professional athletes at your wedding," Payton says. "Maybe we can set Meggy up," she offers with a smile and a wink.

Meghan smiles back, but there's no missing the way she tenses. "That's not necessary," she says politely. But it's what she doesn't say that stands out.

Giving her a small smile, I finish telling them quietly all about our upcoming July nuptials. We're getting married in our backyard, a beach-themed wedding, with very little information being shared. The press has already caught on that Bad Boy Randall is getting hitched again, and the last thing we want is to have them shooting photos of our big day from boats out in the Bay.

"I just hope this baby comes on her due date. That'll give me time to fit into my bridesmaid dress," Jaime says.

"You? I've got to go a month longer than you. I'll practically be giving birth while walking down the aisle," Lexi groans. Her due date comes just mere weeks before our July twenty-ninth wedding.

"At least it's only one baby this time," Payton says.

"Truth," Lexi replies, getting frustrated that her cream is pouring out of her chocolate piece. "This is hopeless. I suck at making candy." She drops her tools on the table and grabs her water bottle.

"I heard that about you," Payton teases, referring to her suck comment.

"Seriously, this time around, my hormones are all over the place, but I'm still horny as hell," she adds, a wicked smile on her face.

"Me too," Jaime adds. "We go out in the driveway all the time and just sit in his truck so I can give him road-head."

"Why do we always talk about this?" Abby asks, a blush creeping up on her cheeks.

"Don't deny that you don't regularly lick the flesh lollipop, Abigail. Yours is bedazzled. I bet that thing's in your mouth more than your toothbrush," Lexi sasses with a pointed look. The color of Abby's face rivals a red crayon as she averts her eyes and tries not to smile. "See. Told you," Lexi replies when she notices her twin's fuchsia face.

My phone vibrates in my pocket, so I gingerly pull it out, trying not to catch anyone's attention. There's an unspoken rule that the guys aren't allowed at sisters' night, but we all know it's crap. I bet most of them have already either sent a text or received a text from their significant other.

> **Sawyer:** How much longer? I miss you. *sad face emoji*
>
> **Me:** Don't give me that sad face. You're probably having a great time with the guys.

The bubbles appear right away.

> **Sawyer:** We're having fun, but mostly talking about you all. We've become lame in our old age, babe. We're not even drinking anymore. *tear face emoji*

Smiling, I type my reply.

> **Me:** Aww, poor babies. Would it make you feel better if sexual favors are promised tonight?
>
> **Sawyer:** You mean more favors than playing teacher/student when we get home???????????? *heart eyes emoji*
>
> **Me:** Definitely. I was thinking we could use that suction cup dong tonight...
>
> **Sawyer:** Keep talking...

Me: Place it on the wall, get us both all hot and bothered... and finally use it for its intended purposes. *heart eyes emoji* *eggplant emoji* *peach emoji*

I can't help but snicker when I hit send.

The bubbles appear and then disappear. It takes a few minutes before I finally see a reply.

Sawyer: N.O.T. Happening. That thing isn't going anywhere near my ass, Alison...

Me: *giggling girl gif*

Sawyer: Just for that, I'm using the red dong on you...

Me: *twerking gif*

Sawyer: You're making me hard.

Me: Can I molest you like I molest cardboard Mr. Randall?

Sawyer: Fuck yes. How much longer?

I glance at my watch before replying.

Me: It's only nine.

Sawyer: So...

Me: I'll be there in a while.

Sawyer: Five minutes *pouty emoji*

Me: It'll be longer than five minutes. We're making chocolates. You can eat some when I get there.

Sawyer: Off your naked body?

Me: Definitely... *smiling devil emoji*

Sawyer: Hurry. *kissy emoji* *red heart emoji*

I set my phone down, a goofy grin on my face, and get back to making chocolates.

"She's so getting some tonight," Payton singsongs to no one in particular, which makes me laugh.

Who would have thought I'd find my happily ever after while drunk in a bar? What started out as an embarrassing disaster turned into one of the greatest moments of my life. It led me to Sawyer. And even though our road wasn't easy, it has been worth it.

The headline will read: "*PLAYER TO SPEND THE REST OF HIS LIFE WITH A TEACHER.*"

Sounds pretty damn good to me.

Another Epilogue

Meghan

I need to get out of here. I'm surrounded by couples, all happy and content. Even my sisters all have that delightful glow illuminating them. And while I'd never begrudge any of them their bliss, it's just killing me.

Every day, I die a little more inside.

Keeping myself busy helps, which I've become a master at. I work; then I go to some after work class like pottery, scrapbooking, painting, or whatever. Anything to keep myself from being swallowed by the silence. By the loneliness. The fear.

The anger.

I've had a few drinks, but I'm not nearly as buzzed as I wish I were. I just can't seem to bring myself to drink tonight, even though all I want to do is forget.

Forget everything.

Forget nothing.

Two years. It's been two years since my life changed that fateful February night when a car crossed the centerline and drove head-on into his car. Two years since I heard his voice and felt his warm skin beneath my fingers. Two years since my world was only him and the life we once shared.

Two years since it all was taken away.

Josh.

The stupid tears threaten once more. It's been a hard night, one I tried to get out of, but they wouldn't let me. They pulled me from the place we used to share and dragged me here. To a place surrounded by couples.

It's not their fault, though. They're trying really hard to help, and in a big way, they have. I have a niece and twin nephews, and two more on the way. I have a parent who knows firsthand what it's like to grieve for the love of your life and is right beside me, offering me as much support as I need, and two grandparents who share enough love to fill the ocean. Focusing on everyone else's happiness gets me through.

But not tonight.

Tonight it just hurts.

Tonight is the anniversary.

Sitting at the table, surrounded by candy I don't even want to eat, I covertly fire off a text under the table.

My reinforcement.

I quickly set my phone on the table and pretend to be involved in a conversation when my cell rings. Nick Adams DDS. "Oh no, it's Dr. Adams. He only calls if it's an emergency," I say, probably way too chipper, as I pick up the phone and press it to my ear. "Hello?"

"You okay?" he asks, his friendly voice instantly calming the turmoil inside my soul.

"Oh no, a tooth emergency? Of course I can come in. I'm at the bakery with my sisters." I pause, which makes him chuckle. "You'll pick me up on your way to the office? I'll meet you out front," I tell him.

"I'll be there in ten," he says before hanging up.

I take a deep breath and clutch my phone to my chest, waiting for the despair, the guilt to settle in. It's there, waiting, breathing like a living thing. I bury it deep inside, while firmly fastening my "I'm fine" armor into place, plastering my always present smile on my face.

This is my life now.

It's all one big lie.

THE END

About the Author

USA Today Bestselling Author Lacey Black is a Midwestern girl with a passion for reading, writing, and shopping. She carries her e-reader with her everywhere she goes so she never misses an opportunity to read a few pages. Always looking for a happily ever after, Lacey is passionate about contemporary romance novels and enjoys it further when you mix in a little suspense. She resides in a small town in Illinois with her husband and two children.

Website: laceyblackbooks.com
Email: laceyblackwrites@gmail.com

Sign up for my newsletter so you don't miss a single sale, reveal or release!
www.laceyblackbooks.com/newsletter

www.ingramcontent.com/pod-product-compliance
Lightning Source LLC
Chambersburg PA
CBHW070848260626
47170CB00007B/2538